The Vampire Wakes

The seven stone coffins stood upright in a half-circle, with that of the Black Princess in the center of the row, flanked by her six warriors. Weird, black wine now gushed over the open sarcophagi, drenching the shrunken mummies within.

The watchers' eyes were fixed fearfully upon the gaunt figure of the Black Princess, where her coffin faced the reopened passage to the outside world. And all saw *her* eyes crack open! Petrified, the entire assembly stared into the ——————————— were Yath-Lhi's eyes.

The wine ——————————— limbs. And like oil it ea——————————— and made soft the leath——————————— yes opened wider and he——————————— apart in a hideous grin. Creaking like rusted hinges, *she stepped forth out of her coffin*!

The Black Princess beckoned with a still-stiff arm, and a man stepped forward, zombie-like, to stand before her. She reached out her hands and touched him, all ten of her fingers, widespread, contacting his shoulders— and the man began to twitch and flop like a strangled chicken. He did not scream, made no attempts at flight, merely jerked and throbbed and fluttered; he withered, deflated, and became a bag of bones in Yath-Lhi's sucking hands.

Look for these Tor books by Brian Lumley

BRIAN LUMLEY

ICED ON ARAN

TOR
HORROR

A TOM DOHERTY ASSOCIATES BOOK
NEW YORK

ICED ON ARAN

Copyright © 1990 by Brian Lumley

Cover art by Tim Jacobus

A Tor Book
Published by Tom Doherty Associates, Inc.
175 Fifth Avenue
New York, N.Y. 10010

Tor® is a registered trademark of Tom Doherty Associates, Inc.

ISBN: 0-812-52422-5

First Tor mass market printing: March 1994

Printed in the United States of America

0 9 8 7 6 5 4 3 2 1

For Unsung Heroes and Wanderers Everywhere.

CONTENTS

ICED ON ARAN

King Kuranes' questers, called Hero and Eldin for short—though neither of them was short, for being ex-waking worlders they were much taller than the average dreamlander, or *Homo ephemerens*, as Eldin was wont to call them—were laboring up the slopes of Mount Aran, above the trees and toward the snow line.

Hero was rangy, springy of step, younger than his friend; Eldin was stocky, gangling, somehow apish in his length of arm and massive strength, and yet not unattractive. They loved each other like brothers but would deny it almost to the death, while defending each other to that same grave limit; they loved as well adventuring, girls, booze and especially their travels and travails as the Lord of Ooth-Nargai and the Skies Around Serannian's special emissaries, agents, and troubleshooters in general—though the latter was something they'd also deny, except when they were broke and needed the work. Like now.

King Kuranes (or "Lord"; he made no special distinction, and only rarely stood on ceremony) was cooking something up for them right now, a job in far Inquanok; for which reason he kept the pair waiting in timeless

Celephais on the Southern Sea while he made his various arrangements from his manor-house seat in that city. Alas, but sitting still on their backsides was something Hero and Eldin didn't do too well; a day or two of total inactivity was normally sufficient to drive them to drink, and from that to other diversions. They'd been drinking last night; had started boasting, and a boozing companion (one Tatter Nees, a wandering balladeer from Nir) had found himself filling the role of adjudicator.

Their bragging had ungallantly covered women, though never referred to individually by name; deeds of derring-do in various far-flung places; finally feats of physical prowess which, if true, would have made the pair the greatest athletes in all the dreamlands! (They weren't, as it happens, though neither were they slouches.) And finally they'd started in on their climbing skills:

"Who was it," Hero noisily demanded, slopping muth-dew in his enthusiasm, "climbed a Great Keep of the First Ones alone and unaided?"

"And who," Eldin thumbed himself in the chest, "scaled the Great Bleak Range, even to topmost ridge?"

"We were together on that!" Hero at once protested. "I did it too!"

"Aye, and stubbed your toe on the top," Eldin reminded, "*and* damned near crashed down the other side to your death. You would have, too, if a friendly little crevice-grown bush hadn't taken pity on you!"

"I was *knocked* over the rim fighting with Yib-Tstll's vast stone idol avatar, as you well know!" Hero was affronted. "And that's something else I do better than you—fight!" He jumped up, rotated his fists menacingly, leaped nimbly up and down and hither and thither like a frenetic boxer—until his head crashed against a low beam, which brought him to an abrupt, shuddering standstill. Then, staggering a little and grimacing a great deal, he collapsed back into his seat.

The Wanderer (as Eldin was also named) and Tatter Nees laughed till they cried, and Hero too dizzy and dazed even to protest.

"Well," said Tatter eventually, "fight and climb all you like, just as long as you don't go climbing Hatheg-Kla or Mount Aran. They're forbidden to mortal men, those two peaks, and the strange old gods who decree such things are pretty unforgiving."

"Eh?" Eldin raised a shaggy eyebrow. "Aran, forbidden? I mean, I know Hatheg-Kla's a bit hairy—old Atal of Ulthar's an authority on that, if ever there was one—but snowy old Mount Aran? A mere hill by comparison with some mountains! What, Aran of the ginkgos and the eternal snows, whose frosty old crown's forever white? Aran, where he rises from ocean's rim to look down on Celephais and all the southern coast? Aran, that most benevolent of crests, forbidden? I didn't know that!"

"Aran?" Hero mumbled, still recovering from self-inflicted clout and gingerly fingering the lump he could almost feel rising on his head. "That molehill! *Hah!* I'd climb it in a trice!"

"Then I'd climb it twice in a trice!" growled Eldin; and more cautiously, "Except it's forbidden. According to Tatter here, anyway."

"Tittle-Tatter!" cried Hero. "I'd run up Aran before breakfast, just to keep myself in trim!"

"And I'd be on top waiting for you," returned Eldin, "having gone up ahead for a breath of fresh air!"

"Now *that's* climbing talk!" Hero declared, sticking out his jaw. "In the morning, then?"

"Tonight, if you like!"

"No, morning's soon enough—and anyway, I've a headache."

"What? What?" cried Tatter. "Madness, and I'm party to it! Only climb Mount Aran—or race to the top, if you will—and tomorrow here's me composing a lyric farewell to two of my dearest friends, which I shall call 'Quest No More, My Fair Brave Lads.' "

"One fair brave lad," said Hero, "and one old ratbag!"

"More muth!" cried Eldin to the somewhat troubled taverner, who knew their reputation. "I want to drink a last toast to a gallant loser, before he burns himself out on the slopes of Mount Aran."

And so it went . . .

Neither one of the questers remembered Tatter tottering them up rickety stairs to their respective rickety beds in a cheap, tiny, rickety garret room. But both of them remembered their oath. Perhaps they regretted it, too, but things didn't work out that way.

Across the distance of the single pace separating them where they lay, as the sun's first rays crept in through a small-paned window, they blinked crusted eyes and tasted mouths like old shoes with dead-rat tongues, and Eldin said: "Hero—*ugh!*—about Aran . . ."

"Forget it—*yechhh!*" Hero had answered, wondering why muth wasn't called moth. "I won't hold you to it. What would it prove?"

"Exactly."

"I mean, you're all those years older than me . . ."

And after a moment, in a somewhat harsher tone: "Exactly—and that much more experienced! So get up, pup! The sun's up and Aran's snows are sweet and cool and waiting."

Which was how they came to be here now.

During the climb they'd been pretty quiet, heads

clearing, thoughts their own, probably wondering what madness had prompted this contest. The only good thing about it was that it was burning the muth out of their systems. Hangovers which might normally last two whole days should be gone by the time they hit the snow line . . .

Mount Aran *was* a mountain, one of the ocean-fringing range of mountains whose roots lay in the Tanarian Hills beyond Ooth-Nargai, but it was not one of those sheer-sided monster mountains like Ngranek or (worse far) Hatheg-Kla. Its lower slopes were green, gentling up through palms and shrubs and ginkgos, then gradually shifting to scree and bare rock, finally crossing the permanent snow line to rise more steeply, but not frighteningly so, to a white rounded peak. In the waking world it would not have had the height to support permanent snow and ice—relatively few mountains do—but these were the dreamlands, and things were different here.

Perhaps the questers thought of these differences as they struggled higher across slopes of loose, sliding shale, using the roots and springy branches of the few remaining mountain shrubs for leverage. Differences like the "timelessness" of Aran and Celaphais, where the seasons never seemed to change and people led inordinately long, almost interminable lives. Hero, considering this, thought: *I'd be bored to death if I thought I was going to live, or dream, forever!* And he grinned at the apparent contradiction in his thoughts.

Eldin saw that infectious grin; it signified the younger quester's emergence from muth-fume, also the resurgence of his natural good-humor. What's more, it might indicate that he was actually enjoying this barmy scramble, which Eldin frankly was not. The Wanderer scowled. "Funny, is it?" he asked, "this foolish contest you've goaded me into?"

"Funny?" Hero parked himself on a boulder, drank deep of the crisp air. "Daft, more like! Actually, I wasn't smiling at your discomfort; I've more than enough of my own. No, it was something else I was thinking of, far removed from the scaling of Aran. As for goading: we goaded each other, I reckon."

Eldin sat down beside him, said: "You see no point in this, then?"

Hero shook his head. "None at all! Let's face it, we've climbed, you and I, in previously undreamed places. And what's Aran but a big hill, eh? Hardly a climb to tax our talents."

Eldin shrugged. "That's true enough—why, we're halfway up already, and not even noon! So why do we do these things, tell me that?"

Hero grinned again. "With nothing to test our mettle, we test each other. Or maybe it's the forbidden fruit syndrome, eh?"

"Because Tatter said we mustn't? You mean like naughty children? Is that all there is to us, Hero?" He nodded, considered it quite possible, gazed down on Celephais with its glittering minarets and caught flashes of Naraxa water where that river cascaded down to join the sea.

Before they'd sat down the Wanderer, too, had been dwelling a little on the timelessness of things: chiefly on Aran's snowy crest, which was the same now as the first time he'd seen it—oh, how long ago? What kept the ice going? he wondered. Why didn't it melt away? Or, on the other hand, why didn't it get so thick it formed a glacier down to the sea? Had it been this way immemorially? And if so, would it be the same a thousand years from now?

"Sometimes," said Hero, breaking in on his thoughts, "I feel weary."

"That's my line, surely?" Eldin snorted. But it pleased him anyway. What? Hero tired? Ridiculous! He was like a workhorse! But if he really was tired . . . well didn't that say something for Eldin's stamina, who must always keep apace of him?

Hero turned up the collar of his jacket. Fine when you were on the move, but at this altitude it quickly got cold when you sat still. *"Brrr!"* said the younger quester, and: "Tell you what, let's go up to the snow, find a block of ice, and ride it down to Celephais. That should satisfy Tatter. And we'll tell him we climbed opposite sides and clashed heads at the very top!"

"Suits me, if you say so," Eldin agreed. "But who cares what Tatter thinks?"

Hero sighed. "That's what makes me tired. Not Tatter especially, but people in general. These reputations of ours, *they're* what really keep us going. And that's the answer to your question: why do we do it. What are rogues if they quit their roguish ways, answer me that? Brawlers, boozers, adventurers: if we stop doing those things, what's left? 'Hey, look! There go Hero and Eldin. They were a couple of bad old boys—in their time . . .' See what I mean?"

Eldin thought about that for a moment, said: "Now I really *do* feel weary! Let's go and collect that ice and get down out of here; we break the mood of the place, change what shouldn't be changed."

They stood up; started climbing, crossed from scree and riven rock to snow and ice. And there, more than two-thirds of the way to the top—

"Ho, there, you lads! Lost your way, have you?"

Startled, the questers scanned about. The thin snow was dazzling in morning sunshine, where it coated

Aran's ice, so that they must shield their eyes from its glare. But up there, fifty yards on to the ice, was a thin small figure, pick in hand, staring at them apparently in some surprise. They moved toward him, saw that he was old, gave each other sour glances.

"A right pair of adventurers, we are!" Eldin muttered under his breath, which plumed now in the frozen air. "What? Come to climb a 'forbidden' mountain—and grandads leaping about all over its peak?"

As they drew closer, so the old man studied them minutely. They could feel his eyes on them, going from faces to forms, taking in every aspect, comparing Hero's bark-brown garb to Eldin's night-black, the former's curved blade of Kled to the latter's great straight sword. And finally: "David Hero," he said. "Or Hero of Dreams, as they call you. And Eldin the Wanderer. Well, now—and it seems you really have lost your way!"

While the oldster had examined and spoken to them, they in turn had given him the once-over. There seemed no requirement for a detailed scrutiny: what was he but an old man? In no way threatening. Still . . .

He was dressed in baggy gray breeks tied at the ankles, his large feet tucked into fur-lined boots that went up under the cuffs of the breeks. His gray jacket was fur-lined, too, and buttoned to his neck. Tufts of fur protruded from button- and lace-holes. Upon his head he wore a woolen cap with a pompom, beneath which his hair and beard and droopy moustache were white as snow. All in all, his attire looked so grotesquely large and loose on him, it seemed to the questers he must be the merest bundle of sticks inside. Certainly his hands were pale and thin, as the petals of some winter-blooming flowers; blue-veined, they were, and very nearly translucent. Likewise his face, framed in curling locks of wintry hair: all pale and shiny as if waxed, or covered perhaps in a thin skim of clear ice. Icy, too, his eyes; indeed, gray and cold as snow-laden clouds, but not unfriendly for all that. And not without curiosity.

"What brings you here?" he finally asked the pair, his voice almost a chime. "Why do you climb Aran?"

"Because it's here!" growled Eldin at once. And: "Do we need a reason?"

The old man held up placating hands. "I wasn't prying," he said. "I've no authority one way or the other. Just making conversation, that's all."

Hero spoke up. "No motive to our being here," he said, "except we thought we'd climb Aran, that's all. But what's in it for you? You'll pardon my saying so, but it seems to me you're a bit long in the tooth for shinning up mountains."

The old man gave them a gummy grin. "A man's as old as he feels," he said. "And who's to say who feels the younger, you or I? Looks to me like you two are feeling as old as the hills themselves right now—if you'll forgive *me* saying so. As to why I'm here: why, I cut the ice for the fishmongers and butchers and vintners in Celephais! The ice of Aran provides my living, you see, as it did for my grandfather and father before me. Cutting it, and carving it, too—though the latter's more properly a hobby, a small self-indulgence, with nothing of profit in it. Obviously I can't take my carvings into town, for they'd quickly melt. Up here, however—why, they last forever!"

"Carvings?" Eldin looked all about. "I see no carvings . . ." Perhaps the old lad was an idiot.

The icemonger grinned again. "Only brush the snow away where you stand," he said.

The ice-slope had been simplicity itself in the climbing, for here and there it went up in uniform ripples, almost like steps, with only a thin, crisp covering of snow to round off their sharp angular shapes. Eldin scuffed at some of these flat, regular surfaces with his boots; saw that in fact they *were* steps, cut with infinite care into the ice of Aran. And, narrowing his eyes toward the peak, the Wanderer saw that indeed the steps would seem to go all the way to the top.

"Steps!" said Hero, following Eldin's gaze, and at once felt foolish. Of course they were steps.

The old man nodded. "To make the climbing of Aran easier, aye."

"But who'd want to make the climbing of a forbidden mountain easy?" Eldin was puzzled.

The old man laughed. "An icemonger, of course! My grandfather first cut steps on Aran's frozen slopes, and after him my father, and now I cut them. You see, the mountain is not forbidden to me. But ice-steps are not the carvings I was talking about, Wanderer. You brushed snow from the wrong place."

The questers looked again.

Flanking the rippling stairway they had ascended, large expanses of the slope showed columnar, lumpy, or nodal structures beneath a thin snow sheath. Eldin got down on his knees to one edge of the steps and brushed away snow with his hands. Hero likewise on the opposite side of the steps. And now an amazing thing, for beneath the snow—

"Wonderful!" said Hero, his voice full of admiration.

A figure reclined there, laid bare by the quester's hands: the figure of a man carved in ice. He sat (or seemed to) on the slope, his back against an ice boulder, hands in his lap, and gazed out through ice eyes far across all the lands of dream. He was middling old, yet looked ages-weary, and his downward sloping shoulders seemed to bear all the weight of entire worlds. His ice-robes were those of a king, which the ice-crown upon his head confirmed beyond a doubt. But even without the royal robes and ice-jewelled headgear, still the figure was unmistakable.

"Kuranes!" Hero whispered, seeing in the ice an image almost of life itself, yet at the same time a Kuranes utterly unknown to him.

"The Lord of Ooth-Nargai, aye," the old ice carver whispered. "My father sculpted this in a time when Kuranes dwelled in the rose-crystal Palace of the Seventy Delights, before he dreamed himself his manor-house and built his Cornish village on the coast. As you can see, the king was weary in those days, and jaded on the dreamlands; see how clearly it shows in his mien? But once he'd builded a little bit of Cornwall here"—he shrugged—"his weariness fell off him. My father had thought he might visit this place, come up and see himself shaped in ice, but he never came. Still, time yet . . ."

Hero was astounded. "The king didn't sit for this?"

The old man gave a curious, brittle little laugh. "No, it was done from memory. My father's skill was great!"

Hero scuffed at a flat, snow-layered area next to the ice-carved king. It was empty, just a flat space cut out of Aran's ice. "Well, if Kuranes ever does come up here," he said, "and if he sits here, why, then he'll be beside himself!" He grinned.

"That was a joke," Eldin drily explained, but the old ice cutter only narrowed his eyes. The Wanderer had meanwhile cleared away snow from half a dozen ice-carvings. In doing so, he'd brought a curious thing to light. While Kuranes figure was carved only once, the rest—and the slope, as far as the eye could see, was literally covered with snow-humped shapes—appeared all to be duplicated. They sat, kneeled or reclined, or occasionally stood there on the slopes of Aran, in perfect pairs like glassy twins cut from the mountain. Two of each, almost exactly identical, strange twinned stalagmites of ice in human form.

Eldin uncovered more figures, Hero too. "I recognize a few of them," the Wanderer mused. "Here's old Cuff the fisherman. He never married, stayed alone all his days. Most people keep young in Celephais, but Cuff grew old. Toward the end he didn't even speak to people, stopped fishing, just sat around on the wharves staring out to sea. People said he was tired of life."

The cold was starting to get into Hero's bones. "I don't know how you can work up here," he told the old man. "It's so cold here even Zura's zombies would last forever!" Snow was beginning to fall: light flakes like confetti cut from finest white gossamer drifting down near-vertically out of the sky. "As for your work," Hero went on, "I can't fault it. But don't your fingers freeze up? These things must take days in the carving! And there are thousands of them . . ."

The old man smiled his thin, cold smile. "I wrap up warm," he said, "as you can see. Also, I'm used to the cold. What's more I work very quickly and accurately. It's in my blood, come down from my grandfather, through my father to me. And sometimes I have advanced knowledge. I get to know that someone else desires to be carved in ice. Come over here and I'll show you something." He led the way nimbly across the snow-slope, knowing every step intimately. Hero and Eldin followed.

As they went, Hero asked the Wanderer: "So what happened to old Cuff the fisherman? Did he die?"

Eldin shrugged. "Drowned, they say. After a storm they found his boat wrecked on Kuranes' Cornish rocks. They didn't find Cuff, though, and he was never washed up. The sea keeps its secrets. Actually, I'd forgotten all about him till I saw him—both of him—up here."

"How about that?" Hero asked the old ice-cutter. "Why do you carve two likenesses of your subjects? And why, pray, only one of Kuranes?"

"Here we are," the old man might not have heard him. "There—what do you think of that?"

"Why, I . . . I'm floored!" Hero gasped.

"Or, maybe, 'flowed'?" said Eldin. "You know: ice-flowed?"

Hero groaned and rolled his eyes, but the old man said, "Flawed, yes! Kuranes, I mean. You asked why only one of him. Because the ice was flawed. When my father set to work on the second image, it shattered. And so there's only an empty space beside him."

The questers said nothing, merely gazed in astonishment at ice-sculptures—of themselves! The carvings were far from complete; indeed, they were the crudest of representations, the merest gouges and slashes in blocks of ice; but just as a great artist captures the essence of his subject with the first strokes of his brush, so were the essences of Hero and Eldin here caught. Perhaps in more ways than one . . .

Hero's gape turned to a frown, then an expression of some puzzlement. "Two things," he said. "Yet again you've only represented us once apiece. But weirder far, why are we here at all? We didn't ask to be sculpted in Aran's ice; and as for your being forewarned about our coming, why, you couldn't have been! We only decided that last night, and even then we weren't sure."

By way of answer, the old man asked questions of his own. "I'd like to be certain on that point," he said. "About your coming up here, I mean. You told me you climbed Aran 'because it was here.' By that do you mean that you automatically do things you should not? Which in this case is to say, because the climbing of Aran is forbidden? Or was it simply that you were bored, tired of mundane dreaming?"

Hero looked at him a little askance. "Mundane dreamers? Us? Hardly!"

Eldin's ice-statue sat, elbow on knee, chin in palm, gazing frostily on Celephais. The Wanderer got down beside it, put his real elbow on the empty knee, adopted the same pose more or less, and stared into the statue's roughly-angled face. "You keep asking us our reason for climbing Aran," he said. "Because we shouldn't, you ask, or because we were bored? Well, actually—if it's that important to you—it was a bit of both. See, we've been a little out of sorts, Hero and I."

"No, no!" cried the sculptor at once. "Don't sit there, but here, right alongside. That's right. Good! Good!" Similarly, he positioned Hero beside his carving, which sat straight-armed, hands on knees, staring bleakly ahead. Then he took out tools from his pockets, began to chip away. First at Eldin's unfinished sculpture, then at Hero's, and so on, back and forth.

"You didn't answer my questions," said Hero, watching him out of the corner of his eye. "How come you've already started work on us? And why only one piece apiece?"

"My friends," said the old man, "you see the work of long, lonely years here. Here are represented years before I was born, and years before my father was born. There are a number of celebrities carved here—like Lord Kuranes himself—but mainly the works are of ordinary men. Now, the carving of ordinary men is all very well, but it is unrewarding. I mean, in another century or so, who will know or remember them, eh? But men such as you two, destined to become legends in the dreamlands . . ."

"You carved us because we're famous!" cried Eldin, beaming.

"Or infamous!" Hero's frown persisted.

"What better reason?" Again the old man smiled his thin, cold smile.

"Something here," said Hero, hearing warning bells in the back of his head (or maybe the tinkling of warning ice-crystals), "isn't quite right. I can't put my finger on it, but it's wrong." And talking of fingers, the old man had just put the finishing touch to Hero's right hand—which even now promptly fell asleep upon his knee, as dead as if hard-bitten by frost. Hero made to rise, stir himself up, but—

"No, no, *no!*" the old man chided. "Now that you are here, at least do me the courtesy of sitting still. Fifteen or twenty minutes at most, and the job's done. And while I work, so I'll tell you my story."

"Story?" Eldin repeated him, watching how he carefully molded his boot from ice—and feeling his real foot go suddenly cold inside the real boot, with a numbness that gradually climbed into his calf. "Is there a story, then?"

"Ooth-Nargai"—the sculptor appeared to ignore him, his fingers and tools alive with activity—"is said to be timeless. For most people it is, but for some it isn't. If all a man wants is a place that never changes, then Celephais in Ooth-Nargai's the spot. But there are those who want more than that, who *must* have change; restless souls whose hearts forever reach beyond the horizons we know. Alas, not all are fortunate enough to be far-traveled questers such as you two."

"Don't get to believing that all quests are fun and

games, old man," Hero cautioned. "Me, sometimes I get heartily sick of them!"

"And me!" said Eldin. "Sometimes I think: wouldn't it be grand just to sit absolutely still for a thousand years?"

"Exactly!" said the iceman. "And if such as you. can become bored, jaded, dissatisfied, how then the little fisherman—"

"Like Cuff?" said Hero.

"—and the potter and the quarrier, who've never seen beyond a patch of ocean or the hot walls of a kiln or the steep sides of a hole in the ground? And so, in the far dim olden times, every now and then a man would climb Aran." He fell silent, concentrated on his work, shaped Eldin's elbow where it joined his knee.

"Eh?" said the Wanderer at length. "I don't think I follow." He felt an unaccustomed stiffness in his arm, the one that propped up his chin, and grunted his discomfort. But other than that he kept still.

"Maybe," the sculptor continued, "in the beginning, they came to broaden their horizons, to gaze across the dreamlands on lands afar, which they'd never see except from up here. Anyway, that's how it started . . .

"Now, my grandfather was no ordinary ice-cutter. He was a passionate man with a passionate skill. And yet he was compassionate, too. And he knew his talent was magical. He could not bear the loneliness, the boredom, the utter ennui of certain of his fellow men, men who grew old and withered despite the timelessness of Ooth-Nargai. Aye, and he could spot such men at once, for sooner or later they'd invariably enquire of him: 'What's it like, up on Aran?' "

"Is there a point to this story?" Hero suddenly asked, his teeth beginning to chatter. "Lord, I'm freezing! Are we daft, sitting here in the snow like this?"

The old man, working on Hero's sculpture, put a final touch to the jaw—and at once Hero's teeth grew still, almost as if they were frozen in position. "A point? Of course! For when he was asked about Aran, my grandfather would say: 'Aran is forbidden! Don't ask about it. It's not for you to know. No one climbs Aran except me, to cut the ice.' "

"Ah!" said Eldin. "It was him started the myth, then?"

"Because of his consuming compassion," answered the sculptor, "yes. He must be sure, you see, that only the most bitter men climbed Aran—only the ones in whom life's animation was dying! The ones without ambition, without aspiration, in whom nothing was left worth dreaming! Those for whom timelessness and changelessness had fused into one vast and dull and slothlike anathema! What matter to them if Aran were forbidden? What matter anything? They'd climb anyway, and damn the consequences! But did you say myth? No myth, my friends. Aran *is* forbidden—except to such as you!"

Eldon's feet and legs were finished, his thighs, too, also the arm and hand which cupped his chin. The Wanderer would now extend a finger to scratch an itch on his cheek, made so to do—discovered he could not! It seemed the blood had run out of his hand and arm, leaving only a cold numbness there.

The old man now returned to working on Hero, rapidly finished arms and shoulders and neck, also hands where they clasped knees. Following which Hero could only watch him from swiveling eyes, for his neck had suddenly stiffened into a cramp, doubtless from holding the same position too long. Except that now . . . now the alarm bells were clamoring that much louder and faster in the younger quester's mind. He'd seen, heard and felt much here, so that what he'd begun to suspect must at least be better than a guess.

He made a real effort to stand up then, and couldn't; only odd parts of him had feeling, remained in his control at all. And even those parts were rapidly succumbing to a cold, unfeeling rigidity. Here he sat beside his image, twinned, one of him carved in ice and the other human—*for the moment*!

And it was then, like a bright flash of lightning in his mind, that all became known to him. "You're making a big mistake." He started to blurt the words out, but stiffly, from one side of his half-frozen mouth. "Eldin and I, we're not bored with anything! Why, we've got more go in us than . . ."

But what they had more go in them than remained unboasted, for the iceman quickly touched Hero's statue on the lips and brought them to a perfect image of life—and simultaneously froze his actual mouth into complete immobility!

Eldin had been watching from the corner of his eye; he'd recognized the panic, now shut off, in Hero's voice. "What *is* going on?" he demanded, thoroughly alarmed. "What in the name of all that's—?"

The sculptor touched the Wanderer's statue's hair, Hero's statue, too, and etched their locks into icy replicas of life. And oh, the *cold* that seeped down from the roots of their hair into their brains then, and what sudden, frozen horror as they knew for a certainty their fate!

Tears flowed freely from the old man's eyes, freezing like pearls and rolling from his cheeks as hail. He knew they had not come here like the others, tired of an endless, changeless existence and more than ready to accept any alternative. But he also knew he couldn't let them go down again. Only turn these two loose, with tales of fabulous ice sculptures on the slopes of Aran, and to-morrow the people would come in their thousands! Of course, that would be the end of it: the selfless services of three generations of master icemen terminated. Services, yes—for surely it were better—

"Hero!" came a distant cry, soft on the tingly, downy air, startling the sculptor like the crack of a whip. "Eldin!"

What? The old iceman looked down the slope, saw a king's courier waving his arms at the edge of the ice. Looking up here, he'd see nothing of the ice statues, just snow and dazzle and the pair of seated questers, dark figures against a glaring background. He would not see the sculptor, not unless he stepped on to the ice—and he was not likely to do that, because the snow-slopes of Aran were forbidden.

Gaping, the old man turned back to the questers. But too late, they were stirring! And anyway, the courier had seen them, for as yet they were not turned to ice. Not quite. Another touch here, a stroke there . . . it had been *that* close! But too late now, too late . . .

And: *Too late!*: the old man's thoughts were imaged in Hero's mind, for he also had heard the courier's cry. Through ears of cold crystal he'd heard it, and his brittle brain had taken it in, and his faltering, freezing heart had given a lurch. Part of him said: *Go away, whoever you are. I've done with all that. I'm ice now, part of the permafrost, a glassy pimple on Aran's frosty face. I'm at peace with everything.*

But another part had been galvanized into a great start, had gasped and drawn air, had shouted (however silently): *No! I am NOT ice! I'm David Hero—Hero of Dreams!* And that part of him had won.

The snow went out of Hero's eyes, Eldin's too, and they creakingly lowered their heads and their gaze, staring down the slope. There the courier capered and waved.

"Hero! Eldin! Are you two going to sit around all day? My master has a mission for you. You're to report to him at once."

Hero stood up. Or rather, he slowly straightened his knees until his backside lifted and his body tilted forward, then straightened his waist until his hands slid from his knees along his thighs. Thin sheaths of ice cracked and fell from various joints and limbs as he moved them, and the first tinglings of returning life told him all would be well.

"I said—" the courier shouted.

"We heard what you said!" Hero shouted back, which came out as a series of croaks.

"Eh?" the courier cocked his head on one side.

Hero cleared his throat, tried again. "You go on ahead. Tell him we're coming." And as the courier shrugged and turned back down toward the tree line: "How'd you know we were here, anyway?"

"I've been looking for you all morning," the messenger called over his shoulder. "Tatter Nees told me where you'd be. But I don't think I'd better report that to my master!"

"Thanks!" Hero yelled.

"Good old Tatter!" Eldin grunted. He'd struggled to his feet and clumsily brushed himself down, sending thin splinters of ice flying as he shook his massive frame. This proved effective, but not a little painful, too. "Ow!" said the Wanderer, and several other things which don't need recording. Then he glanced down the slope at the courier. "Do you know what the king wants with us?" he shouted.

"Something about a job in Inquanok. You'd better

hurry . . ." And with that the courier departed, scrambling away down the slope.

The echoes of their shouting slowly trembled into silence; it stopped snowing; the questers looked first at each other, then all about at the frozen humps under the snow.

"Inquanok?" said the Wanderer presently. "That's a drab, bleak sort of place to go a-questing, isn't it?"

"You'll hear no complaint from me," said Hero. "Not this time. But first—"

It took them only a few minutes to find what they were looking for. The other statues on the slope were under an inch or so of snow; this one, however, carried only the finest dusting. They clambered over the slope toward him, and saw that he was three.

Then, when they'd brushed snow from the other two, they understood. The three were dressed all alike, and they were obviously blood-related, but there were differences which made each one an individual. Grandfather, father, and son. "Son" was the one with only a film of snow. There'd been no time for any more.

Eldin growled in his throat, began to draw his straight sword—and Hero stopped him. "Vandal!" the younger quester softly accused. "What? You'd deface a work of art such as this?"

"Deface?" the Wanderer glared. "I'd destroy 'em, all three! Especially him. Why, he looks halfway pleased with himself!"

"No need, old friend." Hero shook his head. "He's destroyed himself. His time had come, and he knew it. He'd probably wanted to do it for a long time, and we were the one small push he needed to send him over the edge. He must have known we weren't right for this place. When he sensed we were coming, he tried to carve our images and got only the roughest outlines; but he'd done much better with Kuranes, which shows how close the king came at one time!"

Eldin caught on. "We weren't right for this place . . ." he mused. "But the old iceman himself, he was."

Hero nodded. "As for the look on his face: pleased with himself, did you say? Looks more to me like he's just sighed a long, last grateful sigh—and it's frozen there forever."

They made their way back to the ice steps. "And this one?" the Wanderer stood, sword in hand, beside the image of the Lord of Ooth-Nargai.

"Leave it be," said Hero. "If there's a sort of sympathetic magic in these things . . . I'd hate to think we were the ones brought some sort of doom down on old Kuranes. And who are we to decide a man's destiny, anyway? You never know, p'raps he *will* want to come up here one day—and maybe the old iceman has a son of his own, eh? You know: to carry on the line, and the work?"

Frustrated, Eldin returned to his own ice sculpture. "Well, this at least is one destiny I can decide!" he declared.

"That I'll grant you," said Hero, coming up behind. "These really don't belong here at all." With great grunting heaves they wrested their images from their bases and threw them flat.

And with a great deal more courage than skill, the pair steered their amazing sledges down across the ice, less rapidly across scree and rock faces, shudderingly into the heart of the trees on Aran's lower slopes. From there they continued on foot, and as the statues melted behind them, so their steps grew lighter along the leafy way . . .

AUGEREN

David Hero's sudden exclamation—"Eldin!"—caused the older dreamer to start. He'd been dozing by their fire, while Hero had sat lost in his own thoughts, peering deep into the flickering flames.

"Eh? What? Did you call out, lad? Whazzup?" Eldin the Wanderer cast fearfully about in the firelight, saw nothing amiss, shrugged the blanket off his broad shoulders and reached for his sword anyway. "Was I asleep?"

"Eldin!" said Hero again, more quietly this time, and offered a decisive nod of his head.

The other, still only half-awake, frowned his puzzlement. "Of course I am!" he said. "Who'd you think I was?"

"Funk and Wagnalls!" the younger dreamer delightedly slapped his thigh, tossed another broken branch onto the fire. "Or maybe Chambers Twentieth Century?" He held up a finger, grinned knowingly.

Eldin was wide awake now. "Huh!" he scowled. "A joke's a joke and that's understood. Nothing wrong with a bit of horseplay. I was nodding off and you startled me awake. But what's all this Funk and Wagnalls stuff? Not like you to burst out cursing in the middle of the night. Are you sure you're all right, lad? Or maybe *you* were dreaming, too, eh?"

"Dreaming?" Hero stopped grinning. "Not a bit of it. It's just that I remembered something, that's all. From the waking world, I think. A book I used to own—a book of words!"

"Oh? Curse-words?"

"The *meaning* of words!" said Hero. "Eldin!"

"Yes?"

"No, no! Not *you* Eldin. The *word* Eldin."

"Daft as a brush," the older dreamer declared with no lack of certainty. "P'raps I'd best stay awake in case you go for my throat in the night!"

"Look," Hero sighed resignedly. "Names aren't just names, you know—they are also words which contain meanings. My own name, f'rinstance: Hero. Now what's a hero, eh?"

"Someone brave, daring, rescuer of maidens in distress," Eldin shrugged. "Answerer of calls beyond duty, dragon-slayer, quester!"

"Right!" Hero jumped up, strode to and fro. "And when you think of me, Hero, what do you get? I mean, how do I fit the pattern?"

"Loosely," said Eldin. "Mainly chicken, seducer of distressed maidens, dragon runner-away-from, quester at a price."

"Oaf!" Hero snorted.

"Tired oaf," Eldin corrected him. "I was just about to start kipping in earnest, when you—"

"Forget it!" Hero snapped, cutting him short. "What's in a name, eh? I mean, if you don't want to know the meaning of your name—if you see nothing of any importance in the source or lineage of your character—then just forget it . . ."

He came back to the fire, stood over Eldin and

scowled at him for a while. Then he threw himself down in his own place and yanked his blanket over himself. "Good *night*!" he snarled.

Eldin scratched his chin, frowned at the figure huddled on the other side of the fire. Hero had him hooked and Eldin knew it. Now the younger dreamer would probably make him beg for an explanation; Eldin would lose face, which the other would greatly relish. Also, Hero had doubtless dreamed up a silly origin for Eldin's name. Here in Earth's dreamlands "Eldin" was synonymous now with wanderlust, chiefly (Eldin liked to think) because it was *his* name, his dream-name. What he'd been called in the waking world was lost forever now, an entire dimension away. He couldn't remember, and only very rarely felt a yearning to know. Here he was Eldin the Wanderer, and that was good enough. Except—

"Very well," he capitulated gruffly. "So be it . . . What's it mean?" He got up, stretched, stepped round the fire and prodded Hero with a booted toe. "Eh, eh? Since you've started this silliness you might as well finish it. Except, be warned: if you've made my name something oafish, it'll very likely warrant a clout!"

Hero snored loudly.

"What?" Eldin booted him again, heavier this time. "No one goes to sleep that fast! Up, up! I want to know the meaning of my bloody name!"

Hero sat up, gave a deep sigh. "We've a busy day tomorrow," he said. "Trekking in unfamiliar territory, and an unknown monster—a maneater—to track, trap or kill. We should both get some sleep."

"Up, I said!" Eldin repeated. "I *was* sleeping, remember? And anyway, how'll I be able to sleep with this on my mind?"

Hero got up, put his hands behind his back, ambled to

the edge of the firelight and back. "On your what?" he inquired. "Your 'mind'?" He sniffed and cocked a wondering eyebrow. Then he looked over his shoulder into the darkness beyond the fire's glow and shivered. *"Brrr!"* he said, his tone shuddery.

"Eh? Brrr!? Don't change the subject!" said Eldin sharply. "And anyway, it isn't cold tonight."

"Nothing to do with the cold, old lad," Hero shook his head. "Goosebumps."

"They don't, you know," Eldin returned.

"Eh?"

"Geese. I've seen 'em fight, heard 'em honk, watched 'em fly south for the winter. But I never saw a one bump."

"The fact is"—Hero ignored Eldin's wit—"I'm restless. It's this quest of ours—call it a mission—that Kuranes has sent us on. It's like nothing we ever did before. I was thinking about it, rolling his—its?—name around in my head: 'Augeren,' and that started me off on the meaning of names."

Eldin hoisted himself up on to the horizontal branch of a dead, toppled tree and dangled his feet. He snapped off a smaller branch and tossed it into the fire, watched the sparks leap and the flames jiggle. The circle of light expanded a little, and night's shadows drew back.

Hero turned his back on the dark, gazed earnestly at Eldin. "Fact is," he said again, "I don't like this job we're on one little bit. I've a feeling it's a sight more sinister than it seems—and after what Kuranes has told us, that's saying a lot! 'Augeren' ... *brrr!*"

Eldin hadn't said much about their current job until now, but he had given it plenty of thought—and he knew exactly what Hero meant. Not about this silly "meaning of names" business, but about the actual nature of the beast they pursued. Call it a beast, or

"Augeren," or a *Thing*; call it whatever you liked. It still came down to the same thing in the end: it was unknown but seemed all-knowing; it had been experienced (horribly) but never seen; it struck like lightning out of the darkness at totally innocent victims; and it *always* killed. And it ate. But most monstrous of all was *how* it killed and *what* it ate . . .

As for Augeren's hunting-ground:

Between Inquanok and Leng—that northern plateau of ill-repute which sits like some vast and forbidden iceberg at dreamland's one suspected pole—there stands a range of gaunt gray peaks no dreamer has ever been known to scale. Or if someone has climbed them, he never lived to return and report the fact. The range forms an eyrie for Shantak-birds, who build their massive nests on ledges halfway up; while the topmost pinnacles are eaten into by caves which, according to legend, are the gloomy resting-, nesting-, or mating-places of night-gaunts.

Shunned by many, still the gaunt gray peaks are regarded by most as a blessing, a provision of beneficent gods. If men cannot climb them and so proceed into awful, mist-shrouded Leng, likewise no thing of Leng is likely to attempt the feat in reverse. But between the foot of the gray range and Inquanok, there in the misty twilight valleys and foothills where they slope at first greenly, then stonily oceanward—with the onyx quarries of Inquanok on every hand and farms scattered sparsely here and there about—this was the region of the terror. This was where it had started, as if seeping slowly out of Leng and across the gray peaks, until recently it had reached Urg and crossed into Inquanok itself.

As for what "it" was: there was no lack of clues, but paradoxically no jot of evidence to point to any known predator. It was, indeed, the Unknown.

The thing took its victims in darkness. Here the young, favored daughter of a farmer, carried off soundlessly from her bed and never more seen alive; there the young son of a quarrier, snatched from some makeshift shack at the rim of one of the deep quarries and bundled away in the night. A Shantak, perhaps? But how could so vast a creature possibly sneak down against the stars and the moon unseen and enter *into* a farmhouse or quarrier's shack? Low stone houses and wooden shacks do not have doors or windows sizeable enough to accommodate Shantaks, not without considerable structural damage!

What about Lengites, the horned, wide-mouthed, slant-eyed almost-humans known to inhabit or infest Leng? Or even a Lengite-Shantak collaboration? The Lengites were said to tame and even occasionally ride the hippocephalic Shantak; so couldn't one of those squat, cloven-hooved horrors be the raider? Well possible, but unlikely. The men of Inquanok are wont to make slaves of (or do much worse things to) serious wrongdoers of whatever race; in the present circumstances, only let them sniff an almost-human in the vicinity ... he'd be strung up at once, and almost certainly without trial.

Night-gaunts might seem the best bet, but were they really? There was now a body of evidence to show that they were not the monsters previously supposed; quite apart from which they had no faces, hence no mouths, ergo no "appetites" as such. And on that last note they were definitely out, as were Shantaks and almost-humans. Not that these last-mentioned had no feeding habits; indeed they did, and pretty awful ones at that. But the unknown thing's appetite was such as to leave other messy eaters agog, possibly even turned to jelly.

For Augeren, who or whatever he was, ate only bone marrow!

"Bone marrow!" said Hero, as if reading Eldin's thought. "*Brrrr!* To have the juices sucked out of your very bones!"

Eldin felt a shudder go up his spine. "Enough of the *brrrs*," he pleaded. "You've got me at it now! And anyway that last one of yours was over the top—it had four 'r's." He jumped down from his branch, faced his younger companion across the sputtering fire.

The difference in their ages would be maybe fifteen years, perhaps a little more. Eldin could be anything between forty-five and fifty years of age—hardly an old lad—and Hero at thirty was a deal more than a mere teenager. Both of them were prone to gross exaggeration, however, especially with regard to each other. Hero needled at Eldin's maturity as if he were well into advanced senility, and the Wanderer carped at Hero's comparative youth for all the world as if he were still in diapers! To any outsider their constant jibing and mutually acid sense of humor would appear most disconcerting. But it was their way; it meant nothing; they loved each other better than brothers.

In appearance:

Eldin had a scarred, bearded, quite unhandsome and yet not unattractive face which housed surprisingly clear blue eyes. Stocky and heavy, but somehow gangly to boot, there was something almost apish about him; yet his every move and gesture (when he was not merely clowning) hinted at a sensitivity and keen intelligence behind his massive physical strength. He usually dressed in black, while Hero affected a garb of dark brown.

Hero was tall, well-muscled, as blond in dreams as he'd once been in the waking world. His eyes were a lighter blue than Eldin's; but they could darken very quickly in a fury, or take on a dangerous steely glint in a tight spot. His nature in fact was usually easy-going; but while he loved songs a fair bit and girls a great deal, still he was wizard-master of any sword in a fight, and the knuckles of his fists were like crusty knobs of rock. He was very different from Eldin, yes, but the lands of Earth's dreams occasionally make for strange traveling companions.

But they were not entirely disparate; what they had in common was this: they both were infected with un- quenchable wanderlust, and they were both ex-waking worlders. Extinct (extinguished, anyway) on the purely physical plane, they now existed as questers in the lands of Earth's dreams. Only the occasional flash of memory served to remind that there'd ever been a life before this one; and rare as such insights were, still they could prove poignant, so that the pair usually tried as best they might to put the waking world far from mind. They could never go back there; it was a world of uttermost mystery and fantasy to them now. Sometimes they even argued about the very existence of that other, rather more mundane place.

They had been visiting Celephais, down and very nearly out, as usual, when King Kuranes of Ooth-Nargai had called them to his Cornish manor-house there. For years without number Kuranes—himself an ex-waking worlder, now a power in the dreamlands—had been working for political liaison with Inquanok, that most guarded, secretive, misty place, far to the north across the strange blue waters of the Cerenerian Sea. But the men of Inquanok seemed mainly cold and aloof, sharp- featured and suspicious of outsiders, proud of a heritage dating back (according to rumor, in which the dream- lands abound) to certain of the gods themselves. And

truth to tell their features were not unlike those of a ti-
tan and nameless god, carved in ages beyond memory
into Mount Ngranek's stony face. They held to strange,
sometimes dubious worship; their rites called for strict
adherence and their laws were inviolable, carrying
heavy penalties; their Veiled King was rumored to be
un- if not inhuman, as were the priests of the great temple of certain "Elder Ones," who were *not* the whole-
some Elder Gods worshipped by the venerable Atal of
Ulthar.

But Inquanok's merchants were human, certainly, and
its taverners and quarriers, and for a long time now a secret circle of responsible citizens had questioned—
however privately and in whispers—the autocracy of
the Veiled King and his priestlings, always working in-
directly but purposefully toward their overthrow. All the
dreamlands wanted Inquanok onyx; increased commerce
might bring prosperity to many, pave the way for strong
alliances, dispel mystery, open up all the lands of dream
to the onyx city's sailors and merchantmen . . . were it
not for the Veiled King's policy of insularity, the fact
that Inquanok must be a land kept ever apart.

The Veiled King had not been interested in tales of
terror and monstrous abductions and murders from
Inquanok's hinterland; indeed, it seemed doubtful that
such tales had even reached his ears, for in his vast palace and forbidden temple he had little to do with common men and their problems. But as for the common
men themselves . . .

When the daughter of a well-to-do merchant was
taken from her father's rich house on Inquanok's very
outskirts, and left some miles away in the desert for the
drear dawn to discover dead and drained of marrow . . .
that has been the turning point. Local help was nowhere
available: police or other custodians of the law there

were none, for all miscreants were left to the justice of the Veiled King's priests and palace officials. Petitions to the palace were productive of nothing, were not even answered. Privately organized parties of four or five good men would go out into the deserts or other wild places and return days later with nothing to report—or, worse, with one of their number missing. The terror did not restrict itself to children.

But with this last atrocity fresh in the minds of Inquanok's people—the death of this innocent little girl, her body and bones all drilled through and juices sucked out—finally it was time to seek assistance from outside. Kuranes' long-term attempts at liaison and trans-Cerenerian alliance were remembered: a message of entreaty was sent in secret to Celephais, addressed to the Lord of Ooth-Nargai, Celephais, and the Sky Around Serannian himself. In other words, to Kuranes.

And who better? Hadn't he been mainly responsible for dreamland's victory in the War of the Mad Moon? Wasn't it Kuranes who'd successfully defended sky-floating Serannian against Zura of Zura's plot to topple that aerial island to its doom? And didn't he from time to time employ certain sellswords, questers who'd tackle any job at a price? If Kuranes couldn't help, then who could?

"Can you remember," asked Hero now, "what Kuranes told us of this Augeren?"

"He told us several things," Eldin grunted. "None of them pleasant. A young man walking his girl near Urg was buffeted on the head. He came to almost at once, heard his young lady's faint cry of horror from a misty copse, stumbled to her rescue. This, of course, is assumption, for he did not live to tell it himself. But while he ran he yelled for help; several cotters were startled up, came out with lanthorns; there followed something of a hue and cry. The girl was found almost at once, unharmed but shocked witless by something she'd seen, the closeness of her shave. Her young man—he was finished, all bones intact except for one, which alas was his skull. It had been drilled right through, his brain pierced. Doubtless the monster would have sucked his marrow, except for the cotters charging about with their lanthorns. As for the girl . . ."

"Go on," said Hero quietly, his face ruddy in the firelight.

"She had a bruise or two, was otherwise unharmed— physically. But in her pretty head . . . whatever she saw, it robbed her of her senses. And they haven't been returned to her. Afterward she spoke—or drooled and dribbled—of 'eyes' and a 'mouth like a corkscrew,' and of something 'chalk white' and 'powerful'—something that sobbed as it sank a shining proboscis deep in her lover's brain. And it sobbed: 'My name is Augeren. Augeren, aye, and I hate you all!' "

"Lord!" said Hero, barely containing a *brrr*. "How you can lay it on when you're in the mood! But you're right: the things that girl said, however delirious or crazed she was/is, are very, very nasty . . ." He stood up straighter, squared his shoulders. "Hah! But back there in Celephaïs, in Kuranes' manor-house, what did 'nasty' mean to us, eh? What did we care for 'nasty'? What, after some of the things we've been up against?" He slumped. "Except we're no longer in Celephaïs. Two or three miles thataway"—he pointed roughly south—"lies Inquanok the city. Thataway, Urg. And a good day's march thataway"—(due north)—

"The gaunt gray peaks," Eldin cut in. "Home to

Shantaks and their mortal enemies the gaunts, barrier 'twixt sanity and Leng."

"Or once-barrier?" suggested Hero. And quickly continued: "But here's us anyway, outsiders in these parts, paid for in golden tonds and pointed in the right direction—the most dangerous direction, obviously—then turned loose and forgotten. Questers, sellswords, mercenaries: riff-raff, by the lofty standards of these god-descended flint-faced Inquanokkies. And if we succeed, rid the land of this Augeren, what then? Fêted, applauded, even clapped on the back and thanked most sincerely? Not a bit of it! Done our job, that's all. And if we fail?"

"We haven't failed yet," said Eldin. "Our reputations are safe so far."

"Reputations? What makes you think I'm worried about our reps?" Hero narrowed his eyes, cocked his head on one side. "I meant what if we fail in the worst possible way?"

"You mean if he outsmarts us, this Augeren?" Eldin scowled. "Unthinkable! We don't get beaten. Besides, we're two and he's only one."

"How do we know he's only one?" Hero questioned. "He could be an entire damned flock or pack for all we know! He *could* be something out of Leng, grown tired of a diet of horned-ones and now comes to try humans instead."

"Leng-thing? Flock? Pack? *Pah!* And what do we care for overwhelming odds?" Eldin puffed himself up, thumped his chest once. "Why we've laughed in the faces of armies of zombies, almost-humans, termen, the lot!"

"But this," Hero insisted, "is an Unknown Thing or Things that can drill into you and suck you bone dry—literally!"

Eldin puffed himself up more yet . . . and let it all out in a huge *"Pheeew!"* He scratched his beard and sat down close to the fire. "All right, you've convinced me," he said. "Which way's home?"

Hero kicked more dead wood on the blaze, walked round the leaping flames in a wide circle with his hands behind his back, and: "What else did Kuranes say?" he asked the other.

Eldin sighed. "Anyone'd think you weren't there!"

"Ah, but you tell it so well—and I can listen to you and think at the same time."

"Posses can't get near it," said Eldin. "Or rather, they get too near! The minute a posse sets up camp for the night—as soon as they set a watch—*zzzt!*" he made a slicing motion mid-beard. "One gone watchman . . ."

Hero slowly nodded, "All-seeing, aye," he said. "The thing *knows* when folk go out after it. It *knows* what they're up to. All-seeing and yet unseen, except by its marrowless victims and that one poor loony lass it spoke to and drove mad. And then there's one last thing we know about it."

"Oh?" Eldin watched Hero circle the fire and disappear out of the corner of his eye as he stepped round behind him. In the next moment Hero's hand fell like a grapple on Eldin's shoulder, hard as iron, gripping the cords of muscle between neck and shoulder proper. It was so sudden that Eldin gave a violent start.

"Darkness!" Hero whispered hoarsely in Eldin's ear. "It doesn't like the light, strikes only at night."

"Damn me, lad!" Eldin shook himself loose. "Haven't I enough gray hairs?" He stood up, looked all about in the fire's glow. Beyond the firelight was pitch black, made blacker by the very fire itself. Black, silent night, and a thin leprous mist crawling on the ground. Eldin stooped, fed the flames liberally with wood gathered earlier, said: "So what are you leading up to? You said you'd been playing with its name, Augeren. So what did that get you?"

Hero continued to prowl in a circle. "Things linger," he said, "in mind. I suppose hung over from the waking world."

"Déjà vu," said Eldin.

"Eh?"

"Never mind, another hangover. I'm saying I know what you're talking about, that's all."

"I mean," said Hero, almost to himself, "I don't really know if it applies, but 'Augeren' does things to me. Even the first time I heard it, my mind sort of shied away from it. In one tongue, Augen means eyes, I think. And Aug*er*en comes pretty close. So is that what this thing really calls itself: The Eyes?"

Eldin sat down again, pulled at an earlobe. "I begin to see what you're getting at. That girl mentioned eyes, too . . ." He nodded, added: "A seeing eye, gifted with night-vision, seeing in the darkness as clearly as in daylight."

"More clearly!" said Hero. "Light hurts it—frightens it, anyway. It fled the cotters' lanthorns still unfed."

"A fly-the-light then," Eldin was deeply involved with the puzzle now. "A vampire—but a very specialized vampire."

"No taste for blood," Hero supplied, "but bone marrow."

"And . . . equipped to get it!" Eldin snapped his fingers. " 'Auger'!"

"Bravo!" said Hero, but grimly, quietly.

"An auger's a wood-boring tool, isn't it? A borer, anyway. It makes holes to prepare the wood—"

"—or bone—"

"—for nails or screws—"

"—or for a proboscis."

"An auger, yes!" said Eldin. "You turn it this way and that—left and right, left and right—applying pressure, driving the point deep. Boring without splitting the wood."

"Or without spilling the marrow."

"Weird!" Eldin gave a little shiver.

"And that's not all."

"Oh?"

"What about 'augury'?"

"Ah! Yes! Of course! A prognostication, a portent, vision of a rune-caster or soothsayer. From 'augur,' someone who reads the future." He frowned. "Of course, the spelling's up the creek."

"But the meaning applies," said Hero. "No wonder they've never seen him, can't catch him. Not if he can read the future."

"How much of the future?"

"The immediate future, anyway," Hero answered. "Which gave him the edge over the cotters, allowed him to make a narrow escape."

"Ah, yes! He ran from them."

"Or flew, or flopped. From their lanthorns."

"*Hmm,*" Eldin mused. "A far-sighted marrow-sucking chalk-white ESP-endowed *wampir* with a bad case of photophobia."

Hero sat down, found a nice straight piece of dry branch and made to toss it on the fire—then paused. Instead, he took out his knife, began whittling one end into a long sharp point.

"Stake?" Eldin inquired.

Hero said nothing, continued to work.

Eldin took out his own knife, seated himself, followed the other's example with another piece of wood. After a while he said, "I wish *I* could."

"Eh?"

"See the future. Just a little bit of it. Say, through the night to morning. That would be enough—for now, anyway."

In the utter darkness of an old, worked-out quarry, in a cave not two miles away, Augeren sat and communed with the night. One of his eyes was skinned-over, blind, like the vestigial orb of some queer cave-dwelling frog, the other glittered with many facets, seemed almost metallic, insect-like.

Augeren was hungry. In his mouth, his great wedge of a tongue turned this way and that, oscillating the rasps along its sides; saliva dripped from its hollow needle-tip.

In the facets of his glittering eye, myriad mirror-images showed a near-distant scene: a pair of questers, huddled beside their fire. They whittled away and their shavings went into the fire, which in any case would burn all night. Augeren blinked and the picture disappeared, his eye grew dull; he blinked again and a new picture was framed in myriad reflections. Three miles away, toward Urg, a quarrier and his son sat over their small fire in the lee of a mighty boulder and talked in whispers. The father swigged liberally from a bottle of muth-dew, his voice was already slurred. Nearby, a small stock of damp sticks would not last out the night.

Augeren blinked again and the picture was wiped from his eye. He was hungry. He stirred himself. Something ghastly white moved in the darkness. The cave echoed a single sob . . .

* * *

A drear day followed for Hero and Eldin, one which hardly brightened at all past dawn, but continued the same, in gray drizzle and rolling banks of mist, until evening. Then the weather changed (albeit slightly) for the better; the descending sun, falling far to the south-west, seemed finally to burn its way through cloud-layers high and low, drying out the steamy earth; evening's first stars became visible like ghost-lights in the sky, phosphorescent fire trapped high overhead. Or, as Eldin described it:

"It's like lying on your back in a bowl of thin milk, staring up at fireflies floating on the surface."

"Never tried it," said Hero, "but I'm sure you're right. Just as soggy, too!"

They'd put on a change of clothes, were drying out their first sets on a pole over the remains of a cooking fire built in the mouth of a shallow cave. Supper had consisted of roasted rabbit and crusts of dry bread, washed down with tepid tea: satisfying, if not especially savory. Now, as night drew in, the fire was dying into its own embers, and the pair had no plans to replenish it. Its low flicker illuminated the mouth of their cave with yellow light.

One hundred yards away in the same quarry, there was another cave, deeper and darker than this one. But then, there were many caves. The quarry was honey-combed with old onyx works.

"How long has it been?" Hero asked morosely, of no one in particular.

Eldin answered anyway. "Four days and three nights, this being the fourth. On the first night we lost our yak."

"*You* lost our yak!" Hero accused. "Tethering it to the merest twig like that. Ate the twig and bolted, didn't it." It wasn't a question, just a statement of fact. "We were lucky we'd unloaded the beast."

"Trained!" Eldin scowled.

"*Huh!*"

"Trained, I tell you!" the Wanderer insisted. "That damned Inquanokky who sold us the scrawny beast . . . I'll wager he's sold that same yak a dozen times before ever we bought it! And the first chance it gets—off like a homing pigeon. Right now, it'll be back in a field with the rest of the pack."

"Herd," said Hero.

" 'Course you did," said Eldin. "Else you're deaf as a post."

Hero ignored him. "Second night, we *could* have had a room at that farmhouse."

Eldin shuffled a bit where he sat. "Well, we did all right," he said under his breath.

"We slept in a leaky barn!" Hero barked. "Because *you* kept ogling the old boy's daughters—who were ugly as hell anyway!"

Eldin knew it was true so didn't argue this point. Instead he made one of his own. "Now *last* night," he said, "that must have been the worst of the lot! It drizzled on and off and neither one of us got a decent kip, taking turns to watch and all. Dry one minute and soaked the next, turning myself round by the fire to warm all sides—like a chicken on a spit. This morning I felt three-quarters poached! You and your too-fertile imagination. Augen and augers and auguries, indeed!"

"It was uncomfortable, guaranteed," said Hero. "But this morning we both had marrow in our bones, right? It was the fire kept him away—"

"—if he was anywhere near—"

"—and the fact that one of us was alert at all times."

"Eh? Alert?" Eldin looked mildly surprised. "Ah, alert! Oh, yes—of course."

"*What?*" Hero howled, jumping up and nearly cracking his head on the cave's ceiling. "Tell me you're joking!"

"Er, I'm joking. Yes," said Eldin.

"Tell me right now, this moment!"

"But I already—"

"Are you saying you didn't keep your watch? Is that what you're saying?"

"I mean, I didn't lie down, you understand," he held up his hands placatingly. "I *was* sitting up!"

"Sitting up? Sitting up asleep? It's a wonder you weren't *eaten* up! And me lying there, unconcerned, because I knew that good old faithful Eldin was keeping watch!"

"We had a damn great roaring *fire*!" Eldin finally exploded. "Old Augeren's afraid of light, remember?"

"But we don't know that for sure."

"We know it sure enough that tonight we're deliberately luring the bugger by *not* keeping a fire!"

"Tonight's different," Hero said, his disgust visibly mounting. "Tonight we've a cave at our backs. Tonight we'll be awake—both of us—all night. Or will we? I mean, I'm damned if I know whether to trust you any more. I can't believe it, don't *want* to believe it. Sleeping on the job like that. You, my dearest, most faithful—" He nearly choked on that last word, turned away.

Eldin felt bad, stood up. It seemed he'd really done it this time. It wasn't deliberate—never that—but the fire had been so warm! "I mean," he said, "—damn me, lad, but I didn't actually, well, *sleep*. I just probably nodded off a bit, that's all."

Hero kept his back turned, allowed his head to droop tiredly, let his broad shoulders slump. He made no answer, but merely sighed.

"I mean—" Eldin was desperate now, "is there no way I can make it up to you?"

Hero's shoulders slumped more yet.

"I'd do almost anything . . ."

"Anything?" Hero straightened up a little but didn't look at the other.

"Anything, aye," said Eldin gruffly. He put his hand tentatively on the younger quester's shoulder.

Hero turned and grinned—a grin like the jerk of the line that fixes the hook in the fish's mouth. "Very well," he said. "There's an hour yet to full dark. I'm getting an hour's shut-eye while *you* keep watch. Wake me up when the last embers are dead, right?"

"Why . . . you . . . *you!*" Eldin hissed. "Of all the—"

Hero's eyes widened in warning. He tilted his head up and out into the night, said: "*Shhh! Listen!*"

Eldin held his breath, listened, heard . . . something!

"He's . . . that way," Hero whispered, casually stooping, pouring water from the kettle on to the fire's embers. Steam rose up, hissing to match his whispering: *"Probably hasn't seen you, just me. The night wind's from his direction, so he's unlikely to have heard us either. Keep back, out of sight. Let him come. And when he jumps me, you jump him!"*

Hero was right. The older quester stood further back in the cave and to one side of the fire, and the sound—a slithering of pebbles in the dark, a furtive scraping of stone—had come from along the foot of the old diggings. Who or whatever it was, out there in the night, might not have seen Eldin—but he would certainly have seen Hero.

Eldin shrank back, became one with the shadows of the cave. His sword came out of its scabbard easy as silk, soundlessly. All clowning was done now, buffooning and mock-arguments put aside. This was for real. When it came to stealth, Eldin was like a cat in the dark. And when it came to acting, never a one like Hero.

He was acting now, playing the role of the lone traveler, maybe a prospector, making camp out here in the misty night after a long day's panning or grubbing. He stood tall, threw up his arms and stretched, apparently easing his joints. Then he yawned, long and audibly, and scratched himself for a moment before hunkering down and pulling a blanket round his shoulders. He hadn't killed the fire completely; red embers made his face ruddy, glinted on the steel he shielded with his blanket. In one hand a knife, and in the other a sharpened stake!

Eldin couldn't help but admire his partner. Cool as a cucumber, Hero, but sharp as a razor. Why, just listen to him now: whistling away to himself, however tunelessly, and keeping away the night's evil spirits. All except one . . .

There came more sounds: shale sliding, a low panting—a sob! Then—

Something rushed, floundered out of the dark. A ragged thing, long arms reaching. Swift as thought, it fell on Hero!

Hero tried to turn as the thing crushed his huddled figure down. He tried to direct his sharp stake; failed, as desperately strong arms clutched him tight.

Heart in mouth, Eldin pounced.

"Son! Son! Is that you?" the ragged apparition hugged Hero in its smothering embrace. "Ah, my boy—my *dear* boy! I thought—"

Eldin grabbed the gabbling thing's hair and yanked; at the same time, Hero got his muscles bunched under him and came erect. The night-comer was sent flying, sprawling, and in the next moment the questers were on him. Eldin's sword went aloft, twin-gripped in hands like a pair of hams; Hero's stake was poised on high as he slid on his knees in scree and pebbles beside . . .

Beside the prone body of a pale, frightened, red-eyed man!

Still taking no chances, Eldin lowered the point of his sword to the stranger's throat. Hero balanced his stake over the man's heart, applied enough pressure to hold it there.

The red eyes in the white mask of a face went from Hero to Eldin, back to Hero. "Not . . . not my son?" said the stranger, quite obviously a man of Inquanok. Tears welled up in the corners of his eyes. "Then he's surely dead!"

Hero tossed his stake aside, put away his knife, cradled the sharp-featured, strong-backed quarrier in his arms. The man sobbed like a child. Eldin, less certainly, sheathed his sword.

"Dead?" said the Wanderer. "Your son? I don't know about that, but *you* certainly came close!"

"Careful, old lad," Hero's voice was low. "Show some compassion. He's about at wit's end."

"My son! My poor boy—taken by Augeren!" the man sobbed. Blindly he pushed Hero aside, crawled wearily to the fire's embers, let his unashamed tears fall into them. Behind those tears, his eyes were shrouded in horror.

Hero and Eldin stared at each other, followed their visitor to the fire. Hero blew on the embers, got some fresh sticks of dry timber going. As the shadows fled the cave, he said: "You'll be hungry, perhaps?"

"Starved," the stranger answered. "I've spent the whole dreary day searching for my boy." His eyes focused. He looked at Hero and Eldin and slowly his gaze turned bitter. "You'll be the two outsiders, questers come to kill the beast. *Hah!*"

Hero gave him dried meat, filled the kettle from a skin and put it on the fire. "We have to find him, before we can kill him," he said.

"Anyway," said Eldin, "don't go blaming us for your son's disappearance, or death, or whatever. We weren't with him. You were!"

The man hung his head, sobbed between his knees.

Hero gave Eldin a dig in the ribs with his elbow, asked: "Did you actually see this Augeren? Maybe you'd better tell us all of it . . ."

The stranger got himself under control, ate meat and a little dry bread. Then, while Eldin brewed tea and Hero built the fire a little higher, he told his tale.

"I'm not actually a quarrier," he began, "but I do have an eye for onyx. My name's Geeler Maas, and I work for a handful of sculptors in Inquanok who carve figurines and other small, intricate ornaments. They'll accept only the finest onyx, which I supply. I find it in the old diggings, fragments too small to have any real commercial value—to your average quarrier's or merchant's standards, anyway. Sometimes I'll see a piece just lying there; at others there'll be a vein almost worked out, but showing a special luster only an expert can recognize. It's slim pickings, but I'm my own boss. My family eats well enough, anyway. My . . . my family . . ." And his mouth and chin quivered a little.

Hero passed him a small stone mug of hot tea. "Go on," he said, after a moment.

"I was training my son in the business," Geeler at last continued. "My son, Ilfer. One day, Ilfer Maas was going to be a dealer in fine marbles, rare onyxes and agates . . .

"Anyway, this was his fourth or fifth trip out with

me, and he was getting good at it. But pickings were especially poor this time, and we'd stayed out longer than normal. Last night, what with the miserable weather and all, I was in a bit of a mood. I'd got this bottle of muthdew to warm my bones, which I'd drawn from—just a drop, you understand—each night. Alas, last night I . . . may my ancestral gods forgive me!"

"You swigged the lot, eh?" Eldin guessed. "Well, and you'll not be the first who fell foul of muth!"

"When I woke up this morning," Geeler continued, "first light—Ilfer was gone. No sign of a struggle, just his blankets, empty, clay cold. He'd been gone for hours. I thought: 'Maybe he couldn't sleep! Or perhaps he's gone to fetch wood for a fire, or else just stretching his legs.' I called and called for him, wandering here and there, until I was forced to one final conclusion. Augeren had got him! After that . . . I chased about until I was near exhausted, yelled myself hoarse, maybe went a little mad. Then I saw your fire. And for a moment I thought, hoped, prayed . . .

"Did I see him, you ask? No one ever saw him, not and lived to tell, not sanely, anyway. You don't see him, don't hear him, never even know he's there. I know that now. Maybe if I hadn't drained that muth . . ."

"That's the hell of all tragedies," said Hero quietly. "They can never happen to you—until they do. We all think the same, act the same, like so many sheep. And we never know for sure which lamb's next for the slaughter."

"Well," Geeler stood up, "I thank you for your fire, your food, your comfort. But now I must get on. It's a long night ahead, and somewhere in one of these holes I'll find my boy. I may even find Augeren, and if I do—your job will be done for you there and then." He took out a long knife from under his ragged coat, its blade honed to a shimmer. "Whatever that damned thing is, if I find him, he's a goner!"

Hero came to his feet, laid a hand on Geeler's arm. "Easy, friend. Best by daylight. You don't know what you're going against."

"And do you know any better?"

Now Eldin spoke up: "We know that well-armed posses have lost strong men," he said. "And we know that the three of us together—in daylight—must surely do better than you alone by night."

Geeler Maas was fierce now, his teeth a bar of white in the shadow of his face where they ground the words out: "But Ilfer may still be alive! I *can't* wait till morning. I've wasted enough time as it is. Listen, I thank you both, and I know you mean well—but . . ."

"But you're going on anyway," said Hero.

"Your tea and this bite of food I've taken have given me strength. Aye, and I'm back in my right mind now. Oh, I was crazed for a while, granted, but now—all I want is to find my boy. Dead or alive. And if I find him dead—then I'll not rest until I've found Augeren!"

"Take this, then," said Hero. He handed Geeler a sharpened stake, of hard wood and with a point like a needle. "We think he's maybe a vampire, so this should be surer than your knife."

Geeler tucked the stake in his belt, nodded gratefully and began to turn away.

"Where'll you start?" growled Eldin. "And how will you light your way? Best take this." He gave Geeler a prepared torch of oil-soaked twigs tied tight about a green stick. "I suppose you've got flints?"

Again Geeler nodded. "You're good men," he said. "The best. As for where I'll start: right here. This is as good a place as any. This quarry is vast, with many hundred cavelets. I'll go in a circle. Might get back here by first light. Or might not . . ."

"Don't light the torch until you have to," Hero advised. "We think Augeren fears the light. If he's got your boy, and if he sees the torch, he could just up and run."

"A fly-the-light, aye," Geeler grunted. "I've heard that said before. Well then, I'll only light the torch if I find Ilfer. And if I find him dead, then I'll sit till the torch goes out and taunt Ilfer's murderer all through the night—or until he comes for me. And then it'll be him or me." He finished speaking, stood frowning wonderingly at what the questers were about.

Eldin had stuffed a pair of stakes in his own belt, armed himself with an unlighted torch. Hero had done the same, except he'd also applied a little oil to the curve of his Kledan sword, sliding it in and out of its scabbard with scarce a whisper.

"Well, that's us all fixed up then," said the younger quester. "Right, Geeler, which way will you take?"

"Eh? But I—"

"Listen," said Eldin, "this is how we make our living, remember? A daft way, sure enough, but we're good at it. And this is one job we've already been paid, or promised, for. What?—we should let you do it for us? And when it gets out how some onyx fancier has beaten us at our own game . . . We'd never live it down!"

"Damn right!" said Hero. But Geeler knew that wasn't the motive at all. There weren't any motives. They just wouldn't let him try it on his own, that was all.

"I don't know how to thank you," he said, "except—"

"That's thanks enough," Hero gruffly cut him short.

"Now tell us: is this quarry circular or what? How many exits has it got? We got here in the dark."

"So did I," said Geeler, "but I know the place like the back of my hand. Now look, this defile we're in is the entrance; it goes down a gentle ramp to the quarry proper, then widens out. The ground's uneven down there, and the entire dig is shaped like a kidney three hundred yards long overall. The distance between sides is maybe one hundred and twenty yards average. If you can climb you could get out almost anywhere, but it's dangerous by night. There are caves—forsaken explor-atory digs—everywhere in the face, some of them ex-tensive. And there are pitfalls, too, so go careful!"

"Away from the fire," said Eldin, "our eyes will soon grow accustomed to the dark."

"And raw onyx has a certain sheen in the night," Geeler added. "It can take on a sort of foxfire. On the other hand, shadows can seem bottomless. But now we have to get on. I'll go this way." Hugging the wall of rock at the side of the descending ramp, he moved off, was soon swallowed up by the darkness . . .

Hero and Eldin wasted no time.

As Geeler took his departure, they crossed to the far side of the ramp, began their descent along that wall. "Mad as hatters!" Eldin grumbled low in his throat as they went. "We have to be."

"Madder than that," Hero agreed. "What? Hatters are completely sane by comparison! But be quiet now. Quiet and quick turns the trick."

They reached the quarry's floor, began carefully ex-ploring the caves and niches opening on every hand.

At first the work was slow, laboriously careful, even timid. "Like looking for a wasp's nest," Eldin whisper-ingly observed. "And sometimes when you find it you wish you hadn't."

They went together into caves, waited moments until their eyes were somewhat accustomed, explored and finally left together. But apart from the slow drip of seeping water or the sudden scurry of a rat, they found nothing. "Augeren could be five miles from here." Hero quietly stated an irrefutable fact. "Or fifty."

"Why, after all," asked Eldin, "should the monster be right *here*? Why not any one of a million other places?"

They began to work faster, allowing a little distance to creep between them, choosing their own caves for individual exploration as they went. Then, halfway into the quarry, Hero just emerging from a shallow cave while Eldin was deep in a more complex one—

"Here!" came Geeler's hoarse shout from across the quarry. "Questers, here! I've found the boy's jacket!"

"Geeler, wait!" Hero at once called back. "Don't go on alone!"

"What? Eh? What?" came Eldin's startled inquiry, echoing loudly from the bowels of his cave.

"He's found Ilfer's jacket," Hero called back over his shoulder, as he loped silently across the quarry's rock-and boulder-strewn floor. Panting, he reached the opposite wall, called: "Geeler? Geeler? Where the hell—?"

"Hero?" came Eldin's cry, from what seemed a long way away. "Where are you?"

"Over here!" Hero called back. He skirted a massive boulder, saw a movement in the shadows. And: "Geeler?" he called softly. He stepped forward and something turned to face him.

"Geeler?" Hero tried to say again, even knowing it wasn't Geeler. But the word lodged in his throat, came out as the merest squeak. Faint light gleamed on features utterly alien. A monstrous fly's eye glittered; a wet wedge of quivering flesh and bone churned between distended, slavering jaws.

The unexpected, which should *not* have been unexpected, froze Hero's muscles into instant paralysis. For a moment only—but a moment was all it took.

"Hero? Geeler?" came Eldin's shout, and the sounds of his charging close by. "Damn me, a man could break his neck! Where in the name of all—?"

"Here," Augeren grunted around the monstrous organ in his mouth. "Here, behind this boulder. Come quick . . ."

"What? This boulder? Man, it's like pitch just here; can't see a thing!"

"Are you blind? Five paces straight ahead."

"Eh?" Eldin took three rapid paces. With the fourth he wondered what was wrong with Hero's voice. And with the fifth . . . But there was no fifth. His foot came down heavily on thin air. *"Pitfall!"* thought Eldin, twirling. And landing on his shoulder, neck and the back of his head, he thought no more . . . not for some little time.

Hero regained consciousness to a monstrous sight, one so grim that at first he thought he was still asleep, nightmaring within dreams. It was this: propped opposite Hero where he lay, as if sitting there with his back to the wall of the cave, Geeler Maas stared vacantly ahead, sightlessly, slack-jawed. His arms hung by his sides, their hands loosely a-dangle on the stony floor. And he was quite dead. His glassy eyes told that much; he neither twitched nor stirred, not a fraction. But the wound in his forehead, a neat hole, one inch across, and the brain-tissue which had seeped from it and congealed there—these things were even greater authority on his passing. Dead, aye: his robes torn open, the places in his flesh where his bones would be thickest all pierced through by those same holes, their rims caked with dry blood.

And suddenly Hero recalled everything; every detail of what had gone before returned to him in a flash of memory so vivid it hurt almost as much as the egg-sized lump on the back of his head. Galvanized by those memories—especially by what he had seen in the moment before he was clouted—he thrust himself up from the cold floor.

Or at least he tried to. But he was bound hand and foot, hands behind his back, knees bent, and a length of rope tied between wrists and ankles—hobbled, trussed like a chicken!

As realization dawned—the fact that he had been effectively immobilized, and that this, effectively, was Augeren's larder—Hero forced himself to go limp, simply lay there trying to put all in perspective.

Time, of course, was of the essence, for he didn't know when Augeren would be back. Time . . .

And what time would it be right now? How *much* time had elapsed between clout on head and rude awakening? Last night, or presumably the night before last Augeren had taken Ilfer. And drained his marrow. Last night—Hero glanced again across the cave, and grimaced—he'd sucked on Geeler's bones. Since he hunted at night he must feed then, too, when "food" was available. So . . . this gray twilight filtering into the cave from outside: was it morning's light or evening's? It must be morning's, Hero decided, for he'd never known a clout on the head to keep him out of things for more than a night. Which meant that he'd been here, trussed like this, all through the hours of darkness.

Most of that time, of course, he'd been utterly insensible, his muscles relaxed and not wanting to fight their cramped positions. But for quite some time now he'd been waking up; his arms and legs had been wanting to straighten themselves, flex a bit here and there. This was when cramp had commenced, and his current consciousness was exacerbating the condition. He forced himself to relax more yet, began to study his surroundings.

His eyes were more or less accustomed to the considerable gloom, or were at least reacting to what little light crept in from the imminent dawn. But the fact that it found its way in at all seemed to show that this lair or larder was fairly close to the entrance. Augeren (according to earlier calculations, anyway) did not much care for light, including daylight, presumably, and so must be retreating from the dawn to this lair even now. Or else he was already here . . .

For as Hero's eyes swept the cave yet again, noting to one side a low-ceilinged tunnel mouth or exit whose arch and walls seemed softly phosphorescent, so they came to rest on an apparently motionless shape huddled in one corner—which in the same moment *commenced* to move!

The monster, too, was coming awake, probably disturbed by Hero's own stirrings. Foetal, its slumbering position, becoming more nearly manlike as it roused itself and uncoiled. Then it sat up—Augeren sat up—and Hero saw that it, he, was indeed manlike. Man-*like* . . .

And how Hero fought against his bonds then, straining against them until his muscles bunched, standing out like rocks trapped under his skin—until he thought his teeth must break where they ground together with his effort—until, shockingly, the monster spoke to him!

"No use, quester. None at all." The thing's voice was a slide of oily gravel, wet earth falling from a spade.

Augeren stood up, naked and white as some deadly toadstool, half-crouching with a queer forward tilt. Then he dragged a black, ragged robe from a niche, draped himself, came loping to where Hero lay.

Hero looked at him, and sweat seemed to form, as by some hypnotic magic, under his arms, on his face, the palms of his tied hands, his back. Cold, slimy sweat. He looked at Augeren and felt as much as a cricket must feel face to face with a praying mantis. And indeed, there was also something mantis-like about the monster's stance: his hunched forward appearance under the cave's low ceiling, the faceted glitter of his great, bright, all-seeing eye.

"Augeren," Hero found strength to say, and was somehow satisfied to note that his voice didn't squeak. "You're the murdering thing called Augeren."

"Murderer?" The thing stared down at him. "I kill to live, quester. What excuse do you have?"

Hero wouldn't be suckered by that one. "To rid the lands of Earth's dreams of such as you!" he spat the words out. "But I never killed a young boy, or girl, or any thinking being who didn't first try to kill me. I never destroyed one of my own kind."

The monster nodded. He seated himself on a boulder close by—too close, by Hero's standards—and blinked his faceted eye. The glitter went out of it in a moment, returned with the next blink. And, "There you have me," Augeren replied. "For I have killed my own kind. Hybrids like myself, anyway." And the dreamer was startled to hear a sob burst from behind the fleshy probe which was the thing's tongue.

Hero knew he was doomed. It seemed that his only chance—not to gain his freedom, no, but to prolong his life, for a little while, anyway—was to engage Augeren in conversation. At least until the creature decided he'd talked enough. Or until he was hungry . . .

"You're a Leng-thing, then?" the quester hazarded. "From across the gray peaks of the barrier range?" But before Augeren could answer, Hero was stricken with cramp. The pain in his joints and muscles was intense as hot pokers, forcing a groan from his dry lips as he rocked his trussed body to and fro.

Augeren's hands came out from under his robe. Hero had not noticed them before, but the light was marginally stronger now, the luminescence in the cavemouth a little brighter. The hands were human enough—basically—but larger, powerful; their nails were thick as blades, pointed and sharp-edged. Augeren reached out with one of those hands and Hero winced. He wanted to close his eyes, but couldn't for his life.

The great claw of a hand went behind him, sawed at the rope tied between his bound wrists and ankles. It parted, so that his body straightened like a bow when the twine breaks. For a moment that was even greater agony, so that Hero couldn't help but cry out. But then, as the pain began to ease, he closed his eyes, let out his air in a great gasp, allowed his sweat-soaked head to bump down on the hard rock floor.

And at length Augeren repeated: "A Leng-thing? Like the horned ones from across the gray peaks, do you mean? I have sucked the bones of Leng-things dry. They are foul, not to my liking. I am not one of them; I am not their kin; I have not come out of Leng at all. But long, long ago, I was—or my ancestors were—what you are now. I am a half-and-half thing, yes. But a Leng-thing, no."

A half-breed! thought Hero. *But what had been the other half?* Out loud he said: "Who are you; where do you come from, and why do you hate human beings?"

Augeren's strange sob sounded again. Hero couldn't decide if it was a real sob, the sound of genuine grief, or a sort of suction as the monster drew air around that ghastly tool in its malformed mouth.

"Quester," said Augeren, "in a little while I must kill you, as I'm sure you know. The juices of your bones will be rich, and I shall grow strong on them. But I would kill you anyway, for you are correct: I do hate you, all of you. But there's a burden on me and I want it lightened, and perhaps it would be made less if I told my tale. Also, with you there is no need to make a quick end of it. You are tired, tied, helpless; more important, you make no outcry. For much as I hate you, I would hate futile cries for assistance even more. Aye, and you are curious about me. You despise me, perhaps fear me, but still you are curious. Very well, listen:

"For as long as is remembered, the men of Inquanok have kept apart from the men of other lands. They say it is because they are a race apart, that the blood of gods flows in their veins. Also, they are secretive, so that their ways may not be copied by outsiders; they keep their laws and rituals to themselves.

"What is more, for *almost* as long as is remembered there have been Veiled Kings of Inquanok, though commoners have never understood the system of succession, or indeed the origins, of their Veiled Kings. Likewise the priests of these kings, or of the gods they worship; theirs, too, is a cryptic genesis. But the laws of the kings, and the way they are applied by priests and officials, are known and understood very well indeed. Inquanok does not have much by way of crime or sin, for its punishments are severe. Let me explain:

"A thief in Inquanok has the offending hand cut off. If he persists his other hand is amputated. After that he thieves no more. Cheats are 'cheated'—that is to say, everything they own is taken from them, so that they must start over again. Murderers are escorted to the temple, where the Veiled King's priests receive them. They go in but do not come out. Do you understand?"

"The punishment fits the crime," said Hero. "The rest of dreamland's populated regions have similar measures, though rarely so harsh."

"Ravishment, too, carries a harsh penalty," Augeren continued. "Perhaps the most severe. A man accused of rape is stripped naked and banished north."

"North?" Hero frowned. "But . . . nothing lies to the north. Certainly nothing hospitable. Only the quarries, the foothills rising to the gray barrier peaks, with unknown lands beyond and finally Leng. If a man is banished north he usually dies, or lives like a leper in the lee of the gaunt gray peaks, on roots and berries and whatever he can trap. Or climbs and probably falls, else is taken by Shantaks or gaunts . . ."

". . . Or wins through and descends the far side, to face the unknown terrors of whatever wastelands await," Augeren carried it on. "And perhaps gradually ascends to Leng—there to be captured, tortured, finally devoured by almost-humans. Aye, and if he does none of these things but sneaks back into Inquanok . . . then he is taken to the temple."

Hero nodded. "Let no man ravish in Inquanok," he said.

"And yet they do, from time to time," said Augeren. "One tot too many of muth; or a woman whose charms are resistless, a temptress who goads and then cries out in the night; or simply a man who cannot control his lusts. And so, once in a while, another naked rapist will be found plodding north to a fate undreamed. And all such men, you understand, lusty types, and some even bestial."

"Most, I should think," Hero agreed.

"The gaunts get them usually," said Augeren matter-of-factly. "Not Shantaks, gaunts. The Shantaks fear night-gaunts, and many of the latter who dwell on high, in the peaks, are trained, which makes them especially dreadful creatures to the Shantaks. No Shantak-bird would dare take a human attempting to climb the gray peaks. Did you know that gaunts can be trained?"

"I know a youth who trains gaunts, aye," Hero answered. "He has a power over them."

"Others have powers, too." Augeren sobbed again.

Hero found himself morbidly fascinated. "What do the gaunts do with the climbers they take?" he asked. "And what has that to do with you?"

"Certain caverns in the gray peaks are gates to the underworld," Augeren answered. "Do you believe me?"

"I do," said Hero. "Mount Ngranek on Oriab is likewise a gate to the underworld. Down there at the roots of dreamland lie the Vale of Pnoth, Zin's vaults, black seas of pitch, great ruins without name, and many another nameless thing. I know, for I've been there." He couldn't suppress a shudder.

Augeren was impressed. "And returned unscathed! Then you're a quester born for sure! Alas, the quest for Augeren is your last. But tell me: are you still curious about me, or should I simply kill you now and have done? For sure as the dawn draws nigh I grow hungry, and I'd as soon be filled and sleeping through the day as sat here boring you."

The word "boring" got to Hero. "Curious?" he croaked. Somehow he managed to get his knees under him so that he kneeled, scratched his back against the rock wall behind him. "Never more so. Indeed I'm fascinated! So say on, Augeren. Except . . ."

"Yes?"

"First tell me what happened to my friend. The burly fellow? He's a quester like myself, you see, and I just wondered—"

"Then stop wondering. He won't be coming to save you." Augeren's many-faceted eye glittered. "He's dead, your friend. Fell into my trap in the dark. A great pit . . ."

Hero hung his head, felt grief, anguish fill him like a flood. He gritted his teeth, looked up. "And did you . . ." he choked, "did you—?"

"No," Augeren shook his monstrous head. "Why should I climb down there to feed on him when there was the boy's father—or you? I kill, and then I eat. But once a body is cold, then the marrow of the bones quickly—*ah!*"

For Hero had turned his face away, was silently cursing into the hollow of his own shoulder, biting on the collar of his jacket. And Augeren said: "But see, now you hate me as much as I hate you."

Hero controlled himself—a gigantic effort of will—and looked up again. He prayed that the tears in the corners of his eyes didn't show, for he wouldn't give this damned thing that much satisfaction, and said: "Please . . . please go on. The underworld. Men are taken there by gaunts. Why?"

"New blood," Augeren answered at once. "A guarantee of continuity. They are placed where their unnatural lusts will best serve the denizens of the underworld. Especially the Lords of Luz."

"Denizens of the underworld? Monsters d'you mean? Gugs, ghouls and ghasts and such? I don't understand. And just who are these Lords of Luz?"

As Augeren took up the tale again, so Hero commenced sawing at the rope between his wrists, slowly, painfully working its fibers against a projecting edge of the rock at his back: "Do you know what a dhole is?" the monster asked him. Saliva spurted from the corner of Augeren's distorted mouth, driven out by his restlessly churning probe. "But of course you must know, for you've seen the Vale of Pnoth. Actually, I doubt if you have *seen* one, though perhaps you've been close. But to actually *see* a dhole is to die—usually. And yet I have hunted dholes and killed them! Not alone, of course, but as a member of the hunt. However, let that be for now . . .

"Well, there are dholes in all of dreamland's subterranean ossuaries. Wherever bones are tossed or piled or otherwise accrue, there dwell the dholes. They dwell deep down under the roots of the great gray peaks, too. Down there, in the lightless dark, they go about their curious labors, heaping the massive paleogean remains of monsters extinct since a time when dreams were in their infancy, and the dreamlands themselves were new-formed of the subconscious fancies of the first men. For there in a cavern vast as all Inquanok lies a prehistoric graveyard of beasts; and where better to find dholes, eh, than burrowing in the rustling dark of endless leagues and unknown fathoms of bones?

"But let me first describe the geography, however vertical, of the subterranean places—the better for you to understand the rest of my tale.

"If a man be borne by gaunts through the upper orifices of the gray peaks and down through those hollow mountains into the underworld—which indeed is the only way in, for the peaks are like hollow teeth in a skull—first he will find himself in Luz. Luz, therefore, is the uppermost of the land below, inhabited by the elite"—Augeren gave what sounded like a slobbery snort—"of these sunless regions. Beneath Luz, and accessible only through a fissure constantly guarded by the Lords of Luz, lie the Downs of D'haz, where dwell the halflings of which I am one. There, too, in the walls of that mighty, tilted cave of fungi and etiolated grass, dwell the Url. They are worms big as a man—indeed their trunks are like unto the trunks of men, but their limbs are vestigial and they burrow with spadelike snouts. They live on oil seeped by the centuries through the honeycombed rocks which form the walls of D'haz . . . on that, and on a richer diet by far, of which more later.

"Several chimneys go down from D'haz into the great dhole ossuary, whose extent is largely unknown. It must be vast, however, for there dwell dholes in their hundreds, and with them their attendant parasites, whom you might best think of as tick-men."

"What?" Hero stirred a little, used the opportunity to saw again at his ropes. "Tick-men? Are you talking about human parasites—on dholes?"

"Not human," Augeren slowly shook his head. "Though they probably were, once upon a time . . ." And eventually he continued: "Beneath the dinosaur boneyard, on the nethermost level, there lie the Pits of the Unknown Things. Of them, quite obviously, I can tell you nothing—except that they wage constant war with the dholes and live on their flesh. Also, that the dholes in turn live on *their* flesh."

Hero grimaced. "The whole thing sounds hideous," he said. "A much-magnified hell!"

"But as yet you have not heard half!" Augeren answered. And he went on: "The gaunt kidnappers of men—they will take any man curious enough to venture to the foot of the gray peaks, you understand, and not just licentious, banished criminals—are trained by the Lords of Luz. These so-called 'Lords' have bred gaunts especially for the carrying of men down into the underworld. And there, in Luz, the Lords explain to such luckless men what is required of them. It is an ongoing process which has continued since the first Veiled King and his priests came out of the north into Inquanok the city, which occurred in a time immemorial. Since when there have been many Veiled Kings . . ."

Hero cocked his head a little to one side and frowned, sawed at his ropes, covered his sawing by repeating: "The Veiled Kings come from the north, eh? Into which you seem to read a special meaning . . ."

"You will see, quester," answered Augeren. "You will see."

"I see part of it already," said Hero. "I think. But if what you've told me is true, and if I'm correct in what I'm beginning to suspect . . . why do the men of Inquanok accept Veiled Kings at all? And why do they continue to banish men north?"

"But the men of Inquanok do not know of this underworld," answered Augeren. "Indeed, you are the first man to know of it who has not been there. They do not know where the men they banish go to, only that this banishment is the decree of the Veiled King and his priests; and in any case, who are they to question such things? And why should they dream to question the origin of their Veiled Kings, eh?"

Hero lolled against the wall of the cave, worked harder at his ropes. His wrists were on fire now, for he dared move only them and not his arms. He dreaded that, as the light improved with dawn which must surely break at any moment, then Augeren would see the faint jerking of his muscles, his twitching face, the sweat on his neck in the vee of his shirt which was no longer cold or spawned of fear. "Tell me more," he said.

Augeren nodded, but a little reluctantly, Hero thought. "I grow weary," the monster said, stretching.

"Still, I ate well and slept a little in the night, and indeed I have unburdened myself somewhat. And since the tale is begun I might as well finish it." He shrugged. "You have until then. What is a little time, after all?"

"To you, not very much," Hero answered, making light of it. "To me, a great deal."

Augeren did something with his horrific face which might have been a smile. "You are a brave man," he said, "for which reason, when it is time, I shall make a quick end of it. Until then . . .

"This is what the Lords of Luz tell their newly arrived prisoners: that they are to be taken down into D'haz and there penned with female tick-things, taken when their host dholes are slain! There will be progeny—halfling progeny—and as long as this continues, as long as a man can father halflings on the tickwomen, so long shall he live. But if he cannot, or will not . . . then his bones will be broken and him lowered through one of the many chimneys into the dhole ossuary."

Hero was aghast, his mouth a round "O" in his face. "This is monstrous!" he finally declared.

"The entire underworld would seem monstrous," Augeren nodded, "to a man like you, used only to the sane, safe places of the dreamlands." Hero might have argued the point there, but: "Let me tell you more," Augeren continued.

"Halflings like myself—and yet greatly unlike myself—go down into D'haz and hunt dholes. When they kill a dhole the carcass is netted and drawn up through a chimney into D'haz. Like carrion insects, the halflings drag the huge body up ramps hewn in the walls, and into cavern abattoirs there—in fact they are not abattoirs, for the dholes are already dead, so let us simply call these caves blood-houses. There the dhole bodies are pulped until their juices flow down runnels into the rocks, mix with the ages-seeped oil there and—"

Hero gulped, cried out, "I know, I know!" And, stomach heaving at the thought, he said: "The Url worms in their burrows slurp it up! Thus the halflings feed the Urls!" Then, dreading the answer his question must bring, he nevertheless asked, "But *why* do they feed them?" And to himself: *All you gods of dreams, if you really do exist, please give me strength to bear this horror out to its end!*

"Why do halflings tend and feed Urls?" Augeren thrust his face a little closer. "Because the Lords of Luz command it! Any halfling who fails in his duties risks broken bones and a one-way trip to the cavern of the dholes. That is why. And why, you are wondering, should the fate of great, pale, mindless worms be of any concern to the Lords, eh?"

"Why indeed?" Hero felt faint. Augeren's breath was a stench.

"Because the Urls are the next in the chain, the next phase!" the monster hissed. "The next step in the descent to monarchy."

He sobbed in the light which crept ever stronger into his lair; and such was the horror of Augeren's face that Hero fixed his gaze beyond it, on the bare rock wall of the cave, rather than stare continuously into that travesty of a visage.

"Worms?" said Hero, feeling his voice begin to crack under the strain. "The next phase?"

"Indeed!" cried Augeren. "Oh, yes! And now see where human lust and bestiality has brought us, and now ask why I hate you, all of you! For now the halflings—of which I was one, remember, part-tick, part-human being—are made to mate with the Urls!

Aye, and I have already described the punishment if they should fail in their duties, or prefer not to perform them at all."

"But ..." said Hero, frantically, fractionally sawing. "But ..."

"Aye, but—but—but!" answered Augeren nodding. "But only *think* of it! Only *imagine* those pits of depravity! Only let your mind dwell for a moment—a single moment—upon the *issue* of such matings! First the union of men and tick-women. The tick-women are flattish, like elongated lice, or the pale crabs that inhabit cavern pools. Their skins are leathery, and yet their shape overall is humanish! I am the product of such a mating, and yet I am a poor product, a freak. Yes, a freak, but even more a freak—by halfling standards—than you might ever suspect. For there is *too much* of the human side in me! My brothers were more nearly 'normal,' if you can imagine that!

"Ah, quester, but if only you could have seen my mother! Great hands like claws for gripping the sides of her dhole host; six udders on which to feed her brats; two eyes like this single insect orb of mine, which can barely 'see' at all in your understanding of the word; and her mouth, like mine, complete with a drill of cartilage plates with which to penetrate the flensed bones of her dhole host's victims!"

"You're a loathsome thing!" Hero blurted. "But by the many gods of the dreamlands, I almost pity you."

"Save your pity for yourself!" Augeren's voice was wet and panting. "For my tale will soon be told ..." He drew back a little, sobbed and shook and slopped saliva, finally achieved a measure of control. "Now, about the mating of halfling and Url," he said. "Let me tell you of that."

Hero really did not want to know, but if he stopped

Augeren's tale now . . . what then? "Do go on," he said, once more applying himself to his bonds, which by now were surely weakening.

"The female Urls allow it," said Augeren. "Simple creatures, who live only for the present and have little if any thought of possible futures, the fate of Urls gone before means nothing to them. Indeed, they welcome their mating with halflings; for when a female worm is with young she is pampered and fed and fattened individually by the halflings, even lured from her burrow into a granite pen from which she cannot escape. And why is she given this preferential treatment? Why fattened on raw dhole juice? Because the young she will bear will be many, and *very* demanding. So demanding, indeed, that even though she be fat and full of her disgusting milk, still her dominant infant will kill off all the others—as many as ten or eleven—to take their share! Aye, and he grows and grows, very quickly, in both size and intelligence until, for all her brimming udders, still his mother is hard put to feed him. Then, no longer satisfied with her gruel milk, the young human-cum-tick-come-Url draws blood!

"At this stage the mother must be watched most carefully. She knows her child will kill her, and so she will try to kill him. That is not to be allowed! *She* is expendable, but *he* is not. He kills her and, bloated with her blood, is carried aloft by gaunts . . ."

"Into Luz?" Hero stared wide-eyed, trying to comprehend.

"Obviously—where else 'aloft'? Yes, into Luz, which is his birthright—for he is now a Lord of Luz. Or a Lady, of course."

Hero's mind whirled. "But what . . . what *is* he? Or she? I mean, how must they—?"

"How must they look? What is their nature? I will

tell you," said Augeren. "They are uttermost monstrosities! They have the claw hands of ticks, *some* eyes like yours and perhaps several like mine, flattish of body but with many stomachs, so that they may bloat with blood. They are roughly the size of a man, but their limbs—vestigial in their worm mothers—are lengthened into rubbery tentacles which they can coil or flail at will. Some have cartilage drills for mouths, others the shovel face and tube tongues of the worms. Most are pale pink, and *all* are utterly bestial!"

Hero shuddered, licked his lips. "And you call such as these 'Lords'?"

"From now on they are watched closely indeed," Augeren continued without bothering to answer. "Watched and trained. They are watched for aberration, for madness. Oh, they *are* aberrant, each and every one—they *are* loathsome in their habits, their lusts, their greed and their nameless appetites—but if they are also insane, and many are . . ."

"The great ossuary of the dholes?" Hero guessed.

"Of course. Nothing is wasted."

Hero's mind was morbidly at work. "But how, in creatures like these, *how* may one distinguish 'madness'? I mean, is there any sanity in them at all?"

"Madness in the Lords is not measured in depth of depravity but level of intelligence," said Augeren. "Or rather, lack of it. But if they can learn, then they are intelligent—'sane.' If they can follow the rituals they are required to observe, and perform other . . . functions, then they are fit—to serve!"

The way the monster slobbered out these words had the short hairs on Hero's neck instantly erect. "Their . . . functions," he repeated. "Fit to serve. What functions? And 'to serve' whom?"

"Miscegeny is done with now!" the beast went on,

"but still the final phase has not been reached. Still the ultimate abomination is yet to be born. For now Lord mates with Lady! Aye, but of *their* progeny ask me nothing! I do not know. No creature knows. Except the Lords of Luz themselves—*whom you may call priests*!"

Hero's mouth worked but he said nothing. He had expected some such, but still it came as a shock. These things masqueraded as men in Inquanok, and the worst things of all as Veiled Kings!

"And all of this, everything I have told, occurring in darkness," said Augeren, creeping closer, until Hero was sure he must notice his secret sawing. "All of it taking place in pitch black abysses of earth and rock, where even now men mate with monsters, and their halfling children with others more monstrous yet. And what light there is—the glow of certain phosphorescent mosses, or the foxfire of rotting fungi—even that is *too much* light! Things lusting, devouring each other with their lust and simply . . . simply devouring! Can you picture the nightmare of it? You likened it to a hell, but I say it is the *hell* of hells! I could not stand it! By comparison I was clean! I *would not* be penned with an Url, however 'comely' for one of her race! They said I was more nearly human, and indeed I was not *un*like the men I saw down there in D'haz. I talked to them, learned all I could of the outside, the upper lands, and when finally it was my turn to mate . . ."

"You fled," Hero breathlessly finished it for him.

"Aye, crime in itself. Fled—and fleeing I slew. Slew my Url bride-to-be, her halfling keepers, even a Lord. Threatened a pair of stupid gaunts until they carried me out of the underworld entirely and flew me down to the foothills in the night. Then I slashed their throats and so slew them, too. And at last I came upon human beings for the first time—innocent human beings, mind, not the lusty criminals brought down to D'haz by gaunts—and so learned how I could never find a place here.

"For each and every one, when he or she first saw me, cried out in horror! Cried out until my blood boiled over, and I . . . and I . . ."

"Go on!" cried Hero, afraid to let the creature pause.

Augeren nodded, but crept closer still. "Now picture my dilemma. I could not go back—the broken limbs, the boneyard of the dholes—and I cannot go forward. So here I stay, halfway, a half-creature, half mad."

Strands parted behind Hero's back. He worked harder. And to cover his activity: "And have you no plans at all?"

"Only this," said Augeren, "to live until I die. Until others come, perhaps like you, to put an end to me. Or until the Lords of Luz find me and take me back. For escape from the underworld is not permitted, do you understand? What, escape and bring word of that horror into the outside world? The tunnels of D'haz, winding through slimy rock like the tentacles of some terrible cancer, are mazy and widespread. Perhaps they reach even so far as a certain temple in Inquanok.

"Plans? Not really. Only a desire to destroy. To destroy Luz, also to kill as many 'human beings' as I may before my life is done. For aye, I hate you all, and you"—he leaned forward until his terrible face was only inches away—"you, who I perceive to have been a waking-worlder—yours is the type I hate most of all!"

"There are things," Hero gabbled, "certain things, which you have not explained." He shrank back, molded himself to the wall of the cave. "If you will, please go on . . ."

"What things?" Augeren's voice was a low slobber.

Hero's mind raced desperately. He remembered his conversation with Eldin—how long ago? Yesterday?

Impossible! "Eyes!" he cried. "And auguries!" He prayed he had Augeren's attention, and:

"You said your eyes—your eye—can hardly 'see' at all as I understand sight. And yet in D'haz, you must have seen infinitely more clearly than I ever could. Your 'sight' must be far superior. So how *did* you see, down there in reeking darkness?" More strands parted behind his back.

"This faceted eye," Augeren replied, drawing back the merest fraction, "came to me via my leech-like mother, as did my plated, bone-piercing tongue. What I got from my father I cannot say, except for my general shape. Him I never knew, for he gave himself to the dholes before I was spawned. So perhaps he may be held to account for my 'sensitivity,' eh? As for the eye: it detects and interprets not only light of the present but light of the past, even a little light of the future. It is in itself a sense, additional to the five senses of ordinary men. When my ears hear sounds, the eye gives them shape. When my nose detects odors, the eye frames their source. I touch a living thing in the darkness"—he quickly reached out a huge, taloned hand, touched Hero's thigh—"and my eye describes it in its entirety. See!"

Augeren blinked. Hero saw. The glitter of his eye grew filmy, moist, then quickly cleared. And in its myriad facets, Hero saw himself—a hundred selves—mirrored, ghastly pale, shuddering, trapped here in this very cave, with Augeren crouched over him.

"The eye is also my memory," the monster spoke again. "Let me show you. Now I draw light from the past . . ." The eye shuttered again, and when it opened—

Hero saw mirrored in its facets . . . the underworld! He saw Luz, and frightful half-glimpses of Things that moved oddly in the deeper shadows. Another blink of the eye, and the pallid grass Downs of D'haz crept away into gloomy distance, with squalid huts and stone pens everywhere, and fungi forests, and loping halflings about their business in the wreathing mists. Blink, and now upon every hand great banks of bones, for this was the prehistoric ossuary of the dholes. And: "Would you *see* a dhole?" Augeren inquired.

Hero shook his head; said very quietly, "No."

The faceted eye blinked again. A girl ran through misty woodland, panting. She stumbled in her terror, fell, glanced back. Her myriad faces filled with horror, loathing. And before she could scream, Augeren's shadow fell over her . . .

Blink! Ilfer Maas, gagged, bound, sat in a cave much like this one. His eyes were wide over a nose where the nostrils flared in a silent scream. The hexagonal pictures came closer, ran into each other, became one. Ilfer's eyes grew larger, more terrified still. Something white, dripping slime, slid into view. The opening at its top widened, and a needle-sharp shaft struck forth, chopped cleanly, instantly into the youth's forehead. The picture faded.

And Hero's petrified gaze crept from Augeren's eye to his mouth. The quester watched that gristle-plated organ poise before his face, tilt slightly upward, saw its tip opening and something white gleaming within.

"Augury!" Hero croaked. "Future light! You said you could read the future!" He sawed at his bonds, his wrists now sticky with blood.

"Only the immediate future," the monster's voice was a gravelly growl. "Surely you do not wish to see that?"

"I do! I do!" Hero cried. "Also, why do you hate *me* so? A waking-worlder? Aye, I was that—but what is that to you?"

"Don't you know?"

"I no longer know anything!" Hero sobbed, finally unmanned. "I know only what you tell me!"

"Then ask yourself this," Augeren hissed bubblingly. "Ask why all of this must be: the underworld, the monsters mating here, the nightmare existences I have described, which are as real as I am?"

At last Hero knew the answer. It had come to him with the word "nightmare." It showed in his bulging eyes, his suddenly slack mouth.

"Of course!" cried Augeren. "Yes, certainly! All of these things are—Luz and D'haz, the Unknown Things, the tick-folk and Urls, halflings and Lords—*because some monstrous man of the waking world dreamed them!*"

"A madman, perhaps," Hero gabbled desperately. "But I am sane. Or at least I was!"

"Alas," said Augeren, "but quite definitely, I no longer am. But very well, the immediate future; see it now, then see no more."

Blink!

Things snuffling, scrabbling in darkness, squeezing their grotesque bodies through impossible crevices in fractured rock, digging with spade snouts or clawing their way with sharp knife hands. And others lurking behind, goading them on, urging with quivering tentacular arms!

Hero saw all of this in the monster's fantastic eye— and Augeren saw it, too. He drew air in a slobbering gasp. "They're coming for me!" And even as he cried his frustration, so the floor of the cave shuddered, began to settle in a sagging of rotten rock and crumbly soil.

Blink!—and another picture forming:

Hero's ropes parting with a twang, and spattering blood from his torn wrists onto the black rocks; and a hundred Heroes reaching cramped, agonized hands for the daggers tucked away in the cuffs of their right trouser legs.

"Curse you, quester!" shrilled Augeren. Drill mouth working frantically, he tried to grab Hero's shoulders—but Hero jerked on his bloody wrists and the ropes parted, just as he had seen in the monster's eye! He rolled out of Augeren's reach, grabbed for his knife and found it. Augeren was on him, but Hero's knife was arcing up.

Blink!

Light! Blazing, blinding, merciful light! White light shot with red and yellow, flaring light. The light of a hundred torches, burning on—burning in—Augeren's naked eye!

Blinded by a blazing vision, a scene from his own immediate future, Augeren staggered backward into the hole appearing magically behind him in the floor of the cave. Rocks rained down and dust shook itself free of the walls, and a jagged crack shot across the floor, accompanied by a low rumble of shifting mass. Then . . . several things, all happening at once:

The light glaring forth from the many facets of Augeren's eye was supplemented by real light, marginally preceding the blundering bulk and hoarse, worriedly-inquiring voice of Eldin the Wanderer. Hero, in some entirely detached part of his psyche, might have seen, might have heard something of this arrival; and certainly on that ethereal plane he would have exulted that Eldin yet lived and breathed; but his *will* was now focused upon one and only one task: to kill, and send to hell, and so be free of, the monster Augeren. All else was peripheral to consciousness; only that one desire, that single instinct remained.

To this end, even as Eldin roared into the cavelet with

a blazing torch held high, Hero severed the cords binding his ankles; turned upon Augeren, who seemed
jammed in the hole in the floor as in quicksand. There
was blood on the monster's neck and shoulder from
Hero's blind thrust of moments earlier, but Augeren
seemed not to notice. He was screaming over and over
again: "Come for me! They've come for me!"

And as the floor of the cave continued to shudder,
while ominous cracks began to zigzag across walls and
low ceiling, so the monster reached out his huge hands
and grabbed Hero's ankles.

"If I go, quester, then you go with me!" he sobbed.
"One thing to learn of the ways of the underworld
second-hand, but another entirely to actually *experience*
them!" With that he half drew himself up from the
hole—*and was dragged back!*

Then Hero saw the blood—the monster's blood, from
that first blind knife-thrust—on his trousers where they
were being half yanked from him as Augeren sank
snarling into the ever-widening hole, and finally the taut
thread of sanity snapped in him. That nameless, tainted
blood—spawned of reeking pits and inhuman lusts—on
him? In a frenzy of horror, he stabbed at the clawed
hands where they held him, stabbed blindly and savagely, as often as not slicing into his own calf-boots and
leather bindings in his frantic, repetitious attack.

Augeren's head was below the level of the floor now,
leaving his arms and spastically clawing hands protruding, clutching at Hero. But his head came up one final
time, glared its hatred from the blackly glittering, faceted eye. His hatred . . . and his pleading. "Then kill
me!" he choked, as "hands"—and many of them, and
all more monstrous far than his own—reached up to
gain firmer holds on him.

Until now Eldin had seen very little: dark shadows

leaping, dust falling in powdery rills everywhere, Hero's white face, wide-eyed, and something like a great red one-eyed spider, many-armed, that writhed and heaved on the floor where Hero slashed and slashed at it. The Wanderer couldn't know that the "spider" was Augeren's bloodied head, or that of its many apparent arms, only two belonged to the thing itself! The fact that the monster quite obviously threatened Hero was more than enough. Eldin lowered his blazing torch, thrust it straight into the hideously glittering eye. The scream that issued forth then was an entire nightmare in its own right, but Eldin cared little for that. No time for caring or for anything else now, for events were rapidly drawing to a close.

Eldin stepped quickly to where Hero crouched sobbing and stabbing at the sliding rim of the quaking hole in the floor. "Lad?—David?—we have to get out of here, now! Can you walk?"

Hero didn't answer, seemed not to have heard. Up and down went his knife; the blade broke where it struck rock at the edge of the hole, and still Hero's arm pumped like some mad mechanical thing. But what was he stabbing at? The spider-thing was gone now.

As the cave shuddered yet again, Eldin thrust his torch down into the hole and waved it about. It seemed to him that monstrous shapes, distorted faces and figures, drew back down there. Shadows, most likely. But he couldn't be sure.

"Lad?" he said again. And getting no response, he simply kicked the broken knife from Hero's spastic hand. It made no difference: still the younger quester's empty, clenched fist pumped, still he sobbed and raved. Eldin cuffed him hugely on the side of the head, grabbed him in one hand as he crumpled, then half-dragged, half-carried him out of that hellish place and along the exit tunnel to dreary daylight.

Behind them as they emerged, the tunnel went down in a fall of rock, venting pressured dust thick as smoke as that entire section of the quarry face crashed vertically down in massive blocks, filling in the main area of subsidence . . .

Hero came to when he was dumped jarringly on his rump at the top of the ramp. Down below a seething mist lay on the floor of the quarry, with nowhere a sign of what had passed there. Up here, where a pale sun was striving to break through rising vapors, the whole thing might have been a dream within dreams—except that Hero knew it had been real. His chafed wrists and ankles were ample proof of that. Eldin sat close by, panting like a bellows, his wary eyes on the younger man.

At first there was a glazed look to Hero's eyes, but this gradually disappeared as a very little of his color returned. Then he gave a start, sat up straighter, gazed all about. "Inquanok!" he gasped, as if suddenly realizing where he was—and as if the very word tasted bad in his mouth.

Exhausted one minute, he seemed galvanized the next. He shot to his feet, set off at a fast if wobbly pace eastward. They'd hidden their tiny sky-yacht in a copse of evergreens on Inquanok's very border when they first arrived here. Since their invitation to Inquanok had been other than strictly official, that had seemed prudent. Now Hero was obviously in a hurry to get airborne again and out of here. Which would suit Eldin well enough, except:

"What of the quest?" he asked, hastening to catch up.

"It's over," said Hero, his eyes scanning ahead.

"Over?" Eldin's eyebrows shot up. "You mean . . . in that cave back there . . . Augeren?"

Breath burst from Hero's lips in a *hiss*. He turned swiftly, his eyes burning, and bunched up Eldin's jacket front in a tight knot in his two fists. "Don't!" he warned, shaking his head jerkily. "Just . . . don't." Then he turned away, hurried on.

Eldin stayed a little to the rear after that. "You don't intend to report your . . . findings to those Inquaknackers who asked us here?" he carefully inquired after a little while.

"Kuranes can do that," Hero grated, "after we report to him. As for questing, to *hell* with it!"

"This is your last?"

"It is," Hero nodded, "while I've still got my sanity. *If* I've still got it."

Eldin came up alongside but a little apart. "I expect you'll tell me about it," he said; and immediately followed up with: "—in your own time, of course."

Hero looked at him and some of the harder lines fell from his wan face. "That clout you gave me in the cave was probably the greatest favor you've ever done me," he said. "So I'll tell you this much now: Augeren's dead, or good as. And if he's not actually dead at this very moment, then he soon will be. Now then, can the rest of it wait till we're safely up into the clear blue yonder and out of here?"

"Safely?" the older quester raised an eyebrow. "Are there more dangers, then—which I don't know about—here in Inquanok?"

"Enough and more than enough," said Hero, "and we've a way to go yet. How many miles? Ten?"

"At least," Eldin nodded. Then the Wanderer related how Augeren had lured him into taking a stunning tumble, and how that same monster's shrieks of terror had finally snatched him awake at the bottom of a shallow pit. Climbing out, he'd been in time (but barely) to drag his friend to safety before Augeren's lair and the cliff caved in.

Hero listened to all, nodded, made no answer. And shortly thereafter they began to stretch out their pace a little . . .

Two hours later saw Hero breathing easier and Eldin somewhat winded. But the younger dreamer wouldn't pause. At last they crested a rise and saw a spur of foothills projecting from low-lying mists. The sun was brighter now, sucking up the damp air, and away to the north the jagged fangs of gray mountains were seen to penetrate slow-moving clouds: the gaunt gray peaks. Hero looked at them for long moments, finally shuddered and turned away.

"Chilly, aye," Eldin agreed, then saw the look on Hero's face and added: "Or p'r'aps not?"

Hero made no answer . . .

Now, tramping downhill, it was easier going. They angled their route toward a stand of trees, whose tops were just showing green through the mist, in the lee of a second spur maybe three miles away. That was where their sky-yacht was hidden away. When they'd first arrived here and sought out one of the underground movement's leaders in Urg—a burly, bearded trader, oddly hearty for a man of Inquanok—whose name was Heger Nort, he'd promised them to set a discreet watch on their boat and make sure no one stumbled upon it. If he'd kept his word, doubtless someone would be monitoring their approach even now.

But then . . .

"Inquanodes," said Eldin. "Three or four of 'em. Atop that knoll there, see?"

Hero saw. The party waved at them a good deal, urgently, but refrained from shouting; then they came hurrying down the steep side of the knoll to intercept the questers on the plain between the spurs. It was Heger Nort and three conspiratorial colleagues.

"Treachery!" said Nort, without preamble, as they met. "One of our lot was a quisling for the Veiled King—rather, for his priests. Which amounts to the same thing. He must have told the priests there were dubious outsiders—you'll excuse my way with words—in Inquanok. Anyway, he's been taken care of, permanently! But last night a good many priests left the temple in a hurry and set out in all directions, but mainly north. We suspect they'll be looking for you. So we came looking for you too, to warn you."

Hero nodded. "We're grateful. But anyway, our business here is finished now."

"Eh?" Nort looked puzzled. "Your quest's at an end, you say? Care to explain?"

Hero sighed. "It seems I'll have to," he answered. "Very well, I'll give you the gist of it. I'll not say what I personally suspect, but let you make up your own minds. I'll tell it as we go. After that—it's all yours."

And tell it he did. Two miles later they stood all six at the fringe of the firs and the story was finished, at least in outline. But Hero had framed his tale so as to make no direct accusations. During the telling at first there'd been the odd question from the men of Inquanok, but as the story progressed they'd listened in silence, their expressions gloomy, then ghastly, finally outraged and fearful. Eldin, too.

"No wonder," the Wanderer commented as they entered the copse and made their way through the undergrowth to where the sky-yacht was hidden, "no wonder you were so up-tight-lipped about it! I'd have felt the same. But you'll feel better now it's out of your system."

"I won't feel better till we're aloft!" Hero declared. "*Then* I'll feel better . . ."

Assisted by Nort and his friends, they began shifting a camouflage screen of fir branches from the sides of *Quester*; she floated inches above the pine-needle floor, anchored to a tree. And it was then that a whey-faced man emerged from the little vessel's cabin.

"Hum Tassler!" said Nort. "Sleeping on the job, eh?"

"I . . ." said Tassler, his Adam's apple wobbling. "I mean . . ."

Behind him, sprouting suddenly like some strange toadstool from the cabin, stood a priest.

For a moment the tableau held: the men of Inquanok looked shocked, caught red-handed; their faces fell. Hero went deathly white, drew air in a hiss. Only Eldin seemed unaffected. He laid hands on *Quester*'s side.

"Well, then, and what's this?" said the Wanderer heartily. "Piracy? And damn me if one of the pirates isn't a priest! Here's us, a couple of skyfarers come ashore to provision up and make minor repairs, and we're boarded like smugglers the minute we lower the gangway!" he winked at Hero, who for his part stood wide-eyed, nostrils flaring, staring up at the priest on board the yacht.

The priest was masked and hooded, robed in a black cassock that hid all but the curled toes of his black lacquered shoes. Behind his queer mask and under his hood, his flesh seemed a pale pink, but his eyes, where they peered from slits in the mask, were aglitter with avid curiosity—and maybe with more than that. Tall, he was, and his stance peculiar: as if he held himself aloof, away from commen men, or as if he leaned backward. The sleeves of his cassock were abnormally wide, almost bell-like, and yet were cinched at the wrists. Upon his large hands black gloves, so that no part of him showed except for the eye-glitter and pinkness behind the mask. For a few moments he said nothing, but merely gazed down on the men of Inquanok, examining each in turn. Then:

"These two questers, whom you believe to be mercenary sellswords," he began, his voice high and quivering, "are spies of a foreign power. Whether they are here of their own accord or were invited is another matter, one which is to be investigated. For now the Veiled King has ordered that they be taken before him for judgment. Their crime is this: that in order to gain illicit access to Inquanok's mysteries they invented a monster, Augeren. This supposed 'evil creature' is in fact a member or members of a group of subversives opposed to the Veiled King's rule, a traitor or traitors who have committed vile murder in order to justify the presence here of these so-called 'questers.' All shall be dealt with accordingly. I note that you four are with these outsiders, and so assume that you are members of the subversive band. What have you to say?"

"Plenty!" growled Eldin, drawing the priest's attention.

"Careful!" warned Heger Nort in a hoarse whisper. "Their word is law! In private we can work against them and say what we like, but face to face—these priests are powerful!"

"What about my story?" Hero grated from the corner of his mouth. "Are you all daft? Do you think I made it up? You *know* what must be done!"

Sheepishly, sullenly, the men of Inquanok looked at

each other. Heger Nort seemed about to say something, do something, but:

"Well?" said the priest, a sneer, almost a snigger now, in his tittering treble. And when there was no answer: "Very well, perhaps you can make amends for your participation in all of this. Indeed, perhaps your part in it was small. We shall see. Now bind up the strangers at once. We make haste for Inquanok."

"What?" Eldin roared. "I'll tell you where you make haste for, priest—you make haste for hell!" He swept a brawny hand across *Quester*'s gunnel, knocked the priest's feet from under him. Down came the tall, cassocked figure with a squawk of rage, a lank black bundle tumbling over the side of *Quester* and thudding to the pine-needle floor of the copse. As he fell, so Hero stepped forward, and as he scrambled to rise both of the questers caught at the bell-like sleeves of his robe and tore them loose. They had tried to trap his arms and failed, but in so doing *revealed* his arms. All of them!

The thing in black was stunned, but only for a moment. Then three fat, pink, tapering tentacles uncoiled where true arms should be, at each side of the thing's body, whipped out to wrap like ropes about the necks of the questers. With a massive, unbelievable strength, the creature lifted the pair by their necks, commenced to hang them. At the same time the priest's eyes glittered behind his mask, fixed themselves upon Heger Nort and Co. defying them to intervene. Those eyes glared hypnotically at the four men of Inquanok on the ground, but not at the fifth. On the deck of *Quester*, Hum Tassler had been forgotten.

Before the arrival of the others, Tassler had been surprised by the priest and had spent a whole morning in his company; and Tassler knew that there was scant chance of a pardon for him. The priest had said as much. Well, he might as well be hung for a lion as a lamb. He took out a slender dagger, kneeled quickly on the gunnel, stabbed the tall priest high in his back.

The priest gave a shrill, bubbling shriek; his tentacles released Hero and Eldin, whipped backward to engulf Tassler. But the man on the boat had already withdrawn his knife, wrenched the priest's hood back and open, and snatched his black leather mask from his head. Now, in all his horror, the priest stood literally unmasked.

"A Lord of Luz!" choked Hero through a badly bruised windpipe, pointing at the staggering thing. "Now see him for yourselves! Now know who and what these priests of Inquanok's Veiled King really are!"

As Hum Tassler stabbed again at the Lord of Luz and was snatched from the deck and hurled down for his pains, so the men of Inquanok came out of their trance. Then, as one man, they fell to it with a will—and they literally tore the former "priest" to pieces bare-handed. It might have taken quite a long time, if in the end Hum Tassler hadn't managed to slit the hybrid creature's throat . . .

When it was over, and Nort and his friends stood drenched in stinking ichor, staring at the mess, Hero and Eldin took the opportunity to get aboard *Quester*. Eldin went below and started the tiny flotation engine, and as the bags in the keel and under the deck filled out, as Hero cast off. Up went *Quester*, floating lighter than air through the trees, and still the men below stood grim and silent, their eyes fixed on the remains of the thing they'd killed.

Then Nort shook himself, spat on the ground and looked up. "Hero, Eldin!" he called after them. "We've a lot to thank you for. I do so now. Maybe next time you come to Inquanok you won't have to sneak in, eh?"

"That's up to you," Hero called down. "It's all up to you now. But personally speaking, I don't think you'll be seeing us again. Not if I have any say in it."

Eldin came from below, leaned over the side and looked down. "He's right, you know," he shouted. "You Inquanoggins might be happy in this dreary, twilight land of yours, but there are fairer places far for the likes of us."

"The gods our ancestors put us here," Heger retorted as the sky-yacht drifted higher. "They must have had their reasons."

"It's not your blue-blooded ancestry that worries me," was Hero's parting shot. "Not who spawned you but what you, albeit unwittingly, have spawned. Will you see to it, Heger?"

The bearded trader shouted, "If I can, be sure I will."

"Then farewell!" And with that they set sail for Celephais.

A week later they made report to Kuranes at his Cornish manor-house in Celephais, and a month after that he called them to him with some news. There had been a mass uprising in Inquanok: the false temple there had been destroyed until no two stones stood one atop the other, its "priests" were wiped out to a man—or thing. A simultaneous attack on the Veiled King's palace had proven singularly monstrous: eleven good strong men had died before the Veiled King succumbed, and even then the horror had had to be burned. Beneath the palace and temple a veritable nest of maggots had been discovered, with endless labyrinthine tunnels and halls whose purposes . . . but here Kuranes refused to go into detail. And the questers did not press him.

Now, however, he could tell them that their intervention had been a grand success in more ways than they'd previously suspected. Augeren was dead for one thing, and that had been their original objective; but more than that, the rule of immemorial successions of Veiled Kings was at an end, and their priest minions exposed for the sub-human monsters they were. The new government of Inquanok, headed by one Heger Nort, was already changing the twilight land's laws: there were courts now, and a proper judiciary system. No more men, whatever their crimes, would be sent north naked as babes to test the terrors of the gaunt gray peaks. As for priests—legitimate priests, that is—well, there were many temples and so many priests, but a new law in Inquanok said priests would go bareheaded and with shaven pates, and their limbs would be plainly visible at all times.

Even this was not the end of the matter. Heger Nort was talking of organizing a punitive expedition into the underworld, and had asked for Kuranes' help. Specifically, he had stated that if a certain pair of questers—

Which was the point at which Hero and Eldin bade the Lord of Ooth-Nargai good day, and left his manor house with something less than customary decorum.

Now heading, in the twilight of evening, for a favored tavern on the waterfront, they breathed easier, and Hero uncharacteristically opined: "Bollocks!"

"Lot's of 'em," Eldin agreed.

"Not for a king's ransom!" Hero spat out the words.

"And certainly not for a Veiled King's ransom," said Eldin less vehemently.

"That's one quest I'm well and truly *finished* with!"

Hero declared. "I don't even want reminding of it, not ever!"

"Except—" said Eldin.

"Not ever!"

"But you still haven't told me about my name!"

"Your name?" Hero looked taken aback. "Old duffer, d'you mean?"

The Wanderer snorted like a horse. "How old are you, lad?"

"Eh? My age? Dunno, exactly. Thirty-odd, I suppose. Maybe thirty-two. Why?"

"Because if you want to make thirty-three, watch your lip!" said Eldin "But you *know* what I mean— and you'll listen to me *and* answer me even if I have to tie you down first! Back in Inquanok, when we were dissecting Augeren's name, which as it happens was pretty descriptive of the beast himself, you said—"

"—I said I remembered *your* name's meaning from some old book in the waking world," Hero cut in. "Yes, I know. But try as I might—and I have tried, hard—it's gone. I've forgotten it. You know how it is with these flashes from the waking world?"

"Hmm!" Eldin rumbled, plainly disappointed. He caught Hero's elbow and drew him to a halt on the threshold of the tavern. "Forgotten, have you? Now that couldn't simply be a case of convenient amnesia, could it?"

"I swear I've forgotten!" Hero protested. "But if ever I re-remember . . ." And to himself: *Better if you don't know, old lad. Better far.* For Hero remembered Eldin's love of a good warm fire to sit by, the way he always looked lovingly into the flames—and the fact that he invariably kept a pair of flints, his "lucky firestones," close to hand—and the way he'd once burned Thalarion the evil hive city to the ground, not to mention a certain tightwad inn! And he also remembered how the Wanderer had blinded Augeren ...

Oh, yes, a fire sign, Eldin, without a doubt. But letting him know it would be like blowing on embers, wouldn't it?

"Anyway, the hell with it!" said the Wanderer. "There's booze for the buying and my throat's afire." He held open the tavern's swing door and inclined his head. "Shall we?"

"By all means," said Hero, "let's douse the flames. In fact, let's damn well drown 'em!"

And passing in, they let the door swing shut behind them on a perfect night in dreamland ...

End note

> eldin, elding:
> One or that of fiery disposition;
> a firebrand; fuel for a fire. Arch:
> eilding, eldr, fire.
>> Old Scots Dictionary

A DAY IN THE LIFE . . .

One of those perfect summer days, in fact. With the sun searing the sky until it drips down in shades of blue melt and merges with the sea; and the occasional fish leaping almost as if the water were too warm for him, leaving slowly fading ripples; and a solitary cloud, like a dab of cotton wool, drifting almost lonely over the central peaks of the Isle of Oriab in the Southern Sea. In the little villages flanking the seaport Baharna, nets would be drying in the sun, evening meals being given consideration, donkeys standing in whatever shade they could find, and nobody—*nobody* doing anything much.

Neither were Hero and Eldin.

They had vented flotation essence, come down out of the sky and dropped anchor off a tiny uninhabited knob of rock, the peak of some mountain of which the main range formed Oriab, and here as afternoon crept toward evening they'd got out their lines and were now hard at it, fishing. Except "hard at it" probably paints the wrong picture. Later, tonight, they might well be "hard at it," but that's a different story.

They lay, each with his back to the low structure forming the cabin, Eldin to port and Hero to starboard, with legs bent at the knees and feet scarce projecting over the sides. *Quester* was a small sky-yacht and her masters were big men. Both were naked from the waist up, bare-footed, lines tied to their big toes. They were brown as berries, quietly simmering, content as any pair of dreamers could be. Almost. But when Eldin felt sleepy and contented, Hero usually had something on his mind, and when Hero was feeling all at one with the dreamlands, then Eldin would be astir.

In fact he was astir now, inside his head, anyway.

"I had an odd dream last night," he said, breaking a long hot silence, his deep voice drifting lazily over the top of the cabin-cum-galley and settling like a soft lasso over Hero's mind.

Hero said nothing, concentrated on his toe, which hadn't twitched in a half-hour. The fish seemed too idle to bite. He didn't blame them.

"I'll tell you about it later," said Eldin.

"Oh, good!" Hero returned. "I'll look forward to that."

"It's been on my mind, that's all. In fact, sev'ral things have been on my mind."

"What, all at once?" said Hero. "Braggart!"

"Like, f'rinstance"—Eldin ignored his sarcasm—"Inquanok!"

Hero sighed. "How many times do I have to say it?" he asked, bad memories returning in a flood. "Man, I'm still trying to *forget* Inquanok!"

"No, no, *no!*" Eldin protested. "I'm not talking about what happened there. It's a word-game I've been playing, that's all. A mental diversion."

"Oh?" Hero was dubious. "Look, tonight we're dining with Ula and Una in Baharna. Afterward . . . well, won't that be diversion enough?"

"Purely physical!" said Eldin at once. "But this . . . brain food!"

Hero snorted. "All right," he said, "I'll fall for it. What are you raving on about?"

"Tell me," said Eldin: "what would you call the men of Inquanok?"

"Idiots!" Hero replied. "Before our first—and last—visit there, anyway. Since then, not quite so daft."

"No, no, *no*!" Eldin was getting repetitive. "I mean their actual name, as a race. Like a man of Dylath-Leen is a Dylath-Leener, and the men of Serannian are Serannionians."

"And a man of Celephais is a Celephasian, and dwellers in Ilek-Vad are Ilek-Vadians?"

"Exactly!" said Eldin. "So what's a man of Inquanok called, eh?"

"Never thought about it," said Hero.

"So think."

Unseen, on the other side of the cabin, Hero shrugged. "An Inquaknocker, I suppose."

"Eh?" said Eldin. "A bit sexist, that, isn't it? I meant the people of Inquanok as a whole, not just the girls."

Hero couldn't repress a grin. "Then I suppose that rules out Inquaknackers, too, eh? What about Inquanauts?"

"They're not *all* seafarers!" Eldin protested. "Me, I've reached a decision. From now on I call 'em Inqublots."

"Good!" said Hero. "Anything for peace and quiet, that's what I always say . . ."

There was silence for two full minutes. Then:

"Dreams," said Eldin. (Hero groaned inwardly.) "Do you believe in 'em?"

"Now there's a silly bloody question if ever I heard one!" Hero burst out after a moment's thought. "What?

Here's us, dreamers, adrift in the land of Earth's dreams, and you ask me if I believe in 'em? I mean, should I say no, and then express mild surprise when our boat turns to mist, and you and I gradually fade out, and the entire scene turns to shimmering dust-motes and leaves our shrieking, shrinking ids to wander in eternal oblivion?"

"That's a bit strong!" muttered Eldin. "What's more, it's not what I meant. I meant do you believe that dreams are prophetic?"

Hero frowned, jerked his toe as his line went taut, scowled as it immediately slackened. "What's on your mind?" he asked.

"Dreams are," said Eldin. "I mean, they're damned queer things, dreams. There we were, presumably, dreamers in the waking world, fashioning dreams like mad, never believing for a moment that they were real, with people living in 'em and stuff! Then one day we died, I suppose, and came here. And here, what do we do but dream! At least I do, and damned strange ones at that. So—if you see what I'm getting at—I find the whole thing quite fascinating. I mean, they go inward and outward, probably for ever."

"Eh? Inward and outward?"

"What I'm asking is this," said Eldin. "When we were in the waking world, was somebody on some higher plane dreaming *us*?"

"Ah!" said Hero. "And someone higher still dreaming him, d'you mean? And do the dreams we dream now give life to some ulterior world? Like sitting in a barber's chair where there's a mirror fore and one aft, so that you see yourself seeing yourself seeing—"

"Yes!" said Eldin excitedly.

"Or the world as an atom of some greater world, the macrocosm, and every atom of the world a universe in its own right, composed of even smaller universes. Inward and outward."

"Yes, yes!"

"Or two bees looking at each other, reflected in each other's myriad-faceted eyes, and each facet's facets repeating a myriad bee ogles, and—"

"Yes, yes, yes!" Eldin was ecstatic.

"Shouldn't think so," said Hero.

Eldin got a bite and gave his toe a massive jerk. Hero, too, and likewise.

"Well, it's my belief that they *are* prophetic," said Eldin. "Especially the one I had last night." He hauled on his line.

On the other side of the boat Hero had his own fight going. "Lord, have I got a fish here!" he cried.

"A sprat compared to mine!" Eldin's voice was high with excitement.

Hero leaned forward, caught up his line and gave it a steady pull terminating in a yank—and the fish yanked back! It yanked hard. He was hauled upright, flew forward, nearly shot over the side before he could get his balance. Then, as he felt the line tighten again—

—He threw himself flat, face down and head over the side, legs stretched along the gunnel—and had no sooner assumed that position than he heard Eldin's cry of outrage as *his* line went slack and *his* head cracked against the cabin's planking.

"Ow!" said the Wanderer. "But this is a fish with fight in him!"

Hero scowled thoughtfully, tugged tentatively at his line, and—

"There he goes again!" yelled Eldin.

"Whoa!" Hero cried in something of desperation as the other hauled.

"Eh?" Eldin suspected that the *whoa* had been directed

at him. "What? I should desist? Are you joking? But this is a *big* bugger!"

"Too true, he is," Hero readily agreed. "And if you don't stop hauling on that line of yours you're going to *pull his bloody toe off!*"

There was a long, awkward silence; then they cut their tangled lines and watched them slowly sink, and at last climbed to their feet to confront each other—finally collapsing in tears of laughter on the deck. They'd earlier lowered a bottle of wine by its neck into the water; now they brought it up, drew the cork, took long pulls. And:

"Ah, well," Hero sighed after a while. "I suppose it's up-anchor and heigh-ho for—"

There came a flapping of roseate wings and a stir of air as a pink temple pigeon rotated and braced himself for a landing on the cabin's roof. Tied to his leg, a tiny silver cylinder with a cork stopper. Eldin scooped the bird up as soon as it landed, untied the message cylinder, took out the stopper. He began to slide out the tight-rolled scrap of paper curled within, but Hero stopped him.

"Hang on," said the younger quester. "Not so fast. You know what'll happen if we read that, don't you?"

Eldin raised his eyebrows, looked over his shoulder, said: "Who, me? Am I clairvoyant or something? How should I know what will happen if we—?"

"But you do, you do!" Hero cut him short, taking the cylinder from him. "This bird's from Ulthar or Celephais, Serannian or Ilek-Vad. From Kuranes or Atal or some other person of their estimable ilk. And it carries a summons, a command, most likely a quest—for us!"

"So? But that's how we earn a living, isn't it? We *are* questers, aren't we?"

"Not tonight, we're not!" Hero denied it. He drew out the tiny curl of paper, dropped it carelessly over the side of the boat.

"What? *What?*" Eldin went wide-eyed. "But that's . . . that's . . ."

"It's very sensible," said Hero. "If it was important there'll be another bird tomorrow. If it was *very* important there'll probably be two." He took out a scrap of paper and a sharp shard of charcoal from his pocket (he wrote the occasional line of poetry, much to Eldin's disgust) and scribbled: "Sorry, message dropped overboard by fumbling, drunken elder quester before it could be read. Please repeat instructions." Then he quickly rolled it up, inserted it into the cylinder and recorked it, tied it to the patient bird's leg.

"What did you write?" Eldin queried as the bird soared aloft.

"Told him—whoever—that you were drunk and dropped it overboard," said Hero.

"Oh!" said Eldin, nodding affably. And a moment later: "Eh? You did *what*?"

Hero held up placating hands. "This squares it for your lapse," he explained.

"What lapse?"

"We had a choice," said Hero. "In three months' time—*if* Ula and Una still wanted to see us then—you'd have to explain how you messed up tonight by reading that message and going off a-questing instead of a-whatevering. Or tonight you can tell 'em how you saved the day—or night—by dint of your quick-wittedness. I simply assumed you'd prefer the second option."

Eldin thought it over. "Well that's damned decent of you!" he eventually remarked. "Your logic's a bit lopsided, for which I'll probably clout you later, but for now . . . did you have to say I was drunk?"

Hero sighed patiently. "Of course!" he said. "I mean, what sort of idiot would commit such an enormity sober, eh?" He went below, started up the flotation engine.

Later, airborne and dripping water from their keel as they climbed skyward and turned for Oriab, Eldin said: "Anyway, it gives me a chance to check out my dream theory: that they're prophetic, that is. See, this dream of mine took place in Baharna, in Lippy Unth's place, the *Craven Lobster*. We were in there, having a drink, when who should I spot but the seer with invisible eyes."

"Oh!" said Hero. "Him again. You've told me about him before: you look into his eyes and see nothing. You see their rims—craters on each side of his nose—but nothing in 'em. The spaces between the stars, empty voids, nothingness."

"The same," said Eldin, nodding. "Anyway, we went over to speak to him and he looked at us sort of funny."

"With his invisible eyes?" said Hero.

"Right. And then—"

"Well?"

"He fell face down on the table, dead!"

Hero frowned. "And that's it?"

"Not quite. Before he died, he thrust out his hand. In it, a crumpled scrap of paper. I took it, smoothed it out on the table top . . . and woke up!"

Hero took a deep breath, tut-tutted, sighed, said: "You know, sometimes I feel I've spent half my life listening to you say daft things! I mean, what the hell—?"

"But it was so damned *real*!" Eldin insisted. "A prophecy of some sort, I'm sure."

Hero gazed long and hard at the other, detected no

note of humor or leg-pulling, finally narrowed his eyes. "That settles it," he eventually said. "We'll have a drink tonight, by all means, before we meet up with the girls. But *not* in the *Craven Lobster*!"

"You think there's something in it, then?" Eldin was eager.

"No," said Hero, "but I'm not about to take any chances with it either. I mean, why tempt fate, eh?"

Why, indeed?

In the deeps of the Southern Sea, full fathom five and still descending in lazy, undulating spirals, like some mindless, paperish flatfish, Kuranes' message was destined never to be read by mortal man or dreamer. Couched in his own crabbed script—in the clean glyphs of dreams, in which Hero and Eldin were both now fully versed—its legend was this:

> *Hero & Eldin—*
> *Proceed* at once *to Baharna on the Isle of Oriab, and there seek out the seer with invisible eyes in the tavern of Lipperod Unth, which is called the* Craven Lobster. *Speak to the seer and hear him out, but DO NOTHING MORE until you have further instructions from me. To investigate his tale lacking possession of all the facts would almost certainly prove fatal!*
>

Your employer,
Kuranes.

A fish, ogling by, glimpsed the feathery, slowly disintegrating scrap and perhaps thought it a flap of human skin or flake of flesh, or some other item of edible debris from above. It took an instinctive bite—tore off a single word—and swallowed, found the paper not especially palatable, turned away in search of a more substantial meal.

Thus "Kuranes," like Jonah in a different world and time, and on a slightly higher plane, was swallowed by a probably mythical fish. The only difference being that no one made any fuss about it.

A-MAZED IN ORIAB

Fancying belly-dancers (Eldin was a "jiggly-bits" addict), the questers made for Buxom Barba's *Quayside Quaress* on Wharf Street. Because of Baharna's precipitous aspect—its streets were piled almost vertically one upon the next, joined by steep alleyways climbing inexorably wearisome to more lofty and opulent suburbs—safe moorings for sky-ships were few and far between. Emphasis on "safe." Around the lower squares and markets were ample posts where a boat might be anchored (tied fore and aft, so as not to swing about in a sudden gust and collide with other vessels), which was fine for craft with larger crews, when there would always be a man or men aboard. But dodgy to leave a boat like *Quester* trussed thus, for urchins would scamper up the lines to sample whatever goodies they might find in a small, deserted, obviously foreign boat.

For this and other reasons of security, the pair had moored their vessel within the bay, something less than a quarter mile out, to the mast of some old wreck where it projected slantingly from the sea. The unknown hulk was marked as a hazard with a buoy (bearing a notice which read: " 'WARE SCABFISH!") bobbing over the scummy harbor water.

Scabfish were eel-like wreck-denizens with very anti-social habits; if a man should touch one a scab would develop at point of contact, only falling off when new, clean skin had formed beneath. No city brat was likely to come a-swimming here! Nor, for that matter, were David Hero and Eldin the Wanderer.

Since the wind was in their favor they'd gone ashore suspended beneath a spare flotation-bag, venting essence as they neared the wharves and so arriving in Baharna pristine and not a bit damp. And not a little thirsty, either. Leaving their deflating bag in the care of a net-mending pegleg, and paying him a tip nipped from one point of a triangular golden tond for his trouble, they'd headed for the *Quaress*.

Alas!—closed, shut down: no colored lanthorns glimmering, though evening drew toward night, and no swirly music to announce the fact that the belly-dancers were at it. For in fact, they weren't. Disbelieving (What? Buxom Barba absent or remiss on a fine summer night like this, and the city aswarm with sightseers, sailors and other spenders—not to mention the odd quester or two?), Eldin rapped sharply on the carved, suddenly unfriendly-seeming door, yelled: "Wake up in there, Barba—the boys are here!"

"*One* boy, anyway," Hero murmured, "and one elderly buffoon." And louder: "Can't you see she's closed?"

"My heart's *set* on it!" Eldin insisted. "Naked navels all a-wobble!" And: "Ah!" as the door suddenly opened outward.

A sailor emerged, Celephaisian by his looks, wobbly at the knees and decidedly glazed of eye. He was propelled out into the street by an Amazon the questers knew of old. Big and of gleamy bronze, but clad now for the street and not the stage, Zuli Bazooli—who danced with snakes and did other things—showed her teeth in a smile like a bar of light in the shadow of the silent tavern.

"Hero and Eldin!" she exclaimed, holding her sailor aloft by his collar, like a puppet. "So the tide's washed you two up again, eh?"

"Barba's late opening," Eldin frowned, making to enter. Zuli blocked the way.

"Not tonight, my lads," she declared, her voice almost as loud as the Wanderer's own. "With luck, tomorrow—but not tonight."

"Explain!" cried Eldin, all visions of jiggly-bits receding. "Is Barba sick?"

Zuli shrugged, carefully locking the door behind her. "You might say that," she said. "Ship out of Celephais, docked at noon. Six bow-legged lads came ashore, good drinking men all. They challenged Barba to a bout and she took 'em on. I've just put her to bed. We're shut."

"What?" Hero was skeptical. "Buxom Barba beaten in boozing bout?"

"Sounds like a headline!" said Eldin.

"Took 'em on one at a time," said Zuli. "Fatal! As the first five dropped out in their turn, the girls dragged 'em off to spend their money. This one's the last, and he's mine. The Winner!"

"Not much of a winner," growled Eldin. "If you let go of him he'll march straight off the wharfside!" The sailor grinned lopsidedly and did a half-suspended jig.

"You should see Barba!" Zuli declared. "Or maybe you shouldn't. Come round tomorrow. And till then, goodnight." She made off, aiming her sailor before her.

"Damn!" said Eldin with feeling. "I was looking forward to a bit of belly-dancing."

"So get on with it," said Hero. "I'll take the collection."

Eldin might have said something unkind, but Hero was already leading the way through a backstreet and across the teak-boarded skeleton of an ancient wharf. He headed for a boozer's backwater, one of Baharna's seedier haunts, built on century-old ironwood piles and threatening at any moment to slide into the bay. Only the likely lads came here, and hardened, salty old sea-dogs who thrived on sour wine. Underfoot, glinting like oil, black water slapped in wavelets and sent fish-stink sleazing through huge gaps in the ancient planking.

Eldin caught up with the younger man. "The *Craven Lobster*?" His eyes were wide in the encroaching gloom.

Hero glanced up and back at bustling, lanthorn-bobbing Baharna's healthier districts. "Whitby," he mused, frowning.

"Eh?"

"A seaport in the waking world . . . I think," Hero screwed up his eyes in an effort to catch the fleeting memory. "D'you know, this could almost be it?"

"I said," Eldin sighed, "are we going to—"

"—the *Craven Lobster*, yes," said Hero. "For four reasons. One: the *Quayside Quaress* is shut. And two: the town's overflowing with visitors and we'd never get near the bar in a decent place; not without climbing up to the more expensive levels, anyway. Three: we've an hour or two to kill before we meet the girls."

"And four?" the Wanderer prompted.

"Because I hate mysteries," Hero answered with a low growl. "You and your damned dreams within dreams! Come on . . ."

* * *

The *Craven Lobster* was something else. One hundred years ago fishermen had gutted and cleaned their catches there, and fifty years later it had been the property of a pearler, who'd kept his glass-bottomed boats under its protective planking and used the building itself as a sorting and polishing house. With the sea on three sides and a narrow-necked railed catwalk in front, certainly the place had been secure. It had a good roof, which was about as much as could now be said of it. The salt sea, a thousand heavy autumn fogs, time, and the elements had all taken their toll of the *Craven Lobster*; now its wooden walls leaned ominously and were timber-buttressed without. Inside, the bar consisted of a stout square framework in the center of one huge room, from which the proprietor, his wife and massive son could take in the entire place at a glance.

As for the booze; it wasn't good, but it certainly wasn't the worst. Selling it didn't quite constitute a criminal offense. The muth-dew was watered (not a bad idea) and the ales had ailed a bit; the wines were of no readily recognizable vintage, and the spirits all had the same salty tang to them. But on the other hand it was very cheap, and provided a man had a cast-iron stomach and all he wanted to do was drink, he could do it here for a week on one golden tond.

But the *Craven Lobster*'s chief attractions, certainly in high season, were these: there was always room to sit and sup without tangling elbows; you didn't have to shout to make yourself heard; you wouldn't be bothered by ladies of the night or other bar-flies; and the proprietor, Lipperod (Lippy) Unth, demanded and maintained good order at all times. "Fight all you like," was his motto, "and break whatever you like of what's your own. But break what's mine and you'll never know what hit you!"

Lippy wasn't called that because he liked talking—on the contrary, he was far more a man of action—nor did his nickname derive entirely from Lipperod. But when Lippy Unth was annoyed, then he pouted with his great black lips and thrust them out before him like a warning trumpet; and when Lippy looked like that—

The *Craven Lobster* did have a handful of "girls," the very dregs of the city. No one bothered them much and they wouldn't notice anyway, for they were all of a kind: sunken into a sodden alcoholic mire, from which there'd be no return. They would in the end drink themselves to death. While Hero and Eldin pitied them, on occasion they'd remarked how they would rather snuggle up to a school of scabfish. Now and then a sailor would get senseless drunk and go off with one of them, for which all the gods of dream help him!

The rest of the *Craven Lobster*'s clientele: hard men, loners, the occasional Kledan slaver, sea-captains from unknown parts on the lookout for a crewman to shanghai, other seadogs and peglegs and retired pirates gathered to tell their tall tales, which got taller with each telling. And now and then a pair of questers.

Like now, for instance.

Hero held open the door on its spring-loaded hinges, waited while Eldin wrinkled his nose and sniffed suspiciously on the threshold. Then the Wanderer pretended to reel from the vapors and perfumed smoke and writhing reek of the place, and leaning against this supposed exhalation as against a strong wind made his way to the bar. Following in Eldin's wake, Hero tut-tutted at his dramatics. It wasn't *that* bad.

"Ho, Lippy!" Eldin rumbled, thumping his elbows down on the bar.

Hero drew up alongside the Wanderer and gazed at Lippy's huge ebony features. In the frame of his memory a picture formed, in which Lippy's mouth moved and spoke the words: "Of all the gin-joints in all the towns in all the world, you two had to walk—" But the vision was shattered when the real-life Lippy said:

"Ho, Wanderer!" The Pargan proprietor nodded. "You, too, Hero. Long time . . ." That was their welcome, and never a smile. Then, straight to business: "Eldin, we've a couple of Kledan slavers in tonight. Last time you were here—"

"No trouble tonight!" Eldin held up a flat hand. "My word on it."

"I had to have the wall shored up where you tossed that one through it into the sea."

"But I didn't start it."

"That's true, else you'd have followed him. Very well, what's your poison?"

"Ales," said Hero. "Small ones. We've things to do later and I for one don't want a fuddled head." They paid for their drinks, sipped, gazed around the smoky interior. Lippy moved away to tend to someone else, and:

"Well?" said Hero. "D'you see him?"

"Eh?"

"The seer with invisible eyes, of course—or is the rest of him equally insubstantial?"

Eldin narrowed his eyes to a penetrating peer, began to sweep the room with his gaze. "Maybe he's not—" he started, and froze.

"And maybe he is," Hero nodded sourly, following Eldin's rapt gaze. "Is that him?"

For answer, the Wanderer slowly nodded.

The seer with invisible eyes didn't look like much. He sat on a bench, his back toward an open window in the rear wall (a wall of thin wooden boards, which showed signs of recent repair), and huddled over a mug of muth. He seemed skeletal inside a bundle of rags with the hood pulled up, throwing his face into shadow; the only visible parts of him were his scrawny wrists and clawlike hands, which protruded from his tattered sleeves and circled the mug on the wooden table before him. He seemed oblivious of the fact that no one sat very close to him, oblivious of all else, too; but, as Hero and Eldin stared, the figure lifted a bony hand and crooked a finger in their direction. And: "Come," that finger undeniably beckoned, pulling on their strings.

No one else had noticed; Hero and Eldin shoved off from the bar and moved toward the seer. As they went Hero muttered: "He's on the dew, eh?"

"All he ever drinks," Eldin rumblingly returned.

Hero nodded. "No wonder his eyes have vanished!" he said.

"Sit," the seer sighed, still without looking up, as they reached his table. His voice was a rustle of dead leaves. "I've been waiting for you."

The questers stared at each other in astonishment. "Sit!" hissed the seer. "Don't be so obvious! Pretend you don't know me, as I'll *gladly* pretend I don't know you!"

"Little shrivelled friend," said Hero out the corner of his mouth as he sat to one side of the seer, "I really *don't* know you!"

"But *I* do," Eldin growled. "So what's all this with the secrecy bit, eh?"

"Careful!" the seer now looked up a little, the shadows falling away from his face. "We have enemies here!"

Hero looked into the seer's eyes and saw what Eldin had tried to describe: which is to say, he saw nothing. Those eyes were deep as the spaces out beyond the farthest stars. And that was how cold they looked, too.

Hero felt that if he stuck a finger in one of them, then that finger would go brittle as a crystal and snap off in a single instant. "Bottomless!" he gasped.

"Aye, almost," the seer agreed. "They went this way a moment after I was born. They are my legacy. I'm a mentalist and my eyes are my crystal balls—or my crystal eyeballs, if you like! You see, my mother cast runes and my father was a dream-reader."

"A what?" said Hero.

"Oneiromancer," sighed the seer.

Hero frowned, scratched his head. "What the hell's a one-eyed romancer?"

Eldin's turn to sigh. "A piratical tall-tale-teller!" he rumbled. And to the seer: "What's this about enemies?"

The seer glanced dartingly this way and that. "Didn't Kuranes tell you anything? He did send you, didn't he? Or maybe my sendings reached you?"

The questers looked at each other; Eldin gloweringly, Hero half apologetically and with the ghost of a shrug. "Kuranes told us, er, very little," the younger dreamer said.

"Truth to tell," Eldin added disgustedly, "damn all! What's all this about sendings?"

"Dreams!" said the seer. "I've been sending you dreams. Didn't you dream that you'd meet me here?"

"Er, why yes I did," said Eldin. "But I also—"

"*Shhh!*" the seer held up a cautionary finger. "We're under scrutiny. You see those Kledans there?" He nodded almost imperceptibly across the room. "They—"

At which point there came a *phttt!* from the open window, followed immediately by the noise a soft-bodied fly makes thudding against a window-pane. The seer said, "Ah!" and jerked straighter where he sat.

Hero glanced at the window, thought he saw a dark face disappearing there. The seer slumped, fell face down, sprawling on the table. A long feathered dart, the merest sliver of wood and fluff, stood up from the thin rags on his back. Then—

Chaos!

Hero was on his feet, lips drawn back in a snarl, curved sword whispering from its sheath more magically than any wand. He sprang to the window and looked out—and ducked back. A second blow-dart zipped past his ear like an enraged wasp, stuck quivering into a ceiling beam. But out there in the night, pulling away, a pair of burly blacks worked hard at the oars of their boat; and dangling down from the window-frame, a knotted rope suspended from its grapple. In another moment the boat disappeared out of the light from the window, became a shadow, was lost in the mild summer mist.

Meanwhile:

The Kledans the seer had pointed out had come to their feet, started toward the table where their almost-accuser lay face-down, lifeless. "What?" cried one gutturally, in feigned surprise. "Murder? What have you two done to him there?"

The second black said: "How's that? Stuck him with a dart, did you?"

Every head in the *Craven Lobster* was turned now in the direction of Hero, Eldin, and the ex-seer. Then the first of the black slavers closed with Eldin, snarled his enmity and snatched at his knife. An enormous error.

Eldin reached out swift as lightning and grasped the man's knife hand, bearing down on it and holding the knife safe in its scabbard. At the same time he butted the black in the mouth, heard teeth break and lips squelch into tatters. The second Kledan dragged out the dart from the seer's back, turned with it upraised to strike at Eldin.

Meanwhile:

Hero had turned from the window, taken in the scene at a glance. He stepped forward, caught at the descending wrist, deflected and added impetus to the blow. The Kledan stabbed himself in the groin and squealed like a stuck pig.

By now the first slaver was in big trouble: face bloody and only half-conscious, he was whirled for a moment across Eldin's broad shoulders, then released like a shot from a sling against Lippy's recently repaired wall. The *Craven Lobster* shuddered hugely as the Kledan crashed through in a splintering of timbers.

Meanwhile:

The slaver with the dart in his groin had gone to his knees; white froth started from his lips; he was dead before he toppled. The poison on the dart had been *that* effective! Eldin grabbed at the limp body of the seer, tried to sit him up. Useless, the seer flopped off the bench on to the floor. He lay on his back staring blindly up at Hero and Eldin, and as they stared back, so his invisible eyes filled in. There was a scene in them, mobile, like the reflection in a mirror: *moving pictures of Ula and Una, fighting in the grip of a pair of bully-boys who grinned and fondled them detestably!*

Then—

The scene vanished as the seer's eyes turned scarlet and flooded over. Blood dripped from their rims.

By now everyone in the place was on his or her feet, all eyes turned accusingly on the questers. No one had seen the face at the window except Hero, but all had heard the shouted Kledan accusations. The seer was dead, likewise a slaver. Another slaver was either drowning or fighting off scabfish. And there was a damned great hole in the *Craven Lobster*'s rear wall.

It had all taken a handful of seconds; and meanwhile:

Lippy Unth had been holding his breath. Holding it so long his great ebony face had turned more nearly black, then dark green, finally enraged purple. What's more, his huge lips were protruding in such a pout as was never before seen. He swung himself over the bar and landed four-square, more like a bull gorilla than a man, and straightening up advanced shamblingly on the questers where they stood astonished.

"What?" roared Eldin as Lippy charged, scattering tables and benches and customers and anything else that happened to be in his path, tossing all aside like so much chaff. "What? You blame *us*?"

Lippy bellowed like a behemoth, bore down on Hero, who at once took cover under a bolted-down table. Lippy crashed into the table (more shudders from the *Craven Lobster*, and dust falling from ceiling-beams everywhere), sprawled across it, reached down arms like treetrunks and grabbed Hero's ankles. Which was when Eldin picked up a bench and hit him with it. Lippy stopped bellowing, stood up, fell down stiff as a log.

A moment later and Hero scrambled into view; he was white as a sheet from the closeness of his shave. Then the two were fighting for the door, kicking, biting and fending off blows and oaths with more of the same. Somehow they made it unscathed and turned to look back.

A man could die in the *Craven Lobster* (if he did it quietly) and it probably wouldn't be noticed for a while. Slaves might well be bartered there, and no one would turn a hair—not even Lippy, who'd once been a slave himself. But only spill a man's drink, or interrupt the interminable fables of some old legend-monger, or (worse far) interfere with the service . . .

The questers had done all three with great gusto, and the *Craven Lobster*'s clientele did not approve. Amid the reek and shambles of the place a ring of scarred, furious faces slowly became visible. Knives glinted dully, and bronze knuckle-dusters were slipped over the ridges of horny fingers; and out of the sudden lull came an abrupt, renewed burst of violence. Lippy's son, big as his father and just as dangerous, smashed through the narrowing circle and hurled himself headlong upon Hero and Eldin as they backed off.

Nimble as a cricket, Hero stepped aside, tripped him. Gooba Unth said, *"Oops!"* He flew forward, horizontally now, and was smacked soundly, double-fisted, on the side of his head by Eldin. His flight diverted, Gooba struck a doorpost like a torpedo and knocked it loose. The overhead still sagged and the ceiling groaned as it settled a few inches, while beams popped and more dust fell in threatening rills from the higher rafters.

The questers glanced at one another, grinning maliciously through clenched teeth. They looked again at the circle of muttering faces, and their eyes gleamed as they turned them on the remaining upright. "Me or you?" the Wanderer queried.

Hero shrugged. "Be my guest," he said.

As the crowd surged forward like a tide, Eldin dropkicked the doorpost out into the night. Hero ducked through at the last moment, untangled his friend from the moaning heap that was Gooba Unth, and hastened him along the catwalk to the dockside proper.

Behind them, the *Craven Lobster* uttered a curious sigh and several creaks and grunts: the death-rattle of ill-used timbers giving up the ghost. Then, to a chorus of "Timber!" from the duo, the roof settled slantingly as walls buckled and one sadly defunct tavern slid off its piles into the greasy harbor water. Last to go was the catwalk itself.

"What now?" said Eldin.

"We've a date, remember?"

"What? But surely we want to keep the girls out of this—whatever 'this' is!"

"They're already in," said Hero fatalistically. "You saw what I saw, in the seer's dead eyes, didn't you?"

"Yes, but—"

"But nothing. You asked me recently if I thought dreams mightn't be prophetic. Well, yours obviously was—so what are we to make of what the seer showed us in his eyes?"

Eldin made no answer. He didn't have one.

They made their way into a maze of steep, narrow alleys, climbing rapidly through several street levels into brighter, more friendly districts. Cats in the night, they were gray and insubstantial as shadows, fleet and silent as moonbeams. But stepping at last from shade into the welcoming glow of multi-colored lanthorns strung above the stalls and wares and thronging crowd of a street bazaar, they reverted to being just men again, and no one seeing their beaming faces and the elegance of their gestures and movements would ever guess the disorder so recently left in their wake.

"D'you think the law will get after us?" Eldin gruffly inquired, the while smiling at an old lady who fried honey pancakes and shaped them into hearts for courting couples.

"What, for sinking the *Craven Lobster*?" Hero shook his head. "We could end up on the city's roll of honor!"

"No," Eldin grunted, "for killing the seer. Not to mention a Kledan—or possibly two Kledans."

"We didn't kill the seer," said Hero. "And the slavers tried to kill *us*! That was self-defense."

They crossed the street between stalls, avoided bags

of sweets thrust at them by a man dressed as a toffee-apple.

"*We* know that," said Eldin. "But what about that gang of cutthroats we left in the swim back there?"

"Oh, yes?" said Hero scornfully. "And can you honestly see one of that lot reporting the matter to the law? They might eventually be *questioned* about it—I mean, someone's bound to notice sooner or later, the loss of an entire tavern and whatnot—but they'd hardly go volunteering the information, now would they? I'll bet every man-jack of 'em has a record long as your gangly arm!"

Eldin reckoned he was probably right.

By now they'd reached the foot of a wide wooden staircase, set back from the street, that led up an otherwise sheer cliff face to a cavern eatery. In the back, the choicest dishes of dreams were prepared by a team of experts; out in front, on a great balcony under a mighty red-striped awning, said viands and morsels and gobbets were gobbled by Baharna's most demanding gourmets. A hand-painted sign made an arch over the stairway, saying:

THIS WAY TO PAZZA'S PANTRY!

Not the cheapest restaurant by any means, but Ula and Una were worth it.

Ula and Una were the twin daughters of one Ham Gidduf, a rich merchant of Andahad, a small but opulent seaport on the far side of Oriab. They'd shared adventures with the questers before—indeed they'd been with them in the affair of the Mad Moon—and there was an ongoing amorous affair, too, however sporadic. Now, hearing coos and giggles, Hero and Eldin stood at the foot of the stairway and elevated their eyes to the balcony under the awning. Seated at a table on the very rim, their pretty elbows on the ornate stone balustrade, Ula and Una waved down at them.

The questers grinned, waved back, started up the steps. On the way Eldin queried: "Now say, am I all spruce? I mean, will she look right on my arm?"

"You're fine," said Hero. He heaved a sigh of relief. "And obviously they're fine, too. So the seer's vision hasn't come to pass just yet. And if we stay close to the girls—keep our eyes peeled, our swords ready and senses alert—then when it does happen we'll be there to make a quick end of it."

"Yes, yes, all of that's understood," said Eldin. "But are my boots shiny? Is my jacket tucked into my belt at the back? Are my eyes bright?"

"You're a vain old bugger," said Hero matter-of-factly, eyeing the other up and down. "But yes, all of those things are correct—and your seams are straight, too."

"Eh, seams?"

"Er, 'seems all's in order,' " Hero answered, for already the source of his remark was fading in his mind. A revenant of the waking world, he supposed. "Anyway, what about me?"

They reached the landing that opened on to the balcony. Fabulous food smells invaded their nostrils, tickled their saliva glands, activated their appetites. "What about you?" asked Eldin, his mind on other things. With his eyes fixed on the girls, beaming as he went, he began to make his way to them between tables choked with delirious devourers.

"Am I in good order?" Hero growled under his breath.

"Hell, no!" said Eldin, with the merest glance of disapproval. "Disgusting!" Then they were at the girls' table.

Ula and Una, as fine and desirable a pair of ladies as ever the dreamers had lusted after (and "won," however contrived—by the girls themselves—the double "conquest" had been) were obviously delighted that Hero and Eldin had shown up. The girls knew this pair for what they were, questers, and that their adventurings often took them away, at a moment's notice, into far strange parts and ports.

Dark-haired, green-eyed, and delicately elfin-featured (despite their very worldly prominence in other areas) the girls were supple but something a little more than willowy, and they were very plainly excited to be back in the company of these two likely lads. They stood up laughing as the pair closed on them, and:

" 'Lo," said Hero. "Who's who?"

Eldin, on the other hand, bowed low and with a sweep of his arm said: "The brightest stars of night are fallen on Oriab, and come now into Baharna in the shape of these lovely Loreleis. Good even', O fairest of the fair; but pray, before the festivities commence, may we not inquire which witch is which?"

Then Ula threw herself into Hero's arms: "Oh!" he murmured, almost caving in under her onslaught, "and that's you, is it?"

And Una, hanging on Eldin's neck, saying: "Can't you tell us apart yet, great oafs? I've a slightly longer neck than Ula!"

"All the better for necking, my dear," growled Eldin, in good imitation—indeed in perfect imitation—of a great wolf.

"And I'm a bit longer in the leg," admitted Ula.

"Do you mind if we go into that later?" said Hero, which set the girls giggling again. And so the two pairs stood, locked in each others' arms—but only for a moment more. Then the girls glanced at each other, drew back and smoothed down their pretty frills, finally seated themselves and lifted their noses not a little disdainfully. Their green eyes left the faces of the questers, looked elsewhere, settled for gazing out over the lanthorn-lit city.

"Oh?" said Hero and Eldin together. "And what's all this?" They sat down, each beside his lady.

"Do you need to ask?" Una sniffed. She drew her elbow sharply away as Eldin tried to stroke it. The Wanderer raised bushy eyebrows, glanced at Hero and found his likewise peaked.

"Of course we need to ask," said the younger quester, not unreasonably. "Else how'll we get to know?" But in his secret mind:

Have they heard about our diversion in Dylath-Leen?

And in Eldin's: *P'raps someone's mentioned our carousing in Karkellon!*

Hero: Was it my serenading in Serannian?

Eldin: My how-d'ye-do in Hlanith!

And together, out loud: "Our consciences are clear! So out with it—what's your complaint?"

"We are maidens," said Ula, her glance biting where it fell on Hero's handsome, frowning face, "and yet we are *not* maidens!"

"Shh!" said Eldin at once, peering this way and that in only half-feigned alarm. "Last time you two said things like that you brought all Baharna down on us!"

"But it's true," insisted Una, pouting prettily. "You made us women, and yet have *not* made us wives! Are we toys to sit around waiting for the children to come and wind us up? Then dance for them and sing for them and . . . and . . ."

"And do other things for them," prompted Ula.

"That, too," Una gave a sharp nod of agreement,

"—until they're tired of the game and go off to play at something else?"

"I swear you're my only plaything!" cried Hero to Ula.

"So do I!" said Eldin to Una.

"That's not what we meant!" Ula stamped her foot. "We meant simply that . . ." She tried again. "That . . ."

"Not so simple, eh?" said Hero.

"That we can't marry a pair of questers!" Una finished it for her sister.

For a moment the comrades were silent, astonished—but in the next their frowns turned to beaming smiles. And: "Thank goodness for that!" sighed the Wanderer. "For a while there we thought it was something serious!"

"Buffoon!" cried Una. She jumped to her feet and gave Eldin a ringing clout on the ear.

Hero stopped grinning just in time to receive Ula's punch in his eye. Half-deaf (Eldin) and half-blind (Hero), they too staggered to their feet. At which point—

"*Hold!*" came a deep, throaty voice—the unmistakable Voice of Authority—from close at hand. For while the questers had been involved with their lady-loves, there had been several late arrivals at *Pazza's Pantry*.

The girls, furiously miffed and still not aware of anything untoward, made to stalk off, but were grabbed at once by a pair of gray-clad Regulators. As the questers reached for their swords—an almost entirely automatic reaction on their part—so a party of pikemen stepped forward, formed a circle around them. And *Pazza's Pantry* was suddenly still, with not a chomp to break the silence. As the pikes closed threateningly, so the questers relinquished their grips on their swords, looked to see who led this party of law officers.

And there stood the one who had spoken: a slim, pale fellow of aristocratic mien, his gray uniform complemented by a short cloak of moss-green. And green was the color of high officialdom in Baharna.

"What now?" the stranger throatily inquired, his dark eyes made darker by the pallor of his flesh, his face expressionless. "First mayhem and vandalism on an unprecedented scale, and now rowdyism in a public place? You two are for the jump, I fear!"

"Mayhem?" Eldin tried to look innocent. Almost impossible. His scarred, less than gentle features had "rogue" written all over them.

"Vandalism? Rowdyism?" Hero stood up straighter, radiated indignation. "We were sharing a jest with our fiancées here, that's all."

"How *dare* you!" cried Ula, suddenly coming to life and struggling in the grip of her Regulator. "We're the daughters of Ham Gidduf, and he'll—"

The pale police chief turned on her, cut her off with a snarl. "He'll do nothing at all, my dear! There are laws in Baharna, and I enforce them. *I'm* the one who takes care of lawbreakers and their women, not Ham Gid—"

"Man," said Hero quietly, but with something in his voice that attracted the Chief Regulator's attention. "Whoever or whatever you are," Hero continued, his eyes steely as to strike sparks, "and whatever you 'take care' of, 'ware! You've a nasty tongue. These are ladies, not women, and we're King Kuranes' questers, not lawbreakers. Now if you've more noises to make, make 'em and be on your way. And you two," his eyes drilled into the pair who held Ula and Una, knew them at once as the men in the dead seer's eyes, "you two 'gentlemen': be careful how you handle those ladies. You should know that I'm David Hero, Hero of Dreams, and my friend here is Eldin the Wanderer."

Now Eldin spoke, his voice the soft rumble of a pregnant volcano: "Be advised," he said to the bully who held Una's chin aloft, "not to bruise that lass. I'm a very gentle soul and the sight of a bruise on her would give me nightmares for a month. But you'd be lucky, for your nightmare would be of the very shortest duration . . ."

"Treats, too!" said their cold-eyed chief. He glanced around at Pazza's gaping patrons, shrugged uncomfortably. "So you two are the famous—or perhaps infamous—Hero and the Wanderer, eh? Very well, maybe it would be best if we saw about all of this in private." And to his party of Regulators: "Right, lads, bring 'em along!" He stared directly into Hero's eyes for a moment: "Their *women*, too," then turned on his heel.

Hero and Eldin smoldered as they looked at each other, at the pikes, the gray-clad pikemen. Beyond the balustrade was thin air, one hundred feet of it. Only one way into this place, and the same way out. And down there at the foot of the stairs, another party of Regulators. They began to breathe again, letting out the air they'd been holding on to in a great double-barrelled sigh.

"So be it," growled Eldin. "Lead on."

But the Chief Regulator was already leading on, and the questers, deprived now of their swords, could only allow themselves to be poked and prodded along in his wake . . .

In the main, Baharna is built of porphyry, from its wharves to its topmost terraces. Its streets are frequently arched over, by bridges or co-joining buildings, and go up in a great "V" from a central canal which, landward, passes through a tunnel and a series of shallow locks into an inland lake. The land about this lake is mainly desert, for its waters are tidal and therefore impure; but there are several oases and even a village or two, though these stand all on that side toward Baharna. For on the far side of the lake, called Yath, there lie ruins prohibiting the presence of men. They are lonely and silent, those ruins, and all of great clay-bricks: the tumbled building-blocks of some primal city whose name is not remembered. Or which used not to be remembered. Except that lately . . .

Tellis Gan, father of the present Law Officer-in-Chief, Raffis, had been Baharna's Lord Regulator for more than twenty years, as had his father before him. He had seen the city through some strange times and had been much respected in his day. In the Bad Days he'd set himself and his force of Regulators firmly against the squat, wide-mouthed "traders" who came in their black galleys from "somewhere east of Leng," keeping a watchful eye on all their dubious doings in Baharna and Oriab in general; and driving them out *en masse* when their kinship with dreamland's enemies became more fully realized. He had been a great-hearted man, Tellis, earning all the trust of the city's elders and keeping their laws wisely, the way laws should be kept.

When the elders had come down on slavery, Tellis Gan and his Regulators had put an end to the slavers' markets on Silver Street; and when the elders taxed muth-dew for the upkeep of Baharna's twin lighthouses, Thon and Thal, (following which, the muth became subject to much illicit importation) Gan was the man who gave the smugglers short shrift. The populace had faith in him; his Regulators, apparently, had loved him to a man; not once had he used his position except in the interests and to the welfare of his fellow men, and those of Baharna itself.

Alas, but just a year ago, in a brave assault upon a slavers' den, Tellis had been mortally wounded; sad too that it could only be some traitor among his own Regulators who gave advance warning to the Kledans; sadder still, perhaps, that Gan's only son—who would assume his father's rank and position as his birthright—was spoiled and mean, with little or nothing of his father's love for the rightness of things. But so far Raffis Gan had proved himself efficient; as yet he had given the city elders no reason to demand his resignation from office, as was their right; indeed, apart from his love of legend and archaeological matters (his spare-time wanderings in Baharna's hinterland, poking in the old ruins there, especially on the far shore of Yath), he seemed to go about his duties zestfully and with no small measure of enthusiasm.

Too much enthusiasm far, in the case of Hero of Dreams and Eldin the Wanderer. Or at least, from their viewpoint.

Regulating Branch, like most of Baharna's administrative offices—loose authorities at best—was situated over the canal close to the inland-leading tunnel, where light was largely shut out. Built beneath an overhang, in the very face of the cliff, which Baharna's more prosperous terraces and much more precipitous streets and alleys had somehow bypassed or climbed over or simply ignored, its office windows and barred cells looked up in the shadow of the sprawling city that climbed and clung overhead, and down on the darkly lapping water of the canal fifty feet below. Even in midsummer it was cool here; porphyry pillars and stone flags are not the warmest materials, and the constant shade and dankness of the canal lent a murky miasma which touched everything. But there again, Regulating HQ had not been built for comfort. In the old days, the brawnier Kledan barbarians had kept slaves here—fellow blacks, mainly: Pargans, as often as not, and a few Kledan pigmies from the dense interior of that jungled land, who made good houseboys or chimney sweeps or ratters in the sewers—before selling them off in Baharna's markets.

Their buyers had been sea-merchants of Inquanok, horned Lengites (as they were known now), who had only ever bought fat Pargans, even a handful of lords and ladies from dreamland's so-called "more civilized" regions. That was all long finished with, but certainly the inmates of this place had had a very rough time of it. This was the unspoken conclusion of the questers, anyway, as they stood before Raffis Gan's great desk and were made to feel small.

By now they'd been handcuffed and only two Regulators were in attendance, the same pair who'd laid hands on the girls. Ula and Una were elsewhere, however, separated from the questers as soon as they'd arrived here at Regulating Branch. They would find out where the girls were later. But meanwhile:

Raffis had been silent for some seconds, toying with a quill and a scrap of parchment. Now he looked up, focused on the questers and smiled a thin smile. "Do you have, well *anything*, to say for yourselves?" he asked.

"Something to ask!" growled Eldin. "What's the charge?" Suddenly something clicked in the Wanderer's mind: déjà vu, waking-world memories, he didn't know, but words were on his lips before he even realized it:

"What's on your mind, Gan?" he drawled out of the corner of his mouth. "What's the rap, hey? What do you hope to pin on us, eh? You drag us in, cold-shoulder us, stick us in bracelets ... so OK, bring on the bright lights to scorch our eyeballs, the rubber hoses that won't leave tell-tale bruises. Go ahead, have yourself a ball, Gan. But do you think we'll talk? Hell, we've been worked on by experts! You feel angry, Gan? You want to throw something? So throw the book at us! So what?" He grinned coldly, his mouth aslant, twitching.

"Steady, old lad!" Hero whispered, thoroughly alarmed. "He just might!"

Gan was frowning. "Throw the book? There'll be no tome-hurling here, ruffian! As for bracelets: those iron cuffs must needs suffice! But if I also heard you hinting at torture, *that* might be arranged!"

"Gan," said Hero, "my friend was having a little private joke, that's all, but your joke's gone far enough. Just what *are* the charges? Why are we here? You know who we are, also that Kuranes of Ooth-Nargai won't let us rot in one of your cells. Do you intend to risk a diplomatic clash with Serannian, Celephais, Ulthar and Ilek-Vad? Do the city elders even know you're holding us? The way I see it, we *may* have charges to answer—which we will, given the chance—but this show of high-handedness can only do you harm." Hero frowned in genuine puzzlement. "Just what is this all about, Gan?"

The Chief Regulator sighed, narrowed his eyes, sank down a little in his chair. If the questers were acting, then they were very good at it. Could it really be that they were here "by chance"? Coincidence, at this time? Raffis Gan wasn't much given to believing in such coincidences. On their own admittance they were Kuranes' questers, his agents in the lands of Earth's dreams. And had they talked to the seer with invisible eyes "by chance"? And the seer himself known to be another agent of Kuranes! These women of theirs, these twin sisters, Ula and Una Gidduf: hadn't they been right there with this pair of rogues in the War of the Mad Moon? Were they, too, spies for the Southern Sea's coastal cities?

Just how much did Kuranes know? It was important that Raffis Gan find out. He could play this game soft or hard, however they liked it—or didn't. Very well, first hard. "Charges?" Gan straightened up in his chair. "All right, try these for size:

"One: that you, David Hero, or Hero of Dreams if you insist, stabbed a Kledan with a poisoned dart when he went to the assistance of a previous victim, the charlatan mystic known as the seer with invisible eyes. Two: that you, Eldin the Wanderer, hurled a man—another Kledan, as it happens—through a wall into the harbor, where doubtless he drowned. Certainly his body hasn't been found yet. Three: that both of you, making your escape from the scene of these murders, savagely attacked certain of the customers of one Lipperod Unth a licensed waterfront taverner, Unth himself, his son, and numerous innocent bystanders. Four: that to facilitate your escape, you deliberately vandalized the *Craven Lobster*, a tavern, to such an extent that it fell into the harbor! Charges? And how are they for starters? I could lock you in a cell, melt the key and drop it in the canal, and even your best friends wouldn't want to know about it! Kuranes? He'll consider himself lucky to be rid of you!"

Gan looked at Eldin's scarred face and believed he saw the Wanderer's nerves fraying a little. What he actually saw was a growing impatience and frustration, but he couldn't know that. As for Hero . . . the younger quester's eyes had narrowed more yet, were keenly aglint. And:

"You know, Chief Regulator," said Hero, "I didn't

see a man-jack in the *Craven Lobster* I'd ever have guessed was one of yours. And if there had been, he'd know the truth of it, and these so-called 'charges' wouldn't even arise. Also, you couldn't cram half an hour between the, er, incident and the time you picked us up. So how'd you come by your information so quickly, eh?"

Gan went white, got slowly to his feet, leaned on his desk with knuckles shiny where the skin stretched across them. And: "Are you trying to say something, David Hero?" he hissed. "Making some sort of accusation of your own? That sort of tack won't answer the questions I've got lined up for you, and it won't get you anything but a cell to rot in!"

"I think it's already got me something," said Hero, relaxing a little and nodding knowingly. "It's told me something, anyway: that there's a hell of a rotten stink in Baharna's Regulating Branch!"

Gan went whiter still, leaned right across his desk, opened his mouth to say something—and too late saw his danger. In the heat of the moment Eldin hadn't been able to resist. He stepped forward, looped the chain of his handcuffs over Gan's head, dragged him bodily across the desk.

The Wanderer had no plan; perhaps at best he hoped to hold Gan as a hostage, but he didn't get the chance. More used than their boss to the ways of hard men, Gan's pair of Regulator thugs jumped in, brandishing teak truncheons. Eldin was chopped behind the ear and never knew what hit him. He fell into a pit of stars with no sides and no bottom, like a comet rushing through the outer void.

Hero, hurling himself furiously to his friend's assistance, joined him a moment later. There was more than enough room in that interstellar pit for both of them.

* * *

The first thing Eldin saw when he came to was Hero, red-eyed and haggard, glowering at him across the width of a tiny cell. They were both hanging in chains, manacled, feet on the cold stone floor—barely.

"Ow!" Eldin groaned. He wanted to finger the lump behind his ear, but of course couldn't.

" 'Ow'?" Hero echoed him. "Is that all? Only an 'ow'? In that case you're lucky. Me, I don't think my cranium can take much more of you!"

"Not now, lad," Eldin quaveringly protested. "I deserve it, I know, but upbraid me later. Only not now. Give me a chance to think straight first." And, after a moment: "What month is it?"

"September," said Hero, "—or maybe October. It's morning, anyway."

Dawn's light, feeble down here in Baharna's guts, drifted in through the bars in cold, clinging wreaths of mist from the canal. The wall opposite the barred window featured a stout oak door with its own iron-barred hatch. Nothing else. No furniture, no amenities; nothing at all other than stone walls, floor and ceiling. "We've hung here the night?" Eldin turned his head this way and that, tenderly, his eyes slitted and deeply wrinkled at their outer corners.

Hero gave a painful nod. "Certainly feels like it," he said.

"And the girls?"

"Too late to worry about them now. Just hope that Gan's been a bit more lenient with them than he's been with us, that's all."

"*Huh!*" grunted Eldin. "Lenient? What did they do? Come to think of it, what did we do—except long overdue civic duties at a well-earned launching? Slum clearance, I call it—with a bit of pest control thrown in. And all for free. That Chief Regulator, he's got things up his sleeves."

"So many, I'm surprised there's room for his arms!" Hero agreed.

"But what in hell's it all about, eh?"

"Dunno," Hero shook his head—carefully.

There came a fluttering from beyond the bars at the window. Something pink perched a moment, squeezed its way into the cell, soared straight for Hero and settled on his head. A temple pigeon, message cylinder and all. "P-coo, p-coo, p-coo!" it said, complainingly.

"Couldn't agree more, old chum," said Hero, "we're damned hard to find, I'm sure. But see, we're sort of tied up right now." He tried in vain to get his hands on the bird, remove its message.

"Now if only Kuranes would consider parrots," said Eldin, "we'd—"

There sounded footsteps from outside, bolts were thrown back, and the door clanged open on its hinges. It was Raffis Gan and his bodyguards.

Gan took in the scene inside the cell at a glance. "Get that bird!" he snapped.

"Shoo!" Hero yelled, shaking his head wildly to dislodge the bird—which made him feel he'd dislodged his head. "Run, flap, flee, *fly!*—damn you!"

Too late. The bully-boys were into the cell, one blocking the window, the other snatching at the pigeon and knocking it from Hero's head. To give the bird credit, even half-stunned it flapped for the window—straight into the ham fists of the Regulator there. He grabbed it out of the air, twisted its neck till it snapped. And wrenching the silver cylinder from a still twitching leg, the gray-clad lout tossed the poor lifeless body down.

Nostrils flaring, Hero and Eldin looked at each other.

The faces of Gan's sidekicks were already well-etched on their memories, but now the questers committed them firmly, in minute detail. The one who'd killed the bird was squat, thin-lipped, bald, with a head like the sharp end of an egg. The other—the one who'd held Una's head a little too high—was taller, but bandy-legged, bull-chested, with eyes so close-set only the bridge of his nose kept them apart. With Gan, they made a most unlovely trio.

Meanwhile Gan had taken the message-cylinder, removed the tiny wad of paper tucked inside and opened it out. He gazed eagerly at what was written there; blinked, and stared harder. Then his pale lips curled in disgust and disappointment. "Coded!" he snapped. Which told the questers that it was very important and highly secret. It wasn't often Kuranes used the olden glyphs of dream (which Eldin had a knack for) but when he did . . .

Now the Chief Regulator looked up, came forward. "So I was right," he said. "You *are* spying for Kuranes. But what's he after? What is it you're here for, eh?"

Hero shrugged (to the tune of rattling chains) and answered: "Maybe if we could read that message we'd know."

"Oh, you'll read it soon enough," said Gan slyly. "Be sure you will." And suddenly furrows appeared in his pallid forehead. He gave a little start, said: "Has anyone searched these two since we picked 'em up?"

His men looked at each other, shrugged.

Gan made a tutting sound. "Maybe they're carrying orders, instructions! Do it now while they're hung up. And be thorough!" While his men set about their task, the Chief Regulator paced to and fro, shaking his head as he studied Kuranes' glyphs.

Hero, submitting to the search (there wasn't much

else he could do), wondered why Eldin suddenly seemed subdued. True, he *was* subdued, but now there was also a sheepish look about him. Then the egg-headed thug reached into the Wanderer's jacket and brought out a second scrap of paper—at which Eldin groaned, and not from the pain of last night's lump.

"Eh?" said Hero, finding himself suddenly out of his depth. "What? Eldin, is there p'raps something you should have mentioned?"

"Er, I *did* mention it—sort of," the Wanderer cringed. "Aboard the boat, remember? After we'd been fishing? My dream?"

His dream! Hero rolled up his eyes and let his head loll back gently against the wall. Eldin's prophetic dream. Oh, yes, Hero saw it all now. And thinking back on the affray in the *Craven Lobster*, sure enough he remembered how the Wanderer had straighted up the seer's lifeless body—which must have been when he took this scrap of paper from him.

But now Raffis Gan had that fragment, and his normal pallor became that of a dead man as he read it. Wide-eyed, he glared at Eldin, at Hero, even at his scowling Regulator henchmen. And to them:

"Wait outside!" he hissed. And when the gray-clads were out of earshot and the heavy door closed behind them:

"This," Gan ground the words out, "is *not* couched in glyphs. Of course you already know what's written here, but I'll read it aloud for you anyway, so that there can be no further misunderstanding between us. It says:

" 'YATH—YATH-LHI—TYRHHIA—TREASURE'!"

If Gan had expected a reaction he was disappointed. Hero *did* react, but the wrong way. The younger quester was expressionless for a moment, then blinked vacantly, then gave a chain-clanking shrug. "So?"

And as for Eldin: "Puzzling, isn't it?" said the Wanderer. "Hero, lad, that's why I didn't mention it. Oh, I would have done, eventually, but since it didn't seem to make much sense . . . why let it spoil the night, eh?"

Gan's eyes bored into the Wanderer's. "You took this from the seer, right?"

"He . . . *gave* it to me"—Eldin looked uncomfortable—"sort of."

"Kuranes sent you to see the seer with invisible eyes, who in turn gave you this piece of paper," said Gan. "I see . . ."

"Well I don't!" said Hero. "First, Kuranes didn't send us—we came of our own free wills to see the girls. Second, meeting the seer was entirely accidental. If the *Quayside Quaress* had been open, we never *would* have seen him. And third—"

"Yes?" said the Chief Regulator.

But how could Hero tell him about Eldin's prophetic dream? That would be seen to be a deliberate lie—even though it wasn't! "Third, it was the Kledans started the ruckus at the *Craven Lobster*, not us. We only, well, finished it . . ."

Gan nodded, sourly added, "Disastrously!" He held up the coded message taken from the bird. "And this?"

"A message from Kuranes," Eldin shrugged, trying to muffle *his* chains as he did so. "We are the old King's questers, after all! P'raps it says: 'Report to me in Celephais,' or some such. We won't know till we've read it, now will we?"

Gan turned to Hero. "What do you know of Yath-Lhi? Tyrhhia?" Still looking for some sort of reaction, he snapped the words out.

Hero looked blank for a moment. "Nothing," he said, honestly believing that he spoke the truth.

The Wanderer's memory was better, however. "Well, we do know a little," he said.

"Oh?" Gan smiled thinly. "You do know 'a little,' eh? Go on, then, tell me."

"I mean, it's no secret, is it?" Eldin raised his bushy eyebrows. "It's recorded in certain of dreamland's olden tomes, a story out of the immemorial past, a tale told by grandams about roaring winter fires. At best a legend, almost certainly a flight of fancy, a myth."

"Say on," said Gan.

Eldin glanced across at Hero for his approval. "Oh, by all means!" Hero sighed, gave his chains a feeble clank. "Let's have a story, since we've nothing better to do than hang about here!"

"Yath-Lhi was known as the 'Black Princess,' " Eldin began. "Black as Zura of Zura, maybe even worse. But 'black' describing her nature, you understand, and not her color. Back in the pre-dawn dreamlands, when dreams were young, she ruled in Tyrhhia, a walled slave city—the richest city in all the lands of Earth's dreams! For even the spires of Yath-Lhi's palace were of silver—not leaved with the stuff, *made* of it! Anyway—"

"Ah, *now* I remember!" Hero cut in. "Of course! We had some of it from Aminza Anz, up there in the Great Bleak Mountains, that time we found our way into the Keep of the First Ones. Tyrhhia, yes. And Yath-Lhi, the Black Princess. And her maze. I remember how Aminza likened the maze within the keep to Yath-Lhi's maze under Tyrhhia."

Gan slowly nodded. "Now, we're getting somewhere," he said, sarcastically. "And just see how memories catch fire when someone strikes a flint, eh? So maybe you can finish the story, David Hero. What else is there?"

Hero sighed again. "I don't know where all this is leading," he said, "but . . . very well, if it will hasten matters.

"She had very bad habits, this princess. She was greedy, for one thing—enormously so—and she was cruel beyond measure. She sent out her armies in search of treasure, and thus amassed so much of the stuff she'd lie awake nights wondering if it was safe! Eventually she hit upon a scheme, using thousands of slaves to build a subterranean maze deep under Tyrhhia itself. They worked down there under the lash, those poor creatures, and died in droves before the job was done: a labyrinth extensive as the city itself. And at its center— Yath-Lhi's treasure. Only she knew the way in. When she went in to admire her treasure, or add to it, she would have her bearers slain as soon as she led them back out through the maze. Worse, she even killed the labyrinth's architect, her own lover, by having him dipped in molten gold and adding his 'statue' to her monstrous, ill-gotten hoard.

"When she died—the legend doesn't say how, except that in the end she grew old and vanished—her city-nation died with her. Penniless! No one could ever find his way into the maze, let alone discover the treasure at its center." Hero paused, nodded, said: "That's it. How did I do?"

"Admirably!" said Raffis Gan. He gave a derisive snort. "And knowing so much of the old legend, you two, still this note you got from the seer with invisible eyes means nothing to you? Well, we'll see about that."

He approached Eldin—but carefully, staying well clear of his reach—and held up the second piece of paper, the one he'd said was coded. "Well; and what do you make of this?"

Eldin drew his eyebrows close together, peered, read in silence—or would have.

"Well?" said Gan.

"Give me a chance," Eldin grumbled, absorbing everything.

"Word by word," said Gan, impatient. "Let's have it."

"What? Word by word? A direct translation? Impossible! Man, this isn't in code—it's Ancient Dreamlands!"

"Eh?" said Gan, his thin eyebrows shooting up. "The primal tongue? And are you telling me you can actually read it?"

"Oh, damn right he can!" said Hero from across the cell. "What? Why, if he wasn't a quaint old quester, he'd doubtless be Assistant Curator of the Archives in Ulthar!" His sarcasm bounced off Eldin, failed to impress Gan.

"Be quiet, you!" snapped the Chief Regulator; and to Eldin: "Well, what does it say?"

The Wanderer had read and absorbed all. "Hmm!" he said. "Well, it says this: 'To Raffis Gan from Eldin the Erudite—up yours!' "

Quick as thought Gan snatched back the note, crumpled it into his pocket, backhanded Eldin a clout that rocked his head and cut open the corner of his mouth. The Wanderer reacted in typical fashion: he went berserk, or would have if he hadn't been chained to a wall. While he raved and roared, Gan called out to his thugs:

"Come in, you two. I've had more than enough of this!" His bully-boys rumbled in. "Bind their arms securely and shackle their feet, then bring 'em to the well. If they give you trouble—any trouble at all—beat them black and blue!" He stormed out of the cell.

"You've really miffed that one," said Hero to Eldin. "And you had me worried, too, for a minute or so."

"What?" Eldin stopped roaring on the instant, looked with mild reproof upon the younger quester opposite. "You didn't really believe I was going to tell him what Kuranes said, did you?"

While the two conversed, Gan's hoodlums released them one arm at a time from the walls, bound their arms to their bodies with ropes and their thighs together. Against all this restriction of movement, still Hero managed a shrug. "It would've been no stranger than *not* telling me about that note from the seer with invisible eyes!"

"Would you have made anything of it?"

"No," Hero had to admit. "Not then, anyway."

"And now?"

Hero smiled a tight smile, which turned to a grimace of pain as the Regulator with the egg-shaped head cinched a rope up between his legs just a little too tightly. "Hey, I have tackle down there, my man—watch it, will you?" he grunted.

"A pair of real comedians, you two," the man jerked the rope tighter yet. "Quester? Jesters, more like! I've seen carnival dancing clowns who weren't half so funny. No, not a patch on you lads."

"It's you who'll need patching, friend," Hero gaspingly returned, "if ever we meet on terms a bit more even."

"Daydreams within dreams," the other replied, and he laughed and spat in Hero's face. And Hero unable even to wipe the spittle away.

"Ex-waking worlders," Eldin growled his opinion of them. "You have to be. Or else your fathers were Lengites! Lord, there's some real rubbish finding its way into the dreamlands these days. Now how did such a cute and cuddlesome pair of chaps like you two ever get to be roughy-toughy Regulators, eh? I mean, Baharna's police force has something of a glowing reputation, doesn't it? It certainly used to have—under your current boss's father."

The bandy-legged, narrow-eyed thug whirled on the Wanderer and drove a knotted fist into his belly. Eldin said "Oof!" and bent a little, but seemed otherwise unhurt: bindings and good cloth and sheer mass had absorbed the blow like a huge block of rubber. Hero found it surprising that the gray-clad hadn't broken his hand; *Homo ephemerens* weren't normally all that substantial, so perhaps Eldin had been right about these lads being ex-waking worlders. Except that unlike the questers, they worked for the wrong boss. And on the wrong side of the law? That seemed more possible, however paradoxical, by the moment.

"No more arguments, no snide comments, no lip whatsoever!" Narrow-eyes coughed out the words. "You just come along with us to the well and do exactly as you're told," he indicated the door, propelled Eldin in that direction with a boot up the backside, "and hop to it!"

Hopping, as means of locomotion, isn't overly dignified—but it beats boot-propulsion to a frazzle.

Tight-lipped, each one of them promising a terrible revenge, albeit mutely, the questers hopped.

The well . . .

In the old days, when Regulating HQ had been a slave-harboring area, the well had served a triple purpose. It had provided water for the slavers when (often) they were thirsty; a threat if ever (rarely) they should prove rowdy or in any way ungovernable; a last embrace, however dark and dank, on the occasion (regular) of a sudden demise. Housed in a room half virgin rock—literally a cave—and half rough porphyry blocks, located deep under the cliff's overhang where the light scarce filtered at all, the well was now Hero and Eldin's destination. The second of its ancient functions was about to be resurrected. And depending on the outcome, possibly the third.

There was no door to the room of the well, just half an arch of raw rock and half of roughly cemented blocks, containing a yawning cave with uneven floor and inward-curving walls that met overhead in gloom, cobwebs, and spindly aeon-formed stalactites. And in the center of the floor, the well.

As the eyes of the questers and those of their Regulator guards grew accustomed to the gloom, so Hero felt the cold: a continuous stream of icy air flowing up out of the well and passing knee-deep outward and away. Eldin felt it, too, and couldn't quite stifle an audible shiver. Then Egg-head struck flint to a prepared flambeau in its rusty iron bracket on the wall, and at once the shadows were driven flickeringly back. Their guards pushed the questers stumblingly closer to the well's rim.

It had no parapet, that gaping fissure, and so the pair held instinctively back from it. They could see now that it was a natural rent in the bedrock, a split whose ends tapered to mere cracks while its center was roughly oval or almond-shaped—like a half-open eye in an old, seamy face. The eye's iris was jet black, a hole that went down to . . . where?

"Tide's turned," said Narrow-eyes, his voice echoing hollowly. He sniffed, then breathed deep. "Smell the salt?"

Egg-head nodded. "Sea's coming in," he agreed. And to the near-mummified questers: "Sweet water goes

out—well, brackish water, anyway—and when the tide
turns salt water comes in. It's a river, see, underground.
Sunless, never breaks the surface. There's a story how
long ago a troublesome black jumped down there hugging an empty barrel. He was never seen again, but the
barrel surfaced miles out to sea. When the tide's fully
in, you can fish in this hole, and it stinks of weed.
When it's right out, the air comes up fresh as a field of
daisies. Well, maybe not *that* fresh. Whichever, it's always cold: a cold, dark place to die. You fall—or get
pushed—down there, and you drown, of course . . ."

"If you can't swim," said Eldin, after a moment.

"Oh, it's swimming, is it?" said Narrow-eyes quietly.
"In the dark? In the cold, cold, midnight water? There
are many would just let themselves sink. Quicker that
way, you know?" He chuckled low and evilly.

The questers were prodded closer to the hole, found
themselves leaning backward away from it. Then—

Footsteps, and the echoing protests of well-known female voices. Raffis Gan arrived, dragging Ula and Una
after him. The girls were blindfolded, their wrists bound
to their bodies at the hips, else unfettered. Both sounded
very weary, close to hysterics, but seemed otherwise intact and unharmed. Hero breathed a sigh of relief.

"Easy, girls, easy!" he spoke up, anger vibrant in his
voice.

"Hero, is that you?" cried Ula. "Oh, David! The brute
kept us chained and in darkness all night!"

"Aye, well he'll answer for it, never fear," growled
Hero, "when all of this comes out."

"That's where you're wrong, my friend," said Gan at
once. "You see, it's not going to come out!"

"Oh?" said Eldin, from where he stood too close to
the well's rim, his head cocked to one side and bushy

eyebrows arched. "Murder, Chief Regulator? All four of us? And what good will that do you?"

"The Wanderer's right," Hero added with a nod. "How will killing us get you into Yath-Lhi's treasure chamber, eh?" The words had sprung to Hero's lips as by inspiration. Half an idea had taken shape in his mind, triggering a question he couldn't even be sure had an answer. In any case, its effect was immediate and dramatic.

"*So!*" Gan hissed, stepping jerkily forward. "You do know, after all, do you? But how *much* do you know?"

Eldin wanted in on the game. "Everything," the Wanderer growled. "We're not Kuranes' top men for nothing, bent Chief Regulator Gan!"

"Bent?" Gan frowned.

"I meant crooked," Eldin corrected himself, though "bent" had certainly seemed right just a moment ago. Some left-over phrase from the waking world, he supposed. "Like a corkscrew."

Gan was now the whitest they'd ever seen him. Even in the flaring light of the torch, his skin was waxy as a corpse-fat candle. "I was right," he said. "Kuranes sent you to investigate me—my exploration of the ruins on Yath's far shore!"

Now the questers knew it all. At least, with the exception of a few finer details. And now they could think and speak more nearly in Gan's own terms:

"You don't think we're Ooth-Nargai's only spies in Baharna, do you, Gan?" said Hero. "Kuranes will know soon enough that you have us—and how long then before he puts Baharna's Elders in the picture, eh?"

"Maybe the Elders already know about you, Chief Regulator," Eldin worked the knife a bit. "And d'you really think doing away with us will help your case? Better release us now, at once, and make a clean breast of it. It'll mean resignation from your position as boss of the gray-clads, of course, but—"

"Oh, be quiet!" Gan scowled. "Man, don't you know when you're doomed? I couldn't let you go even if I wanted to—and I don't. Resignation? It would mean my job, would it? *Hah!* Let me tell you it would mean my head! Slavery is forbidden here, which means that working a slave to death is murder. And do you know how many Pargans I've had off the Kledan slavers? Or how many of them have died in cave-ins and rock falls or from sheer exhaustion on Yath's far shore? No, my boats are all blazing behind me—but I'm *that* close!" he snapped his fingers, making a sharp crack.

"Should you be telling them all of this, Raffis?" Egghead wanted to know.

"Why not?" said Gan. "They certainly won't live to repeat it. Or if they do live, their own involvement will silence them. Anyway, thinking out loud helps clarify matters. I see things more clearly when I can talk them over." Safely distant from the well's rim, he put his hands behind his back and began a slow pacing, to and fro.

"*Must* we be blindfolded?" cried Una, who'd been remarkably patient for some little time.

"And is it really necessary that our hands be bound like this?" Ula wanted to know. "We're only girls, after all!"

Hero and Eldin knew better: Ula and Una weren't "only" girls at all, but very brave and highly resourceful girls, as they'd long since proven in the affair of the Mad Moon. But Gan had other things on his mind, and the twins were a distraction—to him they *were* just girls.

The Chief Regulator paused in his pacing, said: "Let them see and free their hands—but one of you guard the arch." And as the girls' blindfolds and ropes were removed, he continued to pace up and down. Finally:

"Of course, I know quite a bit about you two, really," Gan stated. "Indeed I spent most of last night catching up on your alleged exploits. Personally I find them farfetched. From what I've seen of you, I'd say you're a pair of buffoons! Luck has doubtless played a great part in your successes. That, and your apparently natural roguish inclinations. But I think you'd agree your luck seems to have run out on you, and I wonder: just how much of the real rogue do you have in you, eh? Questers now, aye, but before that thieves and sellswords, if I've had it aright."

"Oh?" Narrow-eyes was apprehensive. "Well the way I've had it is that they only *play* the fool, these two. You go up against them—or run with them—at your own risk!"

What Gan had said earlier, about the possibility of Hero and Eldin's own involvement in his scheme, had made connections in Hero's head. And threats, it appeared, were about to turn into offers. But as yet it was difficult to see what the questers had that Gan wanted. "What are you getting at?" Hero was suspicious. "What's on your mind?"

"Why, that's obvious!" Eldin snorted. "He's thinking it might be possible to buy us off!"

The Chief Regulator's face twisted into a sneer. "Oh, and is that so unlikely? Every man has his price, Wanderer, as I'm sure you're well aware. And what I can offer is . . . Why, you could buy half of Celephais!"

Hero only scowled—and scowled even harder at Eldin, who seemed to have brightened a little and was actually beginning to look interested!

Eldin pointedly ignored his friend's glower, asked:

"Just what *are* you offering, Raffis Gan? And what is it you want from us in return?"

"Want from you . . . ?" Gan mused. "I'm not quite sure. But let's first get things in their proper perspective. Which is to say, we should talk about choice—or lack of it." He indicated to Narrow-eyes (Egg-head was standing, hands on hips, guarding the exit through the arch) that he should move the questers closer still to the well's rim. Obediently, the bull-chested thug shuffled his near-helpless charges to the very edge of the hole, where they stood licking their lips and peering nervously into dark and unknown depths.

Now Gan grinned, said: "Not much of a choice, is it? You can co-operate, or die. Quite simple, really. So now, in light of your fresh perspective, we can more properly ask what it is that I want. Well, first let's see what you've got:

"Are you, for instance, talented? It would seem so—at first glance, anyway. You did break into a keep of the First Ones, penetrating its mazy ways to the core and setting free the Beings you found trapped in stasis there. Now *that*, I have to admit, is talent—or extraordinary good fortune! Not the setting free of the First Ones, which I can only consider sheerest folly, but certainly the breaking-in and the maze-managing; for making one's way through mantrap labyrinths is at best a hazardous business, as I've learned well enow. Aye, for it's taken me a three-month and all those poor Pargans just to find my way into Yath-Lhi's maze and reach its center! Oh, yes, this maze-maneuvering is a talent indeed. But which one of you has it? Was it you, Eldin the Wanderer, who broke the seals on that lair of the First Ones, or you, David Hero?"

Hero shrugged. "We both did our bit. Keep-cracking isn't so hard. We've a knack, that's all."

Gan nodded, stroked his chin. He seemed fully recovered now from the shock they'd given him. Or perhaps resigned to the idea. "Equally skilled," he murmured. "Both of you. And what of the reading of glyphs, runes, the 'Ancient Dreamlands' in which Lord Kuranes couches his bird-borne directives? Is this another mutual accomplishment?"

"I'm not entirely unskilled," said Hero, "though it's true that in that department Eldin has the edge on me."

"Indeed," said Gan, pausing in his pacing and nodding his interest. And again, more slowly, "Indeed." He casually motioned to Narrow-eyes, who at once moved up closer to Hero. "But in that case I can cut my costs at once, wouldn't you agree?" Gan continued. "If your friend the Wanderer has everything I require, then what need have I of you?" He motioned again to Narrow-eyes, but more certainly, conclusively—*And the thug at once thrust his shoulder into Hero's back.*

Toppling forward, Hero gave a cry of outrage and horror combined. Eldin, too, eyes bulging in disbelief as he stood cocooned. Ula, no longer blind or bound, flew to her man, grabbed wildly at his slowly toppling form. She caught his shoulder, wheeled him sideways so that he'd crash down on the rim and not into the hole. But Gan merely nodded to Narrow-eyes. "His woman, too!" the Chief Regulator snapped.

Again Narrow-eyes pushed, this time at both Hero and Ula, and at the same time Una gave a wild shriek and hurled herself on to the thug's back—but too late! By the time the bow-legged Regulator had dragged the snarling, spitting, clawing girl over his shoulder in a tangle of fiercely kicking, biting, scratching arms and legs and teeth, Hero and his lady had already vanished into the maw of the rock. Only their cries echoed up— those and the distant splash which finally cut them off.

"Hero!" Eldin hoarsely bellowed. "David, lad . . ."

Sobbing, the Wanderer stumbled and hopped forward, made as if to throw himself down after the younger quester. "Stop him!" said Gan to Egg-head, who'd abandoned his position under the arch, the better to see. The stocky gray-clad grabbed Eldin's jacket, turned him from the well.

"What—?" bellowed Eldin, as if astonished by this interruption. His wide, horrified, disbelieving eyes lit on the face of the man who held him. All vacancy and horror went out of the Wanderer's eyes in a moment, were replaced by the red light of revenge. Trussed as he was, still he battered at the squat Regulator with his head and shoulders, knocked the man down, fell on him and bit into his shoulder with square teeth and great jaws like those of a steel trap.

Gan took Una, who had now collapsed in shocked tears, off Narrow-eyes' hands; and as the trapped Regulator began to scream where Eldin held him pinned to the floor as if trying to chew him to death, the Chief Regulator said to Narrow-eyes: "Finish it—but don't kill him! One good clean clout should do it."

Narrow-eyes stepped to where Eldin was snarling through his chomping as he tried to transfer his grip from collar-bone to throat, bent down and struck one perfectly calculated blow with his truncheon. Eldin fled at once into lightning-shot dreams within dreams; but even dreams full of pain were better than the nightmare he'd just witnessed . . .

Hero and Ula plunged deep, came up slow and gasping for air. The shaft of dim light from above blinked out as a swift current caught them up and rushed them head-long into black bowels of rock. Hero floated on his back, turned into that position by Ula, and she swam alongside, one hand in his hair, buoyed up by the air trapped in her skirt and blouse.

"Ula," he finally managed to gasp against the gurgle and slap of black water. "Are you a good swimmer?"

"The best," she answered. "And swimming—*uh!*—will keep me warm, at least for a little while. But what about—*uh!*—you?"

"Now listen carefully, lass," he ignored her query, fought desperately to stay face-up, "and do exactly as I say. See, there's a trick I learned long ago from Eldin: it's called, 'always keep a sharp knife in a scabbard strapped to your left ankle'! The gray-clads started to search us, but after they found a note in Eldin's pocket they searched no farther. Which means I still have my—" Before he could form the word "knife," a wavelet slapped him in the face, set him rolling. He went facedown, gulped brine, was righted by Ula in the next moment. He coughed and spluttered, knew suddenly what it must feel like to drown.

"You'll have to—*uh!*—take a deep breath," Ula said, "while I—*uh!*—try to get it. Then if you go bum-up again—"

"Listen," Hero hastened to instruct, "there's another part of the—*uh!*—trick, and it's the most important!" But she had already floated him ahead, was desperately treading water while groping and fumbling around his feet.

"Thank goodness—*uh!*—they didn't tie your feet together!" she gasped. And: "What's most important?"

"That you don't—*urk!*" Another wavelet had slopped into his mouth, setting him rolling again. Still groping for his knife, Ula managed to right him. "Don't *drop* the—*uh!*—bloody thing!" he finally got it out.

"I've *got* it!" she said triumphantly. "And don't

worry, I won't drop it. Just you take the biggest breath you ever took, and . . ."

And then she was sawing at the ropes while both of them rolled over and over in the water, slicing and sawing and hoping she wasn't cutting him as well as his bonds.

Finally Hero's head surfaced; it was as if his entire face was a mouth. He sucked air eager as a vacuum, gasped: "My arms are free! Ula, I love you! Will you marry me? Or better still, give me my knife."

Almost exhausted, she was glad to hand the weapon over. And floating along beside him as the incoming current rushed and whirled them, and as he sliced himself free of the remaining ropes about his thighs, at last she found strength and air to say: "I may just hold you to that, my lad."

"Eh? To what?"

"Huh!"

Then he was finished, all limbs freed, buoyant now as a cork as he slipped his knife back into its calf-sheath. And: "Rest," he said. "That is, as best you can. Air in your lungs and your head uppermost, but let the current do the swimming. We can't fight it—have to go with it."

"You state the obvious so beautifully," she said, reminding him a lot of Eldin. But no sarcasm in her sweet voice, in this rushing, reeking darkness, just a sense of inevitability—maybe finality. She bantered to keep from breaking down. And as if to confirm his guess: "Not much hope for us, David, is there?"

"Eh?" he tried to sound startled, surprised, even astonished at the thought. "What? No hope? D'you know who you're talking to, lass? Hell's breath has scorched me and the upper atmosphere frozen me blue, but I'm still here to tell of it. I was once turned into a stone statue on the Mad Moon, remember? In my time I've been near-zombified by Zura, husked by Lathi the ter-queen, brain-drained by the black god Yibb-Tstll him-self! And do I carry a single scar to show for it? So here's us doing a bit of midnight bathing together—as well we might. What's so amiss about that, eh?"

Before she could answer, they felt themselves scraped along a low, slimy ceiling sloping down almost to the surface of the swift-flowing water. For long moments it seemed the ceiling must soon sink below the water level, forcing them under, but then the massive, unseen stone surface overhead receded, and with it their awful sensation of claustrophobia.

"Of course," said Hero, to cover his alarm, "we can get along nicely without *that* sort of thing! But doesn't it just go to show how lucky we are?"

"Lucky?" Her voice had an unaccustomed waver.

"Certainly! If Gan had tossed us down here five min-utes later, when the tide was that much farther in, that sump back there would have done for us. And—"

"Whoops!" she cut him off, clinging to his jacket and thrusting frantically with her legs.

"What is it, lass?" he tried to keep the sudden panic out of his voice.

"A—a wall," she breathlessly answered. "Like being in a great pipe. The bore of this sunless river. I've just felt it go slipping past. Hero, we seem to be moving ter-ribly swiftly. And I'm sure we're spinning. Why, I feel quite dizzy—like a twig in a storm-drain! Where will it all end?" Her teeth had started to chatter; Hero's, too, from the bitter cold.

Where? he thought. *I can't say. But when: pretty damn quickly, at a guess!* But out loud: "Where there's life there's hope, Ula my love. And we're a pair of lively ones if ever there was—"

"My sister, Una, will be distraught. My father, too, when he discovers both his daughters are missing." Her voice was beginning to sound drowsy, seemed too comfortable.

"Lord, but you're feeling low!" Hero declared. "I tell you we're not finished, not yet. And as for Una: she's with Eldin. Need I say more?"

"You're both big, brave lads," she answered, her voice drowsier yet, and slowly her grip relaxed where she clung to him. Hero sensed her—no, *saw* her—drifting away from him. Light? From where?

He reached out a leaden paw and grabbed her, drew her close, shouted desperately: "Ula! No sleeping here, sweetheart—not if you'd wake up again!"

"Umm?—*glub!*" as she swallowed a mouthful of brine. Then she was kicking, stirring herself, coughing and choking to clear her pipes.

Hero looked wildly about in the near-darkness—but *near*-darkness, not utter. On both sides walls swept narrowly by, festooned with weed that glowed with its own faint blue luminescence. *"Huh!"* Hero grunted his scorn. "Light, but not the blessed light of day."

"I see it," she said, swimming again, however feebly. "But what is it?"

"Foxfire," he told her.

"Eh?" She was barely sensible. "Foxes, down here? Shouldn't think so."

"You could be right," he said, feeling a numbness start to creep through his cold, cold limbs and body. "And even if there were, they'd be damned hard to set fire to!" And then, more sharply: "Are you sure you haven't been seeing Eldin on the sly?"

She made no answer, but snuggled to him, making it hard to swim. He didn't push her away: maybe it would be better if they simply . . .

Hero's feet, drifting lower in water which seemed to have lost much of its impetus, struck bottom. They came free, struck again. The small shocks transmitted themselves through his body to his brain. Bottom . . .

Bottom?

Disbelievingly, he forced his legs down, felt his feet dragging over an uneven, slippery surface. And wide awake again, once more he stared wildly all about, saw close at hand—*an impossible sight!*

Framed in weeds and eerie blue light, the angular silhouette of stone steps climbed up out of the underground river to a ledge high above the water's sluggish wash. Impossible? Maybe not. Hero reached out trembling fingers and touched hard, unyielding stone—cold and slippery as ice, but stone! And already the turgid current was sweeping them past.

Hero scrabbled at the greasy stone, found a crevice, dug in his stiff fingers. And: "Ula!" he cried. "Shake a leg, lass! Finished? Not by a mile, we're not! Look here—steps ascending out of the water. No wet, weedy grave for us, my girl!"

He drew her closer, thrust her small fingers into the crack he'd found, shifted his own grip higher. And with an enormous effort he drew himself up, dragged Ula after him, dumped her on a wide slab of a step draped in bladderwrack while he sought higher, drier handholds. Then they were out of danger, crawling side by side up the wide stone flight, past the tidemark, finally collapsing in blue-lit sand and shingly debris atop a broad, cavern-enclosed ledge.

Enclosed?—Hero prayed not. No, there must be a way out somewhere.

Not daring to rest now, hugging himself for warmth, the quester stumbled to his feet, forced himself to dance on the spot, getting his hot blood pumping again. From where she sprawled, Ula watched his jigging for a moment, inquired:

"Do you come here often?"

"Only—*uh!*—in the mating season," answered Hero at once. And: "Are you going to be a wallflower all your life? Up on your feet and dance, girl. Then when we're warm—or at least warmer—we'll try to find our way out of here."

He drew her up, rubbed her hands, arms, all her limbs, jostled her into motion, into life. And while Ula danced she, too, gazed about her. "A way out?" she echoed him then. "Hero, I don't see one. This is a cave, surely? A cave, deep underground, on the bank of a subterranean river."

"Oh?" he answered. "And what of those steps, eh? It was built by men, bless 'em, that stairway. And since it's unlikely they came *up* from the river, it seems only logical that they came *down* to it, right? And if they came down, we can go up."

"Right," she said. "Of course. Show me."

He nodded. "I will, at once," and proceeded to examine the cave.

But after a minute or so, following him as he did the rounds: "Not so easy, eh?" she said. And this time Hero made no answer.

There had used to be a way down (or up), that much was obvious. But now, where the irregular ledge-cave narrowed at its rear like a bottleneck, a wall of rough-hewn, massive stone blocks reared from floor to high ceiling. They weren't cemented, those blocks, except where they met the virgin rock, but the face of each measured eighteen inches by twelve at least. Hero rapped on one with the hilt of his knife and it sounded solid through and through. He tried to force the knife's blade between the blocks and it jammed, so that he must needs wrench it free again. *That* was how closely they fitted.

"A hammer," he finally grunted, casting about in the blue-flickered gloom. "That's what I need. And a damn big one, at that!"

"No big hammers, Hero," Ula told him, and the cave echoed her words. "Just you and me and us."

"And the clothes we're wearing," he added. "Ula, take off your dress."

"David?"

He got down on all fours, dug around in the sand and shingle and rubble, found a large rock and weighed it in his hands. Too small. He found another, dug it up, lifted it with some effort. It was rounded, hard and heavy as iron. "Your dress," he repeated. "I need to make a hammock for this boulder."

"A hammock?" But she did as he asked.

"More a sling, really," he said. "And yet not quite. For a sling is for slinging, and this is a shot that will go unslung!" He tore her dress here and there, folded it this way and that, rolled the boulder into its folds, made a stout knot. Then he lifted it and staggered in a circle, hands clasped through the knot. Faster, he whirled, and faster. Round and round—then stepped in close and smashed the thing into the wall knee-high.

The block he'd struck sustained a jagged crack and was knocked back a good six inches. Dust fell in trickles here and there as the gonging of the mighty clout echoed on for several seconds. *"Hah!"* Hero panted. "A couple more like that and—"

"And my dress will be ruined!" Ula said. "But then, it is already—so you'd best get on with it."

Two more enormous smacks and the block was knocked right through the wall. By then a neighboring block in the same tier was hanging loose, so Hero knocked that out, too, and the one above, which required the merest tap. All this work had served to warm the quester somewhat, but Ula was now shivering continuously. Aware that he must find or create some warmth for her, and quickly, Hero got down on his knees and thrust head and shoulders through the hole he'd made. It was dark as night in there, but he groped carefully about with one hand, eventually found something that clanked metallically: chains. Hero knew the sound only too well.

He caught up a loop of the heavy links, dragged it through into the faint blue light of the cave. He hauled harder, and a bundle of disintegrating rags was drawn through—*all wrapped about a skeletally shrunken corpse!*

Hero gave a great shudder and sprang to his feet, and Ula, uttering a small squeak, threw herself into his arms. He got a grip of himself, stared at the mummified skull, which grinned back at him and fixed him with empty socket eyes. Then the skull's grin seemed to turn to a leer and he kicked it aside. The chain ended in a wide band of dull metal about the skeleton's neck, coming loose along with the skull.

Hero shuddered again, said: "*Huh!* Well, that's one who didn't get out of here!"

"Oh, Hero!" Ula whispered, hugging him.

He disengaged himself, pushing the skeletal debris aside with his foot, stooped and climbed through the hole. Ula heard him groping about for a moment or two, then silence. "Hero? Hero, what are you doing?" The edge of hysteria was back in her voice.

"Standing still," his answer came echoing back. "Letting my eyes get used to it in here—not that they're likely to, for it's dark as pitch! Now I'm moving again, but cautiously. Feeling along the wall shoulder high."

"You're what?"

"Looking for . . . *Ah!*"

"Hero?"

"A flambeau and sconce! And a niche in the wall beside them. Containing . . . firestones! Strikers, and bone dry! The two go together, you see? A torch is no good without the means to light it. Someone put these flints here a thousand years ago—or ten, or more—and they're still here, just waiting to strike fresh sparks. But to what? Ula, can you get the rags off our long-dead friend out there without turning them to dust?"

Fighting down her loathing, she did as he instructed, passing scraps of parchment cloth through the hole into his eager hands. A moment later she heard the scrape of flint, and Hero's triumphant "Ho!"—followed at once by a loud gasp, and then complete silence. Yellow, flickering light came through the hole in the wall now. Ula took up the remains of her ravaged dress, pushed them ahead of her through the hole.

She emerged into a place too huge to be taken in all at one glance, straightened up beside Hero, who stood wide-eyed and mouth agape. And following his gaze, finally she saw the reason for his awe and astonishment. Yes, and there was reason galore!

In his nightmare, Eldin the Wanderer read Kuranes' carrier-pigeon message again:

Hero, Eldin—
  I shall be as brief as possible:
  As you will now know, the seer with invisible eyes is one of mine. His specific task in Oriab is to keep covert watch over a place of ancient evil. I refer to the ruins of Tyrhhia, Yath-Lhi's city-seat in

primeval times, which now lies under the desert on the shore of the Lake of Yath. The place is shunned, or was until recently. Old legends die hard, and such are the legends of Yath-Lhi that none have sought to discover or disturb her immemorial resting place—or the vast treasures which, the olden lore has it, lie buried with her. Indeed, only a handful of mages in all the dreamlands even know the location of Tyrhhia, all of whom are now sworn to secrecy. The reason for such zealous, even jealous, protection of the site and its secret is simple: the so-called Black Princess left behind her a monstrous legacy, a curse which remains extant to this day.

Atal of Hatheg-Kla has it that this curse will visit itself first upon him who steals Yath-Lhi's treasure—and then upon the dreamlands in their entirety! For so it is written in the Fourth Book of D'harsis, *whose glyphs only Atal himself has ever deciphered; and D'harsis was one of dreamland's greatest mages—that is, before his daemonic demise.*

But of course all this is by way of reiteration; you will have had it in some detail from the s.w.i.e. himself. As for the requirement:

The activities of Raffis Gan, Baharna's Chief Regulator, have recently become a matter of some concern. The s.w.i.e. has reported to me Gan's "archaeological" interest in the ruins on Yath's far shore, a region whose very aura has in the past sufficed to keep out curiosity seekers, prospectors, searchers after solitude and others of Gan's alleged paleological persuasions. And it would appear that Gan's interest has gone deeper far than that of any mere amateur. I am now driven to the conclusion that he knows the ruins are those of Tyrhhia, and that beneath Tyrhhia Yath-Lhi constructed her treasure-maze, possibly still intact.

What's more, it seems likely that he is using slaves to excavate the ruins; certainly he is in league with a gang of very dubious Kledans, whose penchant for slaving continues unabated throughout dreamland's less civilized lands and districts.

Alas, but all of this is hearsay—I have not one jot of solid evidence. And Gan is, after all, Baharna's Chief Regulator. If the s.w.i.e.'s information is incorrect in any instance, and my own conclusions less than accurate, any unwarranted accusation would constitute a very serious breach of diplomatic etiquette and might well damage beyond immediate repair relations between the mainland (including Serannian) and Oriab. Which is to be avoided at all costs.

To put it in a nutshell: I cannot approach Baharna's Council of Elders without proof positive of Raffis Gan's assumed criminal and at best very suspicious and extremely dangerous activities. Such proof will not be easy to come by: the s.w.i.e. has himself twice narrowly escaped apprehension on the shore of Yath, where Kledan guards apparently patrol a wide perimeter.

And so to the crux of this communication: you two are to obtain this evidence, with dispatch, so that I may then approach the correct authorities from an entirely secure position. The utmost urgency is, of course, imperative. Yath-Lhi was known to be a sorceress of great power; her interest in vampirism—the fact that she herself aspired to leadership of an Undead Legion more mon-

strous far than Zura of Zura's zombies—is con-
vincingly recorded in the Fourth Book. *In light of*
which, who can hazard a guess what ghoulish
guardians she may have left to watch over her lab-
yrinth, or what aeon-slumbering curse Raffis Gan
may yet awaken?

Take care, you two, and may you be successful
in this venture as in all the others I've set you . . .
Kuranes.

"Well, Wanderer?" said Raffis Gan's pale, intense face from behind the thin sheet of smoothed-out paper on which, in a long-dead tongue, the message was written. "Maybe you've come to your senses in more ways than one, eh? And now will you tell me what it says?"

And suddenly Eldin knew he was no longer dreaming. His mind had returned from the sub-conscious realms of his dreams within dreams, and he was back in the dreamlands proper, conscious again following his second clout on the head in . . . in how long? In too short a time, to be sure! Two eggs now, to be counted on the back of his head; and as for Hero . . .

Hero!

Full memory returned in the next moment—memory and the horror it brought.

"Hero!" Eldin hoarsely croaked, trying to sit up. And even as the hope dawned that perhaps that, too, had been part of his nightmare, so it was dashed. The Wanderer found himself chained below decks in some strange vessel, sensed the rush of water beyond the ribs and planking of the hull, saw that he was still Raffis Gan's prisoner. For a moment he strained forward, then collapsed again in his chains and lay there, staring almost vacantly into the eyes of his inquisitor. And:

"Gan," he breathed tonelessly. "You murdered David Hero. Aye, and the girl, Ula Gidduf, too."

Eldin's seemingly vacant eyes were red-rimmed, but the Chief Regulator thought he saw blood in their pupils, too, and so kept well back out of reach. "I put them out of my way, Wanderer, that's all. I had no need of them—but I do have need of you. And my offer still stands: work for me, and I'll not only spare your life but make you wealthy beyond your wildest flights of fancy!"

Again Eldin dragged himself into a seated position; his chains wouldn't allow more than that. "What of Una, the other sister?" he growled.

Gan nodded. "Your woman, aye. I thought you'd ask for her. Well don't worry, she's safe enough. She's aboard, if you'd like to see for yourself. But first things first. And remember, Wanderer, my patience is short and you've already stretched it far enough. I *do* need you, but not so much that I'll take any more of your nonsense. Understood?"

Again the vacant look—a shocked look, Gan thought, of immeasurable loss, weariness, pain—was back in Eldin's eyes, but he gave a slow nod. "Oh, yes, I understand. What do you want of me?"

"This for starters," said Gan eagerly, waving Kuranes' message. "Now, for the last time, will you or won't you translate it for me?"

Una was here, right now, on this boat. What would become of her if Eldin refused? Gan didn't bluff, the Wanderer knew that now.

Perhaps the Chief Regulator saw the question written in Eldin's face. "I'll give her to my colleagues," he smiled thinly. "Myself, the flesh of women isn't much to my taste. But those two . . ."

"Dog!" said Eldin, but it came out the merest whisper. And: "Very well, I'm beaten. Only promise me you'll bring her down here, where I can see for myself she's safe."

Gan nodded. "As soon as I know the contents of this message." He took down a lanthorn from where it swung on a hook above his head, thrust it close to Eldin's face. "And the truth, Wanderer—the whole truth, mind—for be sure I'll know it if you lie to me."

Still Eldin hesitated. "And when I've done this for you, what's to stop you killing me and the girl out of hand?"

"You broke into a great keep, found your way into its core," said Gan. "I'm into Yath-Lhi's maze, but the central treasure-chamber is giving me trouble. Quite apart from my promise, that in itself would keep you alive. There are more glyphs to be read than those on this scrap of paper, you see? And you seem to be the man for the job. You can prove me correct on that point right now. Or you can prove me wrong, and face the consequences. Now read—if you can."

Eldin's eyes slowly left Gan's face, focused once more upon Kuranes' message. "I've told you it's in Ancient Dreamlands?"

"Yes, so you said," Gan was impatient to the point of itching.

"It can't be translated word for word," Eldin lied, "for it wasn't that sort of tongue. It conveys ideas, impressions, that's all."

"Wanderer," Gan ground the words out, "what—does—it—*say*?"

Eldin let his gaze shift from the message, which he knew now by heart, straight into Gan's slitted eyes. "It says: 'Hero, Eldin, 'ware Raffis Gan. He's found Yath-

Lhi's treasure-maze and would rob all the dreamlands of a priceless legacy.' "

"Yes, yes!" said Gan when Eldin paused. "Nothing new in that, is there? Go on." The Chief Regulator licked his lips. Not eagerly, Eldin noted; or at best, eager-anxious.

"That's it," the Wanderer averted his eyes.

"Liar!" Gan snapped. "What? This great long sheet of hieroglyphs, and that's all it says?"

Eldin made to cover up for his apparent error. "Oh, it's not couched that simply, but in essence that's the message. There is a bit more, however." He squinted again at the sheet, his mind working furiously. "Yes, it also says: 'The seer with invisible eyes can show you the way to Tyrhhia's ruins. Go there—but go carefully—and bring me back irrefutable evidence of the Chief Regulator's criminal activity.' "

"Hah!" Gan snorted. "Well, no problem there, Wanderer, for we're on our way even now. What else?"

Inspiration came like a bright flash of light in Eldin's mind. A man in a hurry makes mistakes. Panicked, an animal will fly straight into the trap. And Raffis Gan was an animal if ever Eldin saw one. "What else?" he repeated, and nodded. "A postscript, that's all—and one you'll not much care for."

Gan's pinched face went narrower still and he frowned. "Go on."

"It says: 'If I don't hear from you by return, my next message goes straight to Baharna's Council of Elders'!"

"*What?*" the Chief Regulator whispered, his eyes darting from Eldin's face to the glyph-inscribed tissue, and back to Eldin. "Where, Wanderer? Where does it say that?"

"There," Eldin nodded gravely. "The last three lines there, followed by Kuranes' sigil."

Gan reeled for a moment, staggered until his shoulders came up against low beams. Then he seemed to draw strength from his sturdy vessel, straightened up a little. "So, it's come at last. The Elders have had their suspicions for some time, I fancy, but word from Kuranes will clinch it. At least they'll investigate—and I'm afraid I'm not up to much of an investigation. Then they'll be after me full tilt. We're into the afternoon already; Kuranes will be expecting your answer tonight, but he won't get one—that's when he'll dispatch his damned accusations. The Council of Elders will know all by this time tomorrow at the latest. That gives me less than twenty-four hours to crack Yath-Lhi's treasure-chamber . . ." He began to turn away, checked himself.

"The girl," Eldin reminded him, before Gan could say anything else. "You said you'd send her down to me."

Gan's mind was now on other things. "One last question," he said. "Did Kuranes mention . . . a curse?"

"Eh?" said Eldin, trying to be—just Eldin. "Curse, Kuranes? Why, no. He's not much for swearing, that one. Far too much a gentleman. Though I do seem to remember that on one occasion he—"

"A *curse*, clown!" Gan hissed. "A malediction—a DOOM—a lurking evil connected with Yath-Lhi's treasure."

"Oh, *that* sort of curse!" said Eldin. "No, not a word. D'you believe in such, then?"

"These are the dreamlands, Wanderer," said Gan darkly, "and of strange things dreamed by men in the waking world . . . there's no end or limit to what might or might not be. Gugs, ghouls, gaunts, ghasts, dholes, Shantaks, zoogs, zombies and other monsters and mischiefs—their reality has to be acknowledged, because they *are* real. Encounters are numerous and well documented. But a curse, passed down dim centuries to the present day? No, you're quite right: personally I'm not especially superstitious." A worried look crossed his face; or rather, the one already there intensified. "But there have been an inordinately large number of accidental deaths among my slaves, and even a few Kledans have . . ." He paused, scowled. "There's nothing, you say?"

"Nothing at all," replied the Wanderer blandly. "It seems to me old Kuranes is more interested in the theft or priceless antiquities and a certain Chief Regulator's improper use of powers vested, than in any curse of some mummified princess dead since the dawn of dreams . . ."

"Quite right," said Gan, with a curt nod. And again, under his breath, "quite right." He made his way to where a hatch stood open overhead, hauled himself up and out of sight. Moments later a short ladder came down, then Una followed, tearful as she threw herself into Eldin's shackled arms.

But between Gan's going and Una's coming, the Wanderer had lain there with a strange and savage grin on his scarred face. There was no pleasure in that grin, which was more the smile of a wolf, but there was a deal of satisfaction. And not a little of anticipation . . .

"My father was right," said Ula Gidduf, with a low moan. "I should have stayed home and looked after him. Oh, Hero—Hero, what is this place?"

Hero gulped, opened his mouth, gulped again. Then he found his voice. "It's the biggest damn catacomb in all the dreamlands," he finally replied in little more than a whisper. "Lord, it *has* to be!"

The flaring torch flickered lower as fragile rags went up in smoke; Hero looked about for longer lasting fuel. Some of the crumbling corpses that littered the floor of this huge circular room wore wooden yokes, which were now very nearly fossilized into a peaty coal. Hero had no trouble wresting one of these from a skeletal neck, knocking loose its corroded metal hasps and chains against the wall. Then he gave the yoke a harder clout and it shattered, displaying a core of black, woody fibers. Tilted into the smolder of the foul-burning rags of the flambeau, the splinters of ancient timber very quickly caught fire. And as the flames leaped bright and yellow, so Hero and Ula could take in the full size of the chamber, and the full measure of the singular atrocity long since perpetrated here.

The vault was perhaps one hundred feet across, roughly hacked from the raw rock, with a ceiling maybe fifteen feet high. With the exception of a spiraling stone stairway at its center, apparently passing up into and through the ceiling, and the evenly spaced flambeaux around the walls—and of course its contingent of grotesque mummies—the place was featureless. As for the antique corpses:

There must be at least two hundred of them littered about, some in small piles, some singly, seated with their backs against the walls or lying in various crumpled positions. And it hardly took close inspection to tell what they had been or how they had died. Their yokes and corroded chains and ankle clamps spoke all too clearly, however dumbly, of their once-station, or lack of it, in life; hacked vertebrae, necks, crushed skulls and caved-in chests told the rest. They'd been slaves, and some long-dead master or mistress, for some long-dead reason or upon a similarly extinct whim, had decreed that they be incarcerated and slaughtered here.

Mistress? Hero's nostrils flared. Suddenly, an idea—a suspicion—had formed itself in his ever-bright mind. He put it aside at once; it now appeared there'd be time, after all, to examine it later. And turning to Ula:

"Lass, you're still shivering—from cold or sheer fright I'm not sure—but I reckon our first priority is to warm up our marrows a bit. So—d'you reckon you can help me gather up an armful of these yokes? It's not hard work, but it's not especially pleasant, either."

Ula was made of the right stuff: in a very little while she was naked, drying her clothes over a small bonfire of aeon-old hardwood. Hero left his jacket, shirt and boots with her, went off with a sputtering brand to explore the stairway. He would never be very far away, and he talked to her as he went—a running commentary on his discoveries—but still . . . she averted her eyes from the blind, almost accusing gaze of countless eyeless sockets and got on with drying herself.

"I'm going up the stairway," Hero called back, unnecessarily, for of course she could still see his flickering outline in the flare of his torch, but mainly to help her fight down her fear of the unknown, the darkness beyond the firelight. Not to mention his own.

The stair wound about a central pillar; Hero climbed, passed out of view on the far side, reappeared and pressed on higher. Then:

"Dead end," came his voice, echoing down to Ula, its disappointment plain. "Literally! More corpses at the top, several of 'em chopped in half when the plug fell."

"What?" Ula didn't understand. "Stairs going up to nothing? Plug? What are you talking about, Hero?"

"Oh, these stairs went somewhere once upon a time," he answered, holding his torch aloft and sending shadows leaping. "Up through the bedrock and into her palace, I should think. But she had this great stone plug prepared, you see, and at the end—"

"Hero, you're rambling," she cut him off. "Explain yourself. She? Who, she?"

He came winding his way back down the spiral of stone steps. "Yath-Lhi, I suppose. I mean, it all fits, doesn't it? We were brought inland, on the tide, into this subterranean crypt. We doubtless passed *under* Yath the lake—named all that time ago for the princess herself, and the fact of it forgotten—and so found our way into this antechamber. Here it was she killed her slaves, before sealing it and proceeding to her last resting place."

"Eh?" said Ula, seeming to Hero to sound more like Eldin all the time. "She 'proceeded' somewhere from here? Where, pray?"

"This staircase," he answered across the radius of the vault, "not only goes up, but down!"

He started down the winding stairwell.

"Hero!" Ula cried out at once, starting across the corpse-littered floor toward him. "You're not going anywhere without me!"

He peered at her for a moment, managed a roguish grin, however contrived. "And you're not coming anywhere with me—not dressed, or undressed, like that!"

She glanced down at herself, said, "Oh!" returned to her fire.

Hero joined her. "Very well," he said, "we go together. Are our clothes dry?"

"Mine are," she began dressing. "Yours . . . not quite."

"They'll have to do." He dressed slowly, turning himself before the fire, left his boots till last. And finally: "Ula, I—"

"No need to say it," she cut in. "I know. Up, we'd have stood a chance. Down—we're going nowhere."

Hero reluctantly nodded. "I thought I'd mention it," he said. "Easier to face now we're warm and half-dry. And of course, it's not definite. It just wouldn't do to get too deliriously happy, that's all." He tossed his brand into the fire, took up a fresh one. Ula did likewise.

"Very well," she said. "I'll try not to get carried away. So let's go and have a look at Yath-Lhi's treasure-chamber, shall we?"

"Why not?" Hero kissed her roughly. "Who knows? It might be the last treasure-chamber we ever see!"

"What?" Eldin was astonished, almost shocked. *"What!"* he repeated, this time an exclamation. "A minute ago you were very sweetly crying your eyes out, and now you're—*Una!*"

"Shhh!" she shushed desperately.

"But why are you groping me? I mean, this is hardly the time or the place for—"

"Oaf!" she whispered, anything but sweetly. "I am *not* groping you! Wouldn't that be like taking onyx to Inquanok? Or playing the dingaphon to impress the maestro Gaez Voorpin? Would I dream of groping the Grand Groper himself?"

If anything, Eldin was a little disappointed. "Then what are you doing?"

She sighed. "You haven't noticed that your wrists are padlocked together behind your left thigh?"

"Eh? Why, no, I hadn't, actually."

"My tears were for Gan and his cronies," she said, "so they'd see how helpless I was—while I snatched the key to these padlocks you're wearing!"

"Padlocks? More than one?"

Una sighed again. "Your ankles are padlocked, too."

"So they are!" He clanked his chains a bit. "Don't take any chances, these lads, do they?"

"Oh, they do," she answered grimly, "but with the wrong people! So I wailed and cried a lot to distract them, and in the end they were only too glad to send me down here."

Now her eyes were bright and glinting. "They killed my sister," she said huskily. "Oh, yes, let them see my tears now—but later I'll show them the cutting edge of a sword! Or a knife! Or an axe!"

"I hope you'll leave some for me," Eldin growled. "See, my mind runs to mayhem, too—and if that doesn't work out there's something even nastier."

"The worse the better!" she said, giving him a hug.

"Right," said Eldin, "no time to waste. How many of 'em, up top?"

"Gan and his two, that's all. The rest of the Regulators probably don't know their boss is a bad 'un."

"My feeling exactly," the Wanderer agreed. "Now then, I know we're sailing for Tyrhhia, but what's our e.t.a.?"

"We're more than half-way across Yath now, I reckon," she answered, and shrugged. "Ten to fifteen minutes at most. Maybe even less."

Eldin weighed chains, wrapped his great fists in them. "Just the three of 'em, eh?" he scowled. "Can you whirl a chain, d'you think?" He handed her a very unladylike length.

They crept soundlessly to the ladder, and Eldin stepped up it to try the hatch. Mercifully it wasn't battened: with his head, he pushed it open a fraction and peered out. He recognized the vessel at once: a Regulator patrol boat, small, with a fast, fancy sail. He pushed the hatch open more yet—and gasped.

Una heard him, saw his bulk stiffen on the ladder, tugged at his trouser leg. "What's up?" she whispered.

"Your e.t.a. was a mite off," he answered. "We're already there!"

At that moment the boat answered the helm, swung to port a little, lost impetus. And:

"Ahoy there, Slave-Master Druff!" Gan's sudden hail from for'ard caused Eldin to duck back. "How goes the work?"

"Ahoy, Raffis Gan!" came back the answer, in guttural Kledan tones. "Slowly, I fear."

Eldin peered out again.

One hundred yards away, the shore was thick with reeds, bulrushes, semi-tropical shrubs and small palms. Good cover there. The Regulator vessel was closing on a spindly, makeshift wooden jetty; beyond the jetty, a pair of huge Kledan sky-slavers rolled on a fresh-risen breeze, anchored fore and aft with their keels just clear of the water. Another, approaching from the north, was in the process of dropping down from the sky, her anchors about to dip into the lake. Swarthy Kledans galore were plainly visible on the decks of all three squat, ungainly vessels; they mended crude-seeming flotation bags and tended rigging and sails, fished from the gunnels, busied themselves with unloading. But it was *what* they unloaded that interested Eldin the most.

Small lighters rowed by Pargans, overseen by their Kledan masters, wallowed to their gunnels as they bore piled gunpowder kegs ashore, sat light in the water when they came back empty. Eldin's narrowed eyes went back to Yath's shore. A shallow mist lapped the surface of the lake, but it failed to obscure his view.

Long lines of Pargan slaves, each man carrying a keg atop his head, moved between the lighters and a spot where the shore of the lake sloped back and rose up sharply into a sort of barrow or small hill. Covered by rank green growth, the hill lay approximately centrally in an extensive area of ancient ruins which came right down to the water's edge—the tumbled remains of primeval Tyrhhia, as Eldin was now well aware. The side of the hill facing the lake had been shorn of vegetation down to naked rock; the great black throat of a cave led back into darkness, where a long line of fixed torches receded, descending out of sight: the entrance to Yath-Lhi's maze.

Again Gan's shouting startled the Wanderer. "You haven't found a way into the core? Not even a lead?"

"Nothing!" came back the cry from the deck of the closest Kledan vessel. "The walls seem solid. Some are even suggesting that there is no chamber—just a core of solid rock."

"Fools!" Gan shouted. "I've a man here who can read the glyphs on those walls. We'll be into that treasure before nightfall!"

"Oops!" said Eldin. Catlike for a man his size, he slid out of the hatch and drew Una up after him. Under the mainsail's boom, they could see the lower half of the legs of Gan and his two bullies. "Quickly," Eldin whispered. "Over the side—without a splash, mind you— and make for the shore. Do it in stretches, underwater as best you can, and stick close to me. Go!"

Masked by the sail and the cabin's low superstructure, Una slipped overboard like an eel into the milky water; Eldin followed immediately after her, kicked hard for the bottom and chased Una's lithe shape across the muddy, weedy bed of the lake. They surfaced when they had to, and looked back. The Regulator vessel was visible through a thin shroud of mist. But after diving again, swimming, surfacing a second time, only the outlines of the boat could still be seen. Moments later the lake shallowed out and they were able to half-swim, half-crawl ashore into the weed-draped bulrushes. Heads kept low, they made firmer ground, ran almost crouching through dank fern, bulrush and shrub, away from the cavern entrance and the moored ships.

No one had seen their escape, but it would be discovered soon enough. Five minutes later they thought they heard a burst of angry shouting, wild cries of alert, but by then they were well away.

A quarter-mile along the lake's rim, the Wanderer spotted a tiny island only twenty-five or thirty yards out from the shore. Tall reeds grew in clumps there, and trees, whose knotty roots were bedded in several large boulders, and an outcrop that looked for all the world like a ruined wall. Maybe it was.

"That'll do for now," Eldin nodded. "The mist's clearing. If we can get across there quick, we'll catch the last of the sun and dry out before nightfall." Una made no comment, but at once followed him into the water again.

Ten minutes later they had their clothes spread out over domed boulders at the rear of the island—whose entire circumference was no more than two hundred feet at most—and made do with underclothes as they explored their refuge. There wasn't a lot of it to look at: ruined stone walls crumbling away, bedrock thrusting up, a few boulders and an abundance of greenery. Difficult to believe that, two hundred yards beyond, Yath's shore all was desert and dust.

Totally impossible even to conceive that less than a mile away horizontally, and ninety feet vertically, Hero and Ula were even now exploring Yath-Lhi's treasure-chamber . . .

* * *

Raffis Gan prowled the deck of *Manhunter*, Zubda Druff's slaver, and scowled his frustration into the twilight as the first stars cast their feeble light over Oriab, shining down on the still Lake of Yath. Heavily armed search parties had gone out; come back empty-handed, nothing to report. Eldin the Wanderer and Una Gidduf were off and running (so it appeared) and no hope of catching them now, and the job still to be finished. And Gan had to be out of here by noon tomorrow at latest.

Now, head down and muttering, hands clenched behind his back, he stomped the planking to and fro, waiting impatiently for nightfall.

"Another half-hour," said lean, hard-muscled, ebony Druff from where he hunched on *Manhunter*'s rail and gnawed on a haunch of roasted goat. "That's when the day-shift comes out, exhausted, with nothing to show for their work but blisters. Then *we* go in, with the night-shift, and—and what then, eh? You've made a lot of promises, Raffis Gan, and none of 'em come to pass as yet."

"Shut up, Druff!" Gan cried. He whirled on Egg-head and Narrow-eyes, who stood shuffling their feet, looking surly. "I blame you two! Morons! She must have taken that key from under your very eyes! If you hadn't been doing so much slavering over her and wondering which of you was going to be first . . ."

Druff the Kledan had tossed the remains of his repast overboard. "Gan," he rumbled, slipping down off the rail and fingering the hilt of the curved sword stuck in his silk cummerbund, "we had a deal. We still do have one—at least until tomorrow—but don't you start shutting me up aboard my own ship. You may be or have been, Chief Regulator in Baharna, but out here—"

Gan gritted his teeth, held up his hands placatingly.

"You're right," he said, "quite right. If we start fighting now we can kiss it all goodbye, and that won't do."

Druff shrugged. "It would do for me," he said, "for I can always go back to Kled. But can you go back to Baharna? My task was simply to bring you slaves, a workforce, which I've done and no grudge. For I don't own the slaves you've wasted in that hole. But your backers in Kled do own them, and they'll want paying. If you ran, they'd find you, Gan, no matter where. And I'd probably be the one they'd send after you. So from now on, watch who you're telling to shut up, right?"

"Right, *right*!" Gan snapped again, through clenched teeth. "It's just that I hate it when things go wrong. And I'm sure that that man, Eldin the Wanderer, could have led us right in there. He looked a dolt, right enough, but he does have a reputation for this sort of thing."

"He didn't look that much of a dolt to me," said Egghead ruefully, rubbing at his shoulder. "Not when he was trying to chew my arm off! Well, maybe a dangerous dolt!"

Gan scowled at him, looked away in disgust.

Druff picked his huge white teeth. "Well, he won't be leading us in anywhere now. So it looks like we go back to the original plan, right?"

"Yes," Gan agreed, "we blast our way in! It was a last resort, but that was before there was a deadline."

"Deadline, aye," Druff nodded his shiny black head. "And talking about death, didn't you have certain reservations? About blasting, I mean?"

"I still do," said Gan. "In there, at the central keep where Yath-Lhi stored her treasure, there's an awful lot of rock overhead—you can feel it weighing down on you. Reservations? Too true! So we'll do it one keg at a time, step by step and steady as she goes, and so chew our way right through one of those walls. And like I said, we'll have the stuff aboard your ships and airborne before sun-up."

Druff nodded, turned and strolled away with a rolling, sailor's gait. "I hope so," he growled over his shoulder. "I really do—and not least for your sake . . ."

Gan watched him go, cursed under his breath. Then he turned to his men, said: "Leave me, but stay within calling distance. Get yourselves something to eat, beat up a slave or something. I want to think." He went to the rail, leaned on it and stared out over the dim, gently lapping lake. And he thought back on how it all started . . .

Gan had lived most of his life in the shadow of his father, holier-than-thou, bring-'em-back-alive, go-get-'em Tellis Gan. Tellis Gan the Fearless! And no one had thought of the young Gan as "Raffis" at all: he'd been simply "Tellis' son," and nothing more. "A pale, spotty sort—not a patch on his father." Law and order had been Tellis' life, and Raffis had had it up to here.

Not fitted for any sort of skilled work, he'd early taken to solitary wanderings throughout the land, traveling the length and breadth of Oriab and studying the ancient island's antiquities. His trips had been in large part simply a means of getting out of his father's limelight; but when Raffis' mother had died, he'd blamed his father that so much of his time had been spent in loneliness, away from home and the fragile mother who'd loved him.

From then on Raffis was rarely home at all. To escape the present, he'd begun to explore the past to an ever deeper degree. And one day, in the desert beyond Yath's green border . . . he'd discovered a sheet of beaten silver: a silver tile which, in the present day, he'd known would be made of lead or slate.

And digging deeper in the sand and ruins, he'd found

more of them, a veritable cache of heavy, precious silver, then he'd guessed that this was Tyrhhia. For had not Yath-Lhi's slave city been silver-spired? Yath the lake—Yath-Lhi—the ill-regarded ruins—silver galore—it all fitted, all added up. This *had* to be Tyrhhia. And here, buried deep somewhere under these desert sands, the Black Princess's legendary treasure!

Many the grand dreams within dreams Raffis Gan dreamed then, and many grand schemes schemed. But while he might scorn the laws of Baharna's Elders, which his father supported and enforced so diligently, certainly he was aware of them. Particularly with regard to antiquities, and especially concerning the forbidden, forbidding ruins on Yath's far shore.

And so, working in strictest secrecy, he approached certain ex-slavers, Kledans passing through Baharna, and gave them a message—and an invitation, a proposal—to be delivered to certain offensively rich persons in the fabled, barbarously opulent cities of jungled Kled. In essence his offer was this: he held the key to a fabulous treasure and would share it fifty-fifty; the knowledge was available to whoever could supply as much labor as might be required. Slave labor, of course. And to support his claim that he knew the whereabouts of Tyrhhia, he sent along as a gift (or at least as part-payment in advance) his own weight in ancient silver.

He'd had his answer by return, on the very next ship out of Kled: an introduction to Zubda Druff, who would finalize the arrangements and act as Gan's partner (and his backers' watchdog) until the conclusion of the project. Except . . . there was one major problem. A problem named Tellis Gan.

Baharna's Chief Regulator had a down on all Kledans, but particularly ex-slavers whom he knew, in other less discriminating parts and ports, to be anything but ex. He would not take it kindly if swarms of them suddenly appeared in the streets of Baharna, or even on the Isle of Oriab as a whole. At worst he'd harass them out of their wits, and the very least he'd do would be to investigate. The project simply would not stand up to investigation, not once the dig was under way.

And so, with never a twinge of conscience, Raffis Gan had arranged that treacherous ambush which was directly responsible for Tellis Gan's death. Elevated to the office of Chief Regulator in his father's place, Gan had then subverted a pair of dubious Regulators, sworn them to secrecy, set them up as his thuggish lieutenants; and as soon as he was basically established in his new appointment, he'd finally dispatched an all-clear to his Kledan backers.

Then had come the deep-hulled, wallowing sky-slavers with their miserable human cargoes—not to Baharna, no, but direct to the Lake of Yath itself—and then too the excavation of Tyrhhia had begun in earnest. And while all of this was going on, Gan's Regulators had kept the law in Baharna, with Raffis himself most stringent in the application of those laws that prohibited fishing near Yath's far shore, prospecting in the desert beyond Yath, or the seeking of relics in the (hitherto) unnamed ruins.

As for grandiose dreams and schemes and such . . .

The original deal with the Kledans had been modi-fied. Gan would now take one third of the haul plus a ship, its crew and full complement of slaves. With these he could easily make himself a power in any one of Kled's lush cities, and under an assumed name would doubtless live out his days in untold luxury.

The first Baharna's Council of Elders would ever know of the affair would be when Gan went missing and a Regulator vessel was found derelict upon the shore of Yath. Then they would read Gan's logbook, which would tell a wholly fabulous (but irrefutable) story.

The log would show how, suspicious of Kledan activity, Chief Regulator Gan had discovered slavers excavating the forbidden ruins. It would also record Gan's "plan": to use their own blasting powder to destroy the Kledans and sabotage their extensive diggings. There would be an element of risk in this, of course, but that was all in a day's work ... And that would be all, the final entry.

Subsequent examination of Yath's shore would show a channel blasted from the rim of the lake to the foot of that sloping barrow with its yawning cavern mouth; Tyrhhia's entire subterranean labyrinth would be flooded; numerous bodies of black Pargan slaves—plus a few Kledan corpses, carefully salvaged from several recent accidents—would be found floating in the lake or crushed among fallen rocks. Though the Chief Regulator's body would never be found, it would eventually be assumed that he had died sabotaging the criminal activities of Kledan freebooters. It would be that or admit that Kuranes of Ooth-Nargai was right, and Gan knew that the Elders of Baharna were a proud lot; there would be Gan's family name to think of, and his father's memory to consider. Diplomatic protests would be made to Kled, of course, which would never be answered or even read; there were no kings or governments in the jungle cities where wealth alone was the law and brute strength the only order ...

Gan's reflections ceased. Darkness was fast falling. Out from the tunnel mouth on the shore, a long line of weary slaves came shuffling, their torch-bearing Kledan guards hastening them with curses and cracking whips. The day-shift, coming off duty. But no cries of excitement to herald news of a break-in, of penetration to the treasure-chamber. Gan wasn't much of a fatalist, but he shrugged anyway. Very well, only one course remained open to him. There was an element of risk, but . . . better, perhaps, to be caught in a rockfall than caught here tomorrow by his own Regulators, when the Council of Elders sent them to bring him to justice.

It was a while now since Hero and Ula had descended with their torches the spiral stairwell to Yath-Lhi's burial place, that eerily enigmatic tomb which they'd named "the Booming Chamber." An hour? Two? Maybe three? Time had little meaning down here. It was measured in burning yokes, in the sputtering and flaring of oil long-since turned to resin in its jars, and in the gradually declining level of unbelievable wine, swigged straight from a clay bottle fired and glazed, filled and corked, when dreams were young. But as for treasure . . .

"I understand none of it," said Ula with a shake of her head, after they'd sat together in silence for a long time. They were back now in the chamber of the corpses, which for all its litter of broken human remains seemed friendlier by far than the place below.

"I think I understand some of it," said Hero, "but as for the rest, I've given up trying. I *do* understand my calculations, however—based on the number of yokes we've gathered up, and the lumps of oil I've knocked out of those jars—about how long we'll have light and warmth. Which is to say, for another six or seven hours. And after that we'll be burning corpses. If they'll burn."

Even as he spoke these words Hero could have bitten off his tongue; he realized it must seem that his hopes were fading along with his sensitivity. Which they were, but no good to let Ula know it. And so he added: "Except, of course, that we'll be out of here long before then."

Seated beside him, she shuffled closer, hugged his arm. "Don't be afraid of despair, lad," she said, reminding him strangely, at one and the same time, both of his mother (whom he really couldn't remember, for she'd died long ago, when he was a boy in the waking world) and of Eldin. "As my father used to tell us: when you're right down there's only one way to go—up! Where there's life there's hope, remember?"

"Oh, yes," he nodded, then turned and gently kissed her. "Life! Hope! Of course . . ."

"It's just that they've a long way to go to break through to us, that's all."

"The throw of a knife, actually," Hero replied. "Except knives don't fly too well through solid rock! We must hope Gan's greed is stronger than the barrier between him and what he believes to be a treasure-chamber, eh?" And he gave a sardonic, barking laugh. Then, as Ula snuggled closer yet and rested her head on his chest, he began to think again of what they'd found below.

The spiral of stone stairs had opened into a second and final chamber, at first taken to be circular. But later, examining the walls, they'd discovered the crypt's sides were formed of twenty-three identical panels, three feet wide and ten high, which was the height of the ceiling. There were no joins, however, so that either the twenty-three sides were thickly plastered on the inside, or the entire chamber had been hewn from the solid bedrock. Nine of the almost two dozen panels had shoulder-level brackets holding prepared torches, now fossilized; and on the floor beneath each one of these, large stone jars which had once contained perfumed oil. Hero had seen such in the temples of Ulthar; sprinkled on the flames of ceremonial flambeaux, the oil made a blue, scented smoke. Of course *these* jars had been here countless centuries; there'd be no oil in them now. He'd broken one anyway, and in its base . . . a bowl-shaped block of amber resin! Oil, condensed and hardened by the ages.

All of this, though, had been after Hero and Ula's introduction to Yath-Lhi: the Black Princess herself, and six of her men-at-arms—mummies now in their upright sarcophagi. But *what* mummies!

Seven of them—in coffins of stone stood on end, evenly spaced in a circle and all facing outward from the foot of the stairwell—and Hero and Ula had held their torches high to examine these grim, gargoyle guardians of the place. And they'd seen, too, that Yath-Lhi and her people had been a race of giants. Their slaves had been ordinary dream-folk, aye—small men and women, generally—but Yath-Lhi . . .

Eight feet tall; those stone coffins, with funnel-shaped apertures in their tops, directly over the mummified heads of those within. And though the sarcophagi were massive and at least three inches thick at top, bottom and sides, still there was little room to spare. Yath-Lhi and her men-at-arms, even shrunken by the aeons, were close to seven feet tall. Giants, then, those seven gaunt guardians—but guarding what? The staircase? For of treasures there were none at all, unless one considered the three emeralds Yath-Lhi wore—one on each hip, the other in her navel: a world's ransom.

Or was the Black Princess simply . . . waiting? Had she expected, perhaps, some marvelous reincarnation which never came to pass? Certainly there seemed an air of implacable patience about her . . .

Hero, no midget himself, had gazed up wonderingly into the faces of the seven. And that was another wonder: that after all these years they had faces at all. Or anything else of muscle, sinew, flesh and bone, for that matter. But there they stood, black and wrinkled as prunes, the men-at-arms with their belts and kirtles and swords of bronze; and Yath-Lhi proud and regal, her black hair braided and falling to her shoulders, dressed only in ropes of gold-painted cowries at her loins, with her empty breasts lying flat upon her chest. And in the flickering torchlight it seemed that at any moment their eyes might pop open or blackened tongues wriggle forth from stony lips, and so Hero and Ula had not gazed long upon them.

It had been then, though, staring up at the mummified figures in their stone coffins, that Hero had noticed overhead the necks of seven bottles of fired clay protruding from apertures in the ceiling. There was one bottle for each coffin, its neck directly over the corresponding funnel in the top of the sarcophagus. They must have been incidental to the burial ceremony; perhaps it had been intended that they should drip their contents (some time-forgotten preserving fluid?) on to the heads of the seven after interment, presumably to "anoint" them preparatory to their long voyage down the stream of time. Of course, the bottles would be quite empty now . . .

And yet it seemed to Hero that the age-blackened corks were intact.

Using an upturned oil jar as a stepping stone, and the stone coffin of one of the soldiers for support and balance, he reached up and finally wrested a bottle free of its hole. Its base had been cemented into place, but the cement was brittle as chalk now, and had given in to Hero's persistent tugging. And wonder of wonders, within the bottle's opaque, fragile body—something sloshed!

At which time, frightening the explorers almost witless, had commenced that singular and repetitive sound for which they'd named the crypt the Booming Chamber. But more of that anon.

Finally, all done in the burial vault and eager now to be out of there, the pair carried their prizes of oil-lump and miraculously preserved bottle and contents back up the winding stairs, where Hero smashed the bottle's slender neck against the wall. And if they had been at first astonished to discover anything still liquid in the bottle, picture now their utter amaze at the heady, aromatic fumes which on the instant began to escape from it!

Wine, certainly, but of what rare and incredible vintage? And palatable—they'd nursed the bottle between them from then till now, and one sip at a time had warmed their innards while reducing the wine's level by at least two-thirds. In between, Hero had nerved himself to return below, broken the remaining oil jars, carried their precious fossil fuel lumps back to the tomb of the slaves. He'd tried the rest of the bottles, too, but alas, these had been fixed in their ceiling-holes more securely than the first. Finally he'd again admired (indeed, confiscated) Yath-Lhi's jewelry . . .

As for naming the crypt the Booming Chamber, that had come about like this:

When Hero had got down from taking the bottle from its hole in the ceiling, and just as he'd given it a shake and determined that there was still a full measure of liquid inside, so there had come the first of a long series of thunderous reverberations.

So sudden and startling was the sound, he almost dropped the newly acquired bottle. Ula threw herself into his arms, and as the booming echoes receded she tremulously began to ask:

"What on earth—?" Only to be cut off as a second crash sounded, again filling the chamber with thundering echoes. But as the booming continued regular as clockwork, so reason replaced fear, and the answer dawned: this could only be the work of Chief Regulator Raffis Gan. This place was, after all, Yath-Lhi's tomb; and hadn't Gan boasted that he'd solved the maze, reached the core, and was now seeking to breach the treasure-chamber itself? Obviously the system he employed was that of the battering-ram or -rams; but while the concussions were thunderous, still they caused no more than trickles of dust to fall from the ceiling. Hero's conclusion was that these walls were tremendously thick; the sound of the battering itself carried through them, but nothing of the slaves who worked the machines, or of their overseers. Even in the upper chamber the booming could be heard, so that Hero and Ula had been quite dizzy with it when finally the assault stopped. The pair couldn't know it, but that was when the day-shift had gone off duty, tramping back through the labyrinth to the outside world.

Since when . . . the silence had become more unbearable than the booming! Had Gan given up? If so . . . but that didn't bear thinking about. To *avoid* thinking about it—about dying down here, and becoming a crumbling corpse like the many littered about—Hero now said:

"You were saying? Er, 'what on earth'? Something you don't understand? What, exactly, don't you understand?"

"Several things," Ula answered at once, so quickly indeed that Hero was given to wonder if she'd been thinking along the same lines, and so was grateful that he'd broken the silence. She glanced at him in the flickering firelight. "This wine, for instance. I mean, how could they possibly forget to pull the corks, or prick them, or whatever?"

Hero shook his head. "Maybe it was for them to drink in the afterworld."

"What?" she gave a snort. "And they'd have to go piggy-back to get at it? Undignified sort of afterworld that, isn't it?"

"Umm," said Hero. "I suppose it is, a bit."

"And what of the treasure?" she went on.

"You mean the un-treasure," Hero corrected her.

"The un-treasure, then. Where is it?"

"Don't look at me!" Hero protested. "I was with you."

She obliged him with a grin. "That's the first funny thing you've said in ages! Now I know we'll be all right."

"Must be the wine," Hero scratched his chin. "But actually you're right: I do feel a bit better about things. I mean, what else can happen to us, eh?"

Rather than answer *that* one, she said: "Don't change the subject. We were talking about things we don't understand."

"Like, f'rinstance?"

"Like: why did Yath-Lhi advertise the presence of her burial chamber by building a damn—excuse me—great maze around it? I mean, it was bound to be found. But who'd have tried to search out a simple little hole in the ground, eh?"

"No one," Hero answered. "They wouldn't even want to—unless they thought there was a fantastic treasure buried with her. You know, the more I think about it, the more it seems to me that Yath-Lhi . . . that she wanted . . ." He faltered to a halt, short hairs stiffening on his neck.

"That she *wanted* to be found?" Ula said it for him.

And slowly, oh so slowly, the pair turned their heads to stare wonderingly at each other. At which precise moment the Booming Chamber boomed again. Except that this time it was louder, and the rock beneath their feet gave a small but very definite lurch, and the dust didn't merely trickle, but began to come down in veritable rivulets!

An hour earlier . . .

Eldin had seen the night-shift of slaves go on duty— and he'd seen Raffis Gan, Zubda Druff, Narrow-eyes and Egg-head go with them. His vantage point was a deep, dry ditch crammed with kegs of gunpowder, which ran from the foot of the cavern barrow to the lake, almost. But certainly it *would* run all the way, when this lot went up! Eldin had been obliged to dive into the ditch head-first when the torch-bearing procession had come weaving out of the underbrush toward him. And, as the long snake of slaves had passed by, he'd heard Gan's raised voice warning:

"Careful with those torches, there! Only drop one in that trench and we'll all be blown to blazes!" Which happened to be a thought very close to the Wanderer's own, so that he might even have considered it—were it not for all those poor blameless slaves. He did jiggle his firestones in his pocket a bit, before putting the idea firmly out of mind. Life wouldn't be a hell of a lot without David Hero around, but it would be better than nothing. Oh, he wanted Gan dead, all right, but that wouldn't be much good if he, Eldin himself, wasn't around to enjoy it.

Also, the Wanderer now found himself with a bad case of cat's disease—incurable curiosity. He was curious about two things: Yath-Lhi's curse, and Yath-Lhi's treasure. It might be amusing to steal some of the latter while doing his damnedest to bring down all of the former on Gan. And if he couldn't bring down the curse on him, maybe he would bring down the roof after all.

Which was why, when the slave-gang had tramped out of sight into the barrow's throat, and all that remained of them was the faintest flicker of the hindmost torch, Eldin found a keg with a fuse, tossed it out of the ditch and climbed up after it. With the keg on his shoulder and approaching the mouth of the excavation out of the shadows, he called out to the solitary Kledan guard:

"Ho, there!"

The guard, seated on a boulder, looked up in surprise. "Eh?" he said.

Keeping his face half-hidden behind the keg, Eldin moved closer, grunted, "Keg, see?" He gripped the small barrel between both hands, held it chin high.

Now the guard got a glimpse of his face, jumped to his feet. He drew breath and yelped: "Who—? What—?"

"Keg!" said Eldin again, straightening his arms and ramming the keg forward into the black man's face.

"*Uk!*" said the guard, as his flattened features bounced off the keg and he flew backward, striking the wall of the tunnel with his head.

Eldin, swiftly tucking the keg under his arm, drew back one massive fist to strike a second blow—saw that it wasn't needed. Dribbling spittle and teeth, his brown eyes rapidly glazing over, the Kledan slid down the wall into a seated position.

"There!" Eldin nodded his satisfaction. He took a torch from its bracket on the wall, glared his hatred once at the Kledan ships suspended over Yath, turned into the tunnel, and set off at speed after the column of slaves.

* * *

Swift as a moonshadow, and as silent, Una moved
through the vegetation of Yath's shore—but back toward the excavations, not (as she'd promised Eldin
away from them toward Baharna's safety. He'd told her
she must go back to the city, report to the Council of Elders, tell them all she knew of what had passed. He
would go with her except . . . he had something to finish. With luck they'd meet again; he hoped so, for he
loved her; but for now he had work to do and there
were dangers in it, and it was no job for a girl, and anyway she'd already done her bit. He'd been a little surprised, but glad, when she hadn't argued.

But if Eldin was bent on vengeance, so too was Una
The Wanderer had seen Hero murdered before his very
eyes, and so too had Una seen her sister's cruel death
both of them had scores to settle. Which was why she
hadn't demurred, at least not out loud. Why let him see
in advance that she intended to defy him? That's the
trouble with love: it's fun when the sky is blue and the
sun is shining, but when the crunch comes, then you'll
lay down your life for it. Una had loved her sister—
loved Eldin, too, great oaf—and while she might possibly face life without the one, it would be quite
unbearable with neither.

As for danger: there'd be that, she knew, but on the
other hand who'd be looking for them, she and Eldin?
Those Kledan pursuers they'd seen rushing along the
shore in the afternoon were after a couple on the run,
not a couple in hiding. Which was why they hadn't investigated the tiny island. Eldin and Una wouldn't be
hiding, but hurrying away from here, on their way to report to the authorities in Baharna. So the Kledans must
have reckoned, and doubtless they were still thinking it

when they returned with the twilight, weary and empty-handed. Following which, the fugitives had waded ashore.

Then she'd given Eldin time to get out of sight, watched him disappear in the shadows cast by bulrushes and palms, before following on behind. But bulky as the Wanderer was, few men (much less women) could match his prowess in darkness. A great prowling cat, he'd rapidly outdistanced Una, so that she arrived at the entrance to Yath-Lhi's labyrinth a good ten minutes after his brief altercation with the guard. By then that worthy had fallen over on to his side and was snoring loudly and blowing bloody bubbles. His ravaged face and the great bump on the back of his head spoke less than eloquently but amply of what had gone before.

Eldin's blood was up, no doubt of that, and his mind so full of revenge that he'd overlooked a certain instrument of that emotion, for he'd neglected to take the Kledan's great curved sword. Una weighed it, found it too heavy, settled for the guard's knife instead. My, but the Wanderer was in a hurry! Then, fearlessly and with never a backward glance, she followed in Eldin's footsteps into the tunnel's gloom.

After about a hundred and fifty yards of shallow descent, and when visibility was almost down to zero, suddenly the way turned to the left, and Una saw ahead a flaring torch in its bracket. By its light she paused to tear a great wide hem from her dress (which had been very pretty, but now hampered her movements enormously) before taking down the torch and carrying on into the maze. And after that she went very much faster.

Then, too, she started in on the maze proper; where the way twisted and turned, with side-passages branching off and myriad junctions; with pitfalls, sand traps (all of them sprung now), ominously stained pivoting slabs (now permanently shored up), and other such hazards. But along the way the walls were daubed with yellow arrows, recently painted, and the stone floor was scuffed in a faint telltale track, so that she knew she couldn't get lost in the labyrinth's coils.

And coils they were! Serpentine, and yet in cross-section weirdly angled, the walls of these passages occasionally leaned outward from bottom to top, and at other times narrowed almost to a triangular shape, but they were never straight up and down. On the other hand, all junctions or crossroads looked precisely alike, with corners faceted seemingly in defiance of sane geometric laws. In the dreamlands, of course, the laws of the waking world were often stressed or warped almost beyond recognition, but never so much as here. All in all, the discovery of the way through the maze to the core must have driven Raffis Gan and his Kledan friends almost to the point of madness.

So Una was thinking when she came upon a clay pot of yellow paint with a brush still in it, sitting on the floor close to the wall. At first she passed it by, then retraced her steps and took it up. She looked at it thoughtfully for a moment, then gave a slow smile. So Gan needed painted arrows to find his way through here, did he? And did he also need them to find his way out?

She was about to make certain alterations to her first yellow arrow, when from fairly close at hand there came sounds of shouting and of leather Kledan sandals slapping the stone floor. The Eldin-mauled guard had been discovered! Ducking into a passage to her left, then taking a right, and another left, Una quickly hid herself away—hid herself so well, in fact, that long minutes after unseen slavers had clattered by, she was still trying to find her way back to the maze's main route! But finally she did . . .

* * *

"No more battering-rams," said Raffis Gan. "Too late for that now. Now it's blasting time!"

"Are you sure you know what you're doing?" Zubda Druff was a little claustrophobic: he didn't like darkness, tunnels, or tombs, and he especially didn't like the idea of being buried under millions of tons of rock.

"No," Gan snapped, "I'm not sure I know what I'm doing. But I'm *very* sure of what will happen if we're still here tomorrow! You, there!" he called to a massive Pargan slave. "Get that keg of powder over here—and the rest of you be careful with those torches!"

They were at the central core, which Gan had long since charted. He sat on a wooden stool at a small folding table, a map of the maze spread before him. In design the subterranean labyrinth was like half a disc, with the core almost at the center if the disc had been full. The semicircle—the maze's perimeter—reached almost to Yath's shore, which was represented by a wavy line. The core was shown as a regular geometric figure with twenty-three sides, around which the inner corridor turned full circle unobstructed.

Gan stabbed a finger at the chart. "That's where we are," he told Zubda Druff. "These twenty-three facets"—another stab—"are those walls. And we've had a go at all of them!"

"Tell me something new," said Druff, a little less nervously.

"This core is maybe seventy or eighty feet right through to the other side," Gan continued. "And at its center, Yath-Lhi's tomb and treasure-chamber—which must be fairly extensive, to contain all the loot she took in her time!" He stood up, crossed to the wall of the core, gave it a tap with his knuckles. The wall or facet he'd struck was maybe six feet wide by ten high, which was the height of the ceiling. "I believe," he went on, "that behind one of these facets is a passage leading into the tomb."

"Agreed," said Druff. "The problem is, that whichever panel it is, it's more than three feet thick. Indeed it might be ten or even fifteen feet thick!"

"Now who's stating the obvious?" said Gan. "But you're right: we've battered our way two to three feet into the base of each facet, and we're not nearly through yet. So now you see why I wanted that man, that Eldin the Wanderer, down here to help us out."

"I do?" Druff wasn't convinced.

Gan sighed. "He reads glyphs, understands Ancient Dreamlands—which happens to be the writing at the top of these walls!" He pointed.

Toward the top of each facet or wall, lines of glyphs stood sharp-etched in the flickering light of many torches. "I'm sure," Gan continued, "that these writings contain a clue. The ancients might have been sophisticated in their tomb building, but I think they must have been rather naive in other ways. They were, after all, primitive people. With the Wanderer to read these inscriptions, we might have got a lead on which wall covers the entrance tunnel."

"Water under the bridge now," answered Druff gruffly, tired of words and explanations. "So now we blast until we *find* the right one, right? So where do we start? One wall looks pretty much like another to me."

Gan wryly nodded his agreement. "Yes, they do. So we might as well start right here."

At a point some three feet high in the wall directly before them, a hole had been battered through what looked like solid rock to a depth of about two and a half feet. All about the foot of the wall large chunks of stone, smaller shards and fragments lay heaped and layered with the dust of pulverized rock. At its deepest extent, the hole was just large enough to take a small keg of gunpowder.

"In there," said Gan to the slave with the first keg. "Pack it well in."

But as the huge black moved to obey—

"Raffis Gan! Zubda Druff!" came shouts from along the main passage. "We've caught one of your runaways!"

The thronging slaves were shoved aside by their Kledan overseers, and three more Kledans came into view pushing Eldin the Wanderer before them. Two of his captors held crossbows trained on him, while the third threatened with a whip. The strange thing was that the Wanderer made no protest.

"Ho, Gan!" he rumbled, waving his escort back and coming forward at his own pace. "I thought I'd find you here. And now, about our arrangement: enough wealth to buy Celephais, wasn't it?" Eldin grinned right into Raffis Gan's face.

The Kledans who'd brought him were at first astonished—but in the next moment they'd fallen on him, driving him to his knees. Then Egg-head and Narrow-eyes came on the scene, and the latter snatched a crossbow from one of the Kledans, aimed it straight at Eldin's heart. At which moment—

"Hold!" Gan shouted. He took Narrow-eyes' weapon from him, knocked him aside. "Are you mad? Don't you ever listen to anything that's said? We *need* this man—for the moment!" And to the Wanderer, with his voice falling dangerously low:

"You dare to come in here, looking for me, speaking of 'arrangements'? Do you think you can just come and go as you wish? You ran off, remember?"

"For the girl's sake," said Eldin at once, as the Kledans restrained him. "See, your offer—of great wealth—was too good to refuse. Me, I'd take a chance that you'd honor it, but I couldn't risk the girl. So I got her safely out of it, and then I came back."

"You got her out of it?" Gan rasped. He bared his teeth, drew back a clenched fist. "So that she can run and tell the Council of Elders what a scoundrel I am?"

"No such thing." The Wanderer had it all rehearsed. "Just like you, Gan, when all of this is done, I'd like to disappear. A thousand places in the dreamlands where—with a bit of gold and the odd gemstone—a man might live a full and very pleasurable life. I know of many. And when I was settled in, then I'd send for the girl. That's the plan we made together, anyway. Of course, if she doesn't hear from me within a three-month, *then* she'll go to the Council of Elders. But until then . . . on the contrary, she'll talk to no one."

Gan narrowed his eyes, unclenched his fist, said: "Let him up." And when Eldin was back on his feet:

"Wanderer, your life's still forfeit, for you crossed me and I'm not much for that. There's but one way you can save yourself, one slim chance. And what's more, I'll even throw in a fistful of jewels to see you on your way. That's wealth aplenty to such as you. But this is all on the understanding that you can show us the way into Yath-Lhi's treasure. If you can, good! Only indicate which wall hides the entrance, and we have a deal. I'll blast where you tell me, and if you're right—then your life's your own. But if you're wrong . . ."

"Then we'll blast our way in anyway," growled Zubda Druff, "—but you'll be sitting on the second keg!"

"Talking of blasting," said one of Eldin's captors, "he had a keg with him."

"What's more," said another, "he did a bit of bloody work on poor Guz Umbus as he stood guard!"

Eldin was quick to answer: "I had no time to spare chatting with guards. As for the powder—I reckoned we'd need it. The ancients didn't build their tombs of fine porcelain, you know!"

Gan scowled a little but nodded anyway. "Enough talk, now let's see some action. Wanderer, walk with me. As for you two"—indicating Egg-head and Narrow-eyes—"come with us and watch him. You, too, Zubda, and a couple of your lads. The rest can wait here."

They started round the angled perimeter of the core, passed a massive battering-ram in its frame, examined something of the extent of the work already performed. "We've not been idle, as you can see," said Gan to Eldin.

"You've been a bit heavy-handed, if you ask me," the Wanderer returned. He paused, stared up at an inscription.

"Well?" said Gan.

"She *was* cruel, this Black Princess," said Eldin. "This one tells how, in the tenth year of her reign, she ordered that any of her people found to stand as tall as herself should have their feet cut off. If they stood taller, the order extended to their heads, too!" He walked on, with Gan close behind.

Zubda Druff held up his torch to light the next inscription. Eldin scanned it, growled deep in his throat. "Cruel, aye. It tells how she fed the beggars outside the high walls of Tyrhhia, by throwing down to them criminals tried in her courts—after she'd drawn and quartered them, and soaked their bits in poison!"

Zubda Druff shuddered. "Where's all this getting us, eh?" he asked. But the others had already moved on.

Again Eldin paused, peered at glyphs where they

leaped in torchlight. "Yath-Lhi was skilled in the occult arts," he said. "She hunted down and trapped vampires—of which there were several sorts in those days—and then she drank *their* blood!"

They moved on again, and—

"*Hah!*" Eldin gasped.

"What is it?" cried Gan at once. "What does it say, Wanderer?"

"Simply this," Eldin replied, " 'Let him who would disturb Yath-Lhi's longest sleep first confess his sins'!"

"Wonderful!" Gan's turn to gasp.

"What?" said Zubda Druff. "I don't see how—"

"It's a threat!" Gan cut him off. "Can't you see that? The others were all monstrous boasts, but this is a threat! What she's really saying is this: proceed at your own peril! Because this *is* the panel that hides the entranceway! I'd stake my life on it, just as the Wanderer's staked his. For all her cruelty, she was naive after all, d'you see? Oh, in her day this might have kept your average superstitious tomb-looter out—but today? It's a dead give-away!"

"You back there!" called Narrow-eyes loudly. "Bring up the powder."

And in all the excitement no one noticed Eldin's continued peering at the primal glyphs, or wondered why he frowned. He'd thought to find mention of a curse here, and had found nothing. Gan was right: this was a blatant invitation. The silken-lashed wink of a common slut, leading her night's conquest upstairs to bed. But there *should* be a curse, a warning much more dire than this—unless, of course . . .

And at that very moment, as the keg of gunpowder was lodged firmly in the gash of battered stonework, so Eldin came to the same conclusion as Hero and Ula.

Except that he reached it maybe five minutes before them . . .

When the thundering echoes of the blast had died away and the dust had started to settle, then Raffis Gan and the rest—and Eldin the Wanderer, dragged along with them—returned from their positions of comparative safety and the slaves were set to work clearing blasted debris from the freshly opened passage. For it was clear from the first that indeed there was a passage. Zubda Druff's torch, flickering feebly through thin wreaths of reeking smoke and billowing clouds of fine dust, showed only blackness beyond the heaped rubble now blocking the entrance.

The way was cleared with feverish haste, and the main party entered the short, gently narrowing passageway and gingerly passed along it to the far end. No more than nine or ten paces long, it ended abruptly at an inner wall. But there, standing up from the floor, a great bronze lever set in a slot, with a crossbar at the top forming a "T." Gan got between the side wall and the lever, tried to push it over—to no avail. He swore under his breath, glanced at Eldin. "Wanderer?"

Eldin took Gan's place, gave a mighty shove . . . and slowly the lever tilted. And just as slowly, with a creak and a groan, the narrow end wall—in fact a pivoting panel—leaned away from the men out of the vertical and began to descend; and along its top and sides, widening cracks showed darkness beyond—Yath-Lhi's inner sanctum!

Eldin felt the lever beginning to move of its own accord as the heavy slab gained momentum, let go of it and stepped back. The wall or panel, three feet wide and ten feet high, continued its slow descent to about forty-five degrees, then crashed the rest of the way to the secret chamber's floor.

"We're in!" cried Gan as the echoes of the crash died away. *"This is it!"*

He shoved Egg-head and Narrow-eyes on ahead, with Eldin, Zubda Druff and his Kledans close behind. Then followed a dozen slaves, and finally Gan himself. Torches were held aloft; all eyes searched eagerly for the warm gleam of gold, the fire reflected from myriad gems . . . and all eyes beheld the ring of sarcophagi and their centuried contents, seven stone tombs all standing on end.

"What?" said Zubda Druff. And again, more threateningly: "*What?* And is this your treasure, Chief Regulator? A handful of worm-ravaged mummies?"

Gan opened his mouth, shook his head in wild denial. He tried to speak, tried again, finally said: "No! It has to be here—*has* to be!"

He whirled to glare at Eldin, saw him backing away, his eyes full of terrible knowledge. The slaves were clustering together, muttering, their eyeballs huge and blackly gleaming. They, too, sensed an onrushing something.

"What is it?" Gan whispered, grasping the Wanderer's jacket in both hands. "Where is the treasure?"

"It's somewhere else," Eldin answered, his throat dry as dust. "Only Yath-Lhi is here—the Black Princess, and the curse she brought with her down all the centuries!"

"Curse? But you said—"

There sounded a report like the sharp, clear snap of a whip. Veils of dust fell from overhead. All eyes, elevated, saw thin, precise, converging cracks open in the ceiling; cracks which commenced directly above the fallen slab of the door and elongated rapidly toward the ring of coffined corpses. Some hidden mechanism rumbled briefly; a segment of the ceiling moved, fractionally; the necks of the six clay bottles were shattered in unison, raining their contents downward in a gush of heady wine.

As one man the slaves began to jabber, rushed for an exit only three feet wide. Sensitive to black magic, they knew that whatever was coming was already upon them! They jammed in the doorway, a tangle of flailing black arms and legs and bodies. Outside in the tunnel, and in the maze beyond the tunnel, more slaves and Kledan overseers hearing the uproar, thought it could only be the sounds of excitement at some colossal find. Those inside fought to get out, and those outside struggled to get in.

And in the confusion, no one saw the pair of human shadows which moved together inside the circle of standing coffins—the figures of Hero and Ula who now hugged each other and listened to the babble, and seemed to hear even above that babble the gurgle and rush of weird wine coursing through stone funnels to drench Yath-Lhi and her men-at-arms.

Some of the slaves had carried torches, which now lay guttering on the floor: the light was thus greatly reduced. In the gloom, Eldin made for the crush of bodies in the narrow doorway, but Gan saw him. Whatever was going on here, the corrupt Regulator knew he must quickly regain control. Curse? There was no curse—just a crafty quester and a pack of idiot slaves and confused Kledans. And so:

"Wanderer, wander no farther!" Gan shouted above the hubbub. "I may still have need of you. The rest of you, pick up those torches there. Let's have some light on—"

"WAKE!" a monstrous croak interrupted, silenced him at once, sounding not in his ears but in his head. In the heads—the minds—of all the others, too, including

Hero and Ula. In their inky dark cave of coffins, the younger quester gazed horrified at the lady-love he held in his arms. It had been their plot—hatched in the minutes between gunpowder blast and break in—that Ula should project her female voice in imitation of Yath-Lhi, hopefully scaring off the tomb-looters and making possible an escape. For a moment Hero thought she'd done just that, and almost scared *him* witless, too! But only for a moment. For then:

"WAKE!" came the croaking, grunting mental command a second time—and all in the chamber knew now where it came from, and to whom it was addressed. It was Yath-Lhi, speaking with the mind of a sorceress, raising her soldiers up from the sleep of aeons and commanding their attention!

Within the ring of sarcophagi, Hero and Ula clung more tightly yet, and outside it . . .

All eyes were wide, fixed fearfully upon the gaunt figure of Yath-Lhi, where her coffin faced the recently opened passage to the outside world. And all saw *her* eyes crack open! Petrified, the entire assembly—slaves and masters, blacks and whites alike—stared into the pits of burning sulphur which were Yath-Lhi's eyes.

The wine covered her, dripped from her mummified face and sagging breasts, shone like oil on her wrinkled limbs. And like oil it eased those wrinkles, soaked into and made soft the leather of her flesh. Her breasts filled out, her yellow eyes opened wider yet, and finally her lips cracked apart in a hideous grin. "WAKE!" she commanded a third time—and, creaking like rusted hinges, *she stepped forth out of her coffin!*

Worse, her men-at-arms opened their eyes and stepped out with her—five of the six, anyway. But the sixth—he whose life-giving dark wine of sorcery Hero had stolen—he awoke only to uttermost horror! Yath-

Lhi's voice, her commands, had been mental, telepathic: the voice of the sixth soldier was entirely physical; a whistle of dust whooshing out through collapsing lungs and throat, a crunch of bones brittling into shards, a *hiss* of flesh seething into vile vapor as bronze garments and weapons clanged to the floor in a settling heap of fossilized debris. But all who heard it knew it had been a scream, a long despairing cry fleeing back through countless ages ...

The frozen tableau broke, and frenzy grew apace as the crush at the door seemed to congeal into a sea of flesh. But Yath-Lhi's reborn mind-power was greater than that, would not permit flight.

"HOLD! BE STILL!"

The telepathic command rang out from her reverberantly, formed a sphere that filled all the nearer passages where they converged upon the core, silenced the uproar and stilled the panic on the instant.

Hero and Ula, too, they heard it—saw its result as the milling crowd in the crypt froze, then began untangling themselves, finally stood in silent ranks with their glazed eyes turned inward upon Yath-Lhi. Her five men-at-arms moved closer to her, two on one side, three on the other. All six, they gazed outward upon the spell-stricken invaders of their tomb. And:

"FRESHLY AWAKE," said the Black Princess, "WE ARE STILL WEAK. SUSTAIN YOURSELVES, MY WARRIORS."

She beckoned with a creaking arm, and Zubda Druff stepped forward, paced zombie-like, to stand before her. She reached out her hands and touched him. A touch merely, all ten of her fingertips, widespread, contacting his shoulders simultaneously—and the slaver began to twitch and flop like a strangled chicken. He did not scream, made no attempt at flight, merely jerked and throbbed and fluttered; and before Hero and Ula's eyes he withered, deflated, became a bag of bones in Yath-Lhi's sucking hands.

Finally she released him, a canvas sack that crumpled to the floor—its only resemblance to a man lay in its general shape and the black, blindly-staring marbles gazing out from a shriveled skull—and waited while her men-at-arms took similar sustenance. They, too, chose blacks, one a Kledan and the others Pargan slaves, and each went to his maker as unprotesting as Zubda Druff. And all the while, Raffis Gan and the rest stood frozen, and those in the outer corridors, too, like statues under the spell of the vampire Yath-Lhi.

And yet Hero and Ula, they were untouched by that spell. They saw and comprehended all that occurred but, hugging each other and trembling, they were blessedly immune. Half-fainting, Ula clung to her man; and him propping her up lest she fall, his hand over her mouth lest she cry out. Even Hero himself, he could not have told how he held silent, how fearful he was that at any moment Eldin would be called to that same fate as Druff and the slaves. For in that event, what could he do but leap forward, snatch a sword from one of Yath-Lhi's warriors, have at her and them until . . . until whatever.

But it did not come to that.

"ENOUGH!" said Yath-Lhi in the minds of all. "FOR NOW, ENOUGH."

No longer black and mummified but having metamorphosed into a color like marble, and being now fully mobile, she turned on her heel through one-third of a circle, took in all before her at a glance. And at last her sulphur eyes settled on Raffis Gan.

"YOU! I PERCEIVE YOU BROUGHT THESE DOGS IN HERE—TO RAVAGE MY TOMB OF ITS TREASURES, EH?" Laughter welled up from her black soul, was cut short in a trice. "VERY WELL, NOW YOU CAN LEAD THEM OUT AGAIN!"

Out! thought Hero, aghast. *This vampire princess— out, free, loose in the unsuspecting dreamlands!* No, it must not be. This thing, this exodus from the tomb, must be stopped. But how? Spring forth and Yath-Lhi would merely point and turn all those under her spell, even Eldin, against him! And then what of Ula? Hero couldn't bear the thought of Ula as a bag of bones . . .

Orderly as a small army, single-file through the narrow doorway, all in the tomb filtered out into the maze beyond. Raffis Gan led the way, stiff-legged, arms like lead at his sides, eyes glazed and staring straight ahead. Behind him slaves and Kledans in no set order, with Yath-Lhi and her soldiers central in the column, then more slaves, Kledans, and finally Eldin the Wanderer bringing up the very rear.

The *official* column. But behind Eldin, all unobserved, twin shadows moved apace with the procession, drawing courage and strength from their anonymity.

LEAD THE WAY OUT!—Yath-Lhi's command repeated in Gan's numb brain. THE WAY OUT!—which the ex-Chief Regulator knew as well as any other man: WAY OUT!—for all he had to do was follow the yellow arrows painted on these walls. And the column wound through bowels of rock, coiling like a snake along a route of many angles toward the Lake of Yath.

"We're unaffected!" Ula whispered in Hero's ear, the merest breath of sound as she grabbed him in the shadows and drew his head down to her lips. "How?"

"The wine!"

"*Ah!*—eh?"

"It's all I can think—that it somehow put us outside her power, protected us."

"What do we do about Eldin?"

"First we try to reason with him. Difficult at the best of times! Come on, let's catch up, join the column."

"What!?" She was alarmed.

"Let's play at zombies," said Hero, and he stooped and picked up a guttering torch from where it had fallen from the nerveless fingers of a slave.

For all the stiff-leggedness of the ensorcelled procession, still it was making good speed. Striding awkwardly at the rear, it took Hero and Ula some little time to draw level with Eldin, who walked perhaps four or five paces behind the next hindmost. Ula took up a position on his left, Hero on his right. They couldn't talk to him, nor even whisper now, for fear of being overheard. And so, trying as best they could to match his lumbering gait, they gently took hold of his elbows. Gently wasn't good enough; he just kept right on forging ahead.

Hero dug his heels in, Ula too—and still Eldin strained forward. The column ahead had reached a crossroads, was turning sharp right. Hero nodded grimly to Ula, straightened up, resumed his stiff-legged striding. She did likewise.

The slaves immediately in front were beginning to turn the corner, now less than five paces away. *One*, Hero counted to himself. *Two*, he offered up a prayer to whichever gods of dream might be listening. And—*three*! He stepped behind Eldin, let go a massive belt with the stock of his torch to the back of the Wanderer's neck.

And *still* the hypnotized quester took another step—before crumpling. They caught him, lowered him gently as possible to the stone floor, turned him on his back. "Eh?" the half-stunned Wanderer inquired, the pain-wrinkles under his bushy brows opening to reveal crossed eyes. And: "What the bl—?" the rumbling started; was cut short as Ula sat on his face.

"Umf?" said Eldin, squeezing the query out round firm buttocky curves. He groped about, grabbed Hero's jacket front with one great hand and yanked him close. *"Umf?"*

The zombie column had passed on, hopefully out of hearing. "Shh!—you umfing great lump!" Hero hissed. And: "Ula, get off him—I think he likes it!"

"Eh? Eh? Eh?" demanded Eldin, as Ula demurely stood up. Sprawled on his back, he still wasn't all there. "Why are we whispering?" he wanted to know. "Last thing I remember, I—" His eyes widened. It was as if he saw them for the first time, as if he saw ghosts, and in the next moment he came bolt upright. "Hero! Ula! You're dead! No you're not—and neither is Yath-Lhi!" He grabbed Hero's arm. "I saw her!"

"We've all seen her," said Hero. "The trick now is not to see her again, and for her not to see us!"

"She was dead," Eldin babbled on, "and yet she—"

Shaken by its collision with the Wanderer's neck, Hero's torch had sent up a last burst of sparks before snuffing itself out. But it wasn't that alone which had cut the Wanderer short—it was also the flitting shadow with burning eyes which, in the fading glow of the torch's smoldering, all three had seen rushing upon them!

Hero almost had the knife out of its sheath on his calf when the shadow fell on him. Its breath was sweet where it kissed him.

"Hero!" Una breathlessly whispered. "Ula—sister— and . . . and *Eldin!*" She fell to her knees beside the Wanderer, hugged him, toppled him flat again. Wild, crying, unable to believe, Una threw herself from one set of arms to the next. "Alive!" she cried. "All alive!"

Eldin groaned, struggled into a sitting position again, gingerly fingered his neck. "Speak for yourself, lass," he said. "Me, I'm not so sure!"

"HOLD!" came a telepathic command in Hero's mind. It wasn't directed at him, and it wasn't from close at hand, but he heard it anyway. Eldin, having heard nothing, used his huge lungs as bellows, aiming gust after gust at the torch's embers. They came alive again, but flickeringly. And in the fitful light: Ula, too, had heard Yath-Lhi's mind-voice, if her face was the judge.

"There's a fresh torch back here," said Una, pointing. "Come on, quickly. This is the way out!"

"*Shh!*" said Hero and Ula together. And in their minds:

"THIS IS *NOT* THE WAY! I MAY HAVE SLEPT FOR AGES, AYE, BUT AT LEAST I KNOW MY OWN LABYRINTH. NOW *I* LEAD THE WAY!"

Wide-eyed, Ula gazed at Hero. "Gan took her the wrong way?"

Una was gleeful. "They followed *my* arrows! I changed them, you see?" Then she frowned. "Are you two all right?"

Hero looked at her, at Eldin, too. "You didn't hear it?"

"Hear what?" the Wanderer was bewildered.

Hero and Ula exchanged knowing glances. "The wine," said Hero.

"And that clout on the neck you gave him," she nodded. "We were made as one with her through receiving the wine—"

"Stealing it," Hero put in. "And 'one with her' only on a telepathic level."

"—and Eldin's hypnosis was broken by the clout!"

"Something certainly was," the Wanderer growled. "And that was you, was it?" he glowered at Hero.

"I saved your soul," said Hero, "so don't go complaining about a stiff neck!"

"We'd better get out of here," said Ula. And to Una: "Sister, you were obviously outside her sphere of ensorcelment—thank goodness! Now where's that torch you mentioned?"

Behind them, as they found the brand and brought it to life, there came the tramp, tramp, tramp of zombie feet slapping stone in unison. Then:

"Ula's right," said Hero. "Time we weren't here. Una, lead on—and don't spare the elastic!"

On their way out, as they put distance between themselves and the marching menace behind them, Hero and Ula took turns to tell what happened after Gan had them thrown down the well at Regulating HQ. It was all very quickly told; likewise Eldin and Una's adventures from then till now. By which time they'd covered three-quarters of the distance to the outside world.

"And what then?" Eldin asked. "When we're out, I mean? We can't just walk away and forget it. There's that bag of worms back there to think about. Are we simply to let Yath-Lhi out into the clean, sane air of the dreamlands?"

"Sane?" said Hero. "Yes, I suppose it is, compared to the Black Princess and her boys! So what's your plan?"

"My plan?" the Wanderer was taken by surprise. "I have a plan?"

The questers strode out while the girls trotted alongside, hard put to keep up the pace. "You must have had some sort of plan when you came bursting in here," said Hero. "You could have reported all of this in Baharna, but instead you came back. So what did you have in mind?"

"Gan's blood, that's what I had in mind!" said Eldin darkly. "I planned to get in, grab Gan, gut him and get out again—if I could. If not . . . I thought you and Ula were dead, remember? So this was to be my revenge, and I didn't really stop to consider how to achieve it. I even had an idea to block his way out—by bringing down the tunnel right there at the entrance—and I borrowed a keg of gunpowder to do just that. But there were all of those innocent Pargans to think of. So in the end I settled for Yath-Lhi's curse. I realize now, of course, that I wasn't thinking straight; I thought the curse would direct itself only at the one who sought to steal Yath-Lhi's treasure. As to the *nature* of the curse— well, who could have foreseen that?"

Hero nodded. "All of which was to say, you don't have a plan—right? Well, neither do I. So it's a case of wait and see . . ."

"Floor's sloping upward," Una took the opportunity to put in. "There's one last turn up ahead, and then—"

"Whoa!" said Hero as they reached the final bend in the gradually rising shaft. As they all skidded to a halt he inclined his head toward the corner. "You may not have heard Yath-Lhi's mind-voice, but I'm sure you can hear that!"

"Damn right!" said Eldin.

Faint but clear, the distant sounds of shouts and screams, of cannon-fire and bloody battle, echoed down to them. And superimposed on the background hubbub, the sound of running footsteps and of shouts inside the entrance tunnel itself!

"Revolt?" Eldin hazarded. "The slaves have turned on their Kledan masters?"

"I do hope so!" cried Una.

Hero stuck his head round the corner, saw three figures, Kleedans, racing toward him. The leader had a torch held high, was shouting: "Druff—Zubda Druff—*treachery*!"

"Hear that?" Hero said over his shoulder.

"What sort of treachery?" Eldin wanted to know.

"He'll have to shout louder than that," said Ula with a little shudder, "if he wants to speak to Zubda Druff!"

"Here they come," said Hero. "Three of 'em. They won't be expecting us. Eldin, are you fit?"

"Never fitter!" the Wanderer snorted. He positioned himself in the center of the corridor, went into a crouch and leaned slightly forward. "Let 'em come!"

They came, rounding the corner two fore and one aft—and met instant chaos. Una had the torch; she thrust it directly into the face of the slaver on the left. He had a beard and his head was a mass of tight black curls; all went up in flames, which he beat at with both hands, screaming and dancing to and fro. The man on the right collided with Eldin, which was about the same as running into a brick wall full tilt. The third was able to fetch a skidding halt, was reaching for his curved sword when Hero stepped forward and hit him. He at once joined Eldin's victim, groaning on the floor. Meanwhile, Ula had tripped the Kledan with the burning beard and hair, and Una had bashed him on his smoking head with her torch. As quickly as that, the confrontation was over.

"For a minute there," said Eldin, eyeing the two girls, "I felt we were back on the Mad Moon battling moonbeasts!"

"FASTER!" said an eerie voice in the minds of Hero and Ula, not talking to them but possibly about them. "I SMELL DANGER!"

"Let's go," Hero snapped. He, Eldin and Ula relieved the Kledans of their swords, went at a run the rest of the way up the ramp to the entrance. But even before they reached the mouth of the excavation in the barrow where it overlooked Yath, Una had tossed her guttering torch aside. No need for that now. Beyond the entrance, night's blackness was shot with gouts of fire and flaring white balls of light!

At first it was difficult to see just who was fighting whom; but as the four emerged at the run from the barrow on to the slightly elevated level area at the head of the ramp, so they were engulfed in a roiling crush of men locked in hand-to-hand combat. A slave uprising? Not a bit of it: it was gray-clads against Kledans, and it seemed the Regulators were here in force.

Hero at once cut down a huge, roaring slaver, snatched up and tossed the dead man's sword to Una—and then they were in the thick of it. But this was a weird scrap! One minute they were surrounded by gleaming, burly blacks, and the next a hail of Regulators came literally dropping out of the skies. "I knew Baharna's gray-clads had the rep of being fly-boys," Eldin rumbled, "but this is ridiculous!"

The questers and their girls gazed aloft into fire-streaked skies. Sky-ships were up there, locked in combat. Out over the lake, flanked by a pair of vessels who poured shot after shot into her, a blazing, badly listing Kledan ship settled for the calm water; another slaver ran south-east for Kled, but lumberingly, half her sails shot away. The third slaver was almost directly overhead, exchanging panicky cannon-fire with what looked like a staid old merchantman. And it was this last vessel which discharged Regulators, who swarmed expertly down ropes and rope ladders dangling from the decks to drop yelling into the fray.

Hard, trained fighting men, these—trained indeed by Tellis Gan in better days—and now a knot of them formed a protective ring about the questers and their ladies as the tide of battle swept by them. Hero glanced at Eldin, said: "Difficult to know whose side we're on, isn't it? But we can't fight 'em all." And to the senior Regulator, a sergeant: "You, there—we surrender!"

"You'll be Hero," that worthy replied, accepting his sword. "And Eldin the Wanderer, and Ula and Una Gidduf, right? Damn me, all four of you alive! That's a turnup!" He grinned a tight grin. "Well, surrender all you like—but actually we're here to rescue you!"

"What?" Hero's jaw dropped. "You're not Gan's men?"

"Raffis Gan, you mean?" the other scowled. "Don't shame us more than we're shamed already, quester! The dog didn't fool all of us, you know."

As he spoke, more ropes came dangling from on high, empty ones this time. And: "Can you climb, all of you?" said the sergeant. "Right, then—up you go!"

Hero and Ula got aloft, climbing rapidly; but before Eldin and Una could follow the merchantman gave a lurch and rolled under the impact of a fusillade from its Kledan adversary. The ropes and ladders were all set swishing and jerking; the two ships straightened up, backed off; all on the ground were momentarily cut off. But on board the rescue ship:

"Ula!" cried Ham Gidduf, tears of relief in his eyes, lifting his daughter gently over the rail—then reaching down great arms for Hero. "And you!" he scowled into Hero's face as he dragged him unceremoniously on board.

"NOW *I* COMMAND!" came a newly familiar voice in Hero's head, Ula's too. "ALL HEAR—ALL OBEY! BE STILL, AND HEED THE WORDS OF YATH-LHI!"

Gunners aboard Ham Gidduf's ship had just loosed half a dozen balls from hastily rigged cannons into the

Kledan a moment before Yath-Lhi's mind-command. One shot at least must have hit the slaver's magazine, for with a tremendous roar and gout of fire she reeled and almost broke asunder in the sky, then slowly began to settle earthward.

"BE *STILL*, I SAID, AND LOOK AT ME!"

The Black Princess had cast her monstrous hypnotic mind-spell, and none could deny it. All aboard the merchantman looked; Hero and Ula out of morbid fascination, everyone else because they had to. On the ground all fighting had stopped; in the air, the cannons no longer roared; Kledans, slaves and Regulators alike all gazed now upon Yath-Lhi and her men-at-arms where they stood on the elevated ground before the entrance to the excavated barrow. A few rocket-flares were still settling to earth. They'd been fired aloft by slavers and Regulators both, each to illumine the other, but now they shed light on the unnatural, frozen tableau before the mound—frozen except for Yath-Lhi and her reborn retainers.

"NOW I SPREAD MY VAMPIRE INFLUENCE ABROAD," the primal princess announced. "AND ALL OF YOU SHALL BE MY DISCIPLES AND CARRY MY WORD—AND MY POWER—WITH YOU. I SHALL TOUCH YOU, AND YOU SHALL BE ONE WITH ME. AND WHOSOEVER *YOU* TOUCH, HE TOO SHALL BE MINE. THUS YOU GO FORTH—INTO THE MOUNTAINS, THE OCEANS, THE WARM PLACES AND THE COLD, THE JUNGLES AND THE CITIES—AND MULTIPLY."

"The beginning of a monstrous plague," Hero groaned under his breath.

And Ula, horrified, answered: "Only look at my father!"

Ham Gidduf gazed down on Yath-Lhi, his eyes glazed, his whole countenance and being rapt upon her.

"They're all the same," said Hero. "All except us . . ." He ducked down behind the gunnel, moved toward a small cannon slung in a makeshift cradle between capstans. The cannoneer, a gray-clad, stood there like a statue, robbed entirely of his will, cannon loaded and taper smoldering in his hand.

"Hero!" gasped Ula. "Oh, David—look!"

"BUT YOUR PRINCESS HAS FASTED THROUGH ALL THE AGES AND KNOWS A GREAT HUNGER," Yath-Lhi spoke again. "AND IT WOULD SEEM ONLY RIGHT THAT THOSE WHO SPRUNG HER TRAP SHOULD NOW SUSTAIN HER FOR THE GREAT WORK AHEAD. I WHO HAVE MERELY SIPPED WOULD NOW SUP. AYE, AND IT SHALL BE A FEAST!"

Hero gulped, his Adam's apple bobbing. "Gan's turn," he said.

"Narrow-eyes and Egg-head, too," said Ula in a very small voice.

"I had plans for all three, I admit," Hero added, "but nothing so terrible as this."

Unprotesting, Gan and his bullies, as well as one Kledan and two Pargan slaves, went to their makers, flopping and fluttering as the sucking hands of Yath-Lhi and her soldiers drained the life and soul out of them. And in a very little while, six shuddering sacks crumpled to the packed earth of the barrow's entrance.

"MORE!" said Yath-Lhi—her telepathic voice a drooling croak, her appetite now ravening—as she and her soldiers turned toward the closest knot of people. Which just happened to be composed of Regulators, Eldin the Wanderer, and Una Gidduf. And with a deal

more animation now, the ex-mummies stepped menacingly toward that group, their deadly hands reaching.

"Hero!" cried Ula, white-faced as she stared down on
all of this. "Hero—*what now*?"

Hero snatched the taper from the hypnotized Regulator gunner, realigned the cannon. "It took ten seconds'
sleep and a headache to shake the Wanderer out of it
last time," he said through gritted teeth. "So let's give
'em *all* a headache, and see what effect that has, eh?"
And he lowered the taper to the touchhole.

Then, because he was no cannoneer and chary of loud
bangs, Hero stepped back—which was as well. The cannon made a noise like frying bacon, then went off with
a deafening roar and bounced about in its cradle. Smoke
poured from its muzzle, and the night sky thrilled to a
wh-eee of displaced air. The cannon had been charged
with twin balls fastened together by a length of chain: a
deadly whirling device which now slammed into the almost vertical face of the barrow, directly over the mouth
of the excavation.

Great slabs of rock thundered down on to the staging
area, were buried in a landslide of smaller rocks, soil
and sand. Yath-Lhi and her party staggered this way and
that under the shuddering and roaring of the avalanche;
likewise the others in her vicinity, gradually unfreezing
as the sudden assault upon their senses began to sub-
side. Several Kledan overseers had disappeared under
the fallen mass; the rest had been safely forward of the
danger area.

"All of that from a small cannon?" Ula's jaw hung
open.

"That rock face must have been very brittle," Hero
answered. "It was like taking a hammer to a slab of
slate!"

Ham Gidduf had given himself a shake, was now

leaning over the rail shouting: "Una, grab a ladder. And you, great thug—give the girl a hand!"

On the ground Eldin came to life. He grabbed up Una, thrust her aloft to where rope ladders dangled.

"Oh-oh!" Hero's eyes stood out like marbles. He'd suddenly noticed that the crippled Kledan ship, its hull and sails gouting great sheets of flame, was foundering directly toward the trench of piled gunpowder kegs. "Ham!" he yelled, jabbing his forefinger down toward the danger.

The barrel-like, rock-hard merchant gave a gasp, then roared: "Engineer—let's have some elevation! Full-throttle on the pumps and fill those flotation bags brim-full, d'you hear?"

Below decks, the thumping of the ship's flotation engines became a rumble of thunder; slowly, the merchantman lifted, agonizingly slowly. On the ground Eldin made a desperate flying leap—caught hold of a rope and held on for dear life as he was whisked aloft.

"WHAT?" Yath-Lhi was still confused. Someone had ignored her mind-command, had slipped the telepathic leash? Someone had actually threatened her? She turned this way and that, gazed here and there. Regulators, Kledans and slaves, all had now seen the danger, were scurrying to put distance between themselves, the death-filled trench and the tunnel entrance to the labyrinth.

"WHAT?" the Black Princess repeated, her mental fury lashing outward. "WHO DARES DEFY THE—?"

At which point, the blazing slaver's keel crashed down into the trench, and shattered masts hurled fire everywhere.

Night became day as the trench dug itself that much deeper. First one keg exploded, then another; five together, then ten. A mighty chain reaction of an explosion! Even on high, Ham Gidduf's ship reeled, and reeled again from a succession of concussions. Yath-Lhi and her party, isolated now on the elevated ramp in front of the half-blocked entrance to the labyrinth, staggered to and fro, fell, got up and fell again.

On board the merchantman, Ham Gidduf gave a cry of joy and hauled his second daughter to safety, hugged her almost to breaking point. Eldin, smoldering a bit round the hem of his jacket and looking like a chimneysweep, was left to fend for himself. He came sprawling over the rail, choking on upward-sweeping sulphur belches from the inferno below, singed and coughing, and cursing for all he was worth. Hero had meanwhile got hold of a spyglass, and now commenced a running commentary on the scene below:

"That trench isn't just a trench!" he breathlessly reported. "This seems to have been the one area in which Gan planned well. Where the ground rises toward the barrow, the trench becomes a tunnel. Right now it's blasting away like a great cannon, hurling out ball after ball of fire!"

Eldin joined the younger quester. "There it goes!" he rumbled. "The level area in front of the barrow is falling into the tunnel. The channel to the lake is almost complete."

"And there go Yath-Lhi and her lot, clambering up the sides away from the hot stuff!" said Hero. "They're not very good at it—still very stiff from their sleep of ages."

"They're also too late," Eldin pointed out. There came a final mighty blast and tons of earth were tossed skyward right at the water's edge. Yath lake boiled down the fire-fashioned channel, lapped at Yath-Lhi's heels where she and her five soldiers scrambled desperately in raining rocks and smoking earth.

"Too late?" Hero repeated his friend. "What do you mean, too—?" By which time he could see for himself.

"Vampires, of a sort," said Eldin. "And you know what running water means to a vampire. For Yath-Lhi it has to be even worse. What is she, after all, but a bag of century-old dust? A good torrent will cleanse a fouled gutter every time, Hero my lad!"

"NO!" Yath-Lhi's mind-shriek echoed up to them. "NO-*Ooooo*!" They watched her melt down into the swirling, gurgling waters. She and her five guards crumbled and sloughed away like snowmen in a great furnace. And a moment later:

"Gone!" said Ula with a shudder, hugging Hero's arm.

"The Black Princess, all gone," Una agreed, sighing her relief against Eldin's great chest.

"Aye," said their father, gruffly, "and the renegade Raffis Gan gone with her. And these accursed ruins swamped forever. Well, we've all a bit of explaining to do, I think. So now you four had better come along with me to my cabin."

Down below, Yath continued to send a surging brown stream gurgling into what would soon become a weedy, watery labyrinth of aeons . . .

As for explanations: there weren't so many after all.

Glibly, the questers had started to tell how they'd come to Oriab to see Ula and Una—

"Only to 'see' them?" Ham scowled dangerously.

"Well, actually, er, to make plans," Eldin engaged in some mental scrambling, searching for a way out.

"Marriage plans!" Ula gleefully seized the main chance; and, "Soon!" Una clinched the thing.

Hero had then cast murderous side glances at Eldin;

the Wanderer had choked up and reddened a bit; Ham Gidduf had positively beamed!

"How soon?" he'd wanted to know.

"In the, er, future—" Hero had answered. And guided by Ham's rapidly changing expression: "The far—er, not-so-far, er, would you believe near?—future." With Eldin hurriedly adding: "But just plans at this stage, of course . . ."

And then the questers (smiling fixed, frozen smiles) and the girls (joyously hugging their arms) had listened to Ham's side of the adventure.

He'd had business in Baharna and decided to look up his daughters at their tiny house in an upper-class hillside suburb. They'd not been at home, but a busybody neighbor had heard that just last night they'd been arrested "with a pair of gentlemen friends, loutish fellows, apparently" by the city's Regulators—arrested and "taken in"! Ham had exploded, gone to see a friend of his on the Council of Elders who lived in the vicinity; together they'd stormed Regulating HQ, and there . . .

Two young ladies? And their men-friends? Yes, Chief Regulator Gan had brought them in—for questioning, presumably. Odd, for there was no written record of charges . . . Er, but they had spent the night here, yes. And less than an hour ago Gan had taken them away with him in the official launch. Something about discreet investigations . . . ? This information from the Duty Sergeant. But Ham had wanted to know: "Did Gan take all of them with him—all four?"

The sergeant made hasty, flustered inquiries, and: "Er, actually, only two. One male, one female."

"That 'female' was one of my daughters!" Ham had started to thump the desk. "Which means that my other daughter, her sister, is still here! *Here*, locked up like a common criminal! Where?" Accompanied by the now completely unnerved sergeant, Ham and the Elder Councillor had then searched the place cell by cell and top to bottom. To no avail. But at least Ham had seen the severity of the cells, and he knew that his daughters had spent the night in one of them . . .

Then, just when the powerful merchant was on the point of violating several city ordinances, an experienced junior officer, Inspector of the Watch, had come forward. He'd spoken to the two VIPs in private, voiced certain fears, made certain cautious half-allegations.

"It's probably my job on the line if I'm wrong, I know, but . . ." And he'd told something of a tale about Gan's peculiar obsession with the ruins on Yath's shore, and of the Chief Regulator's apparent friendship with—or at least his relaxed attitude toward—an inordinately large number of visiting Kledans.

Ham Gidduf's high-ranking friend had found all of this very interesting and not a little disturbing, and again in confidence, he too had voiced his concern. He didn't know just how Ham's daughters fitted into the picture, or their quester friends (Kuranes' men, weren't they?— good sorts, if a bit unorthodox), but for some time now Gan had been acting strangely and, indeed, was under a gathering cloud of suspicion. No charges had been brought against him as yet, he was not being investigated, but . . .

What?!—Ham Gidduf's daughter in the hands of a man who rubbed shoulders with Kledan slavers?

Now Ula's and Una's father was a man of action; while the Elder went off in a hurry to seek advice from his fellows on the Council, Ham went and spoke to the captains of three of his ships, unloading their cargoes at that very moment on Baharna's docks. Likewise, he approached the captain of a warship out of Serannian, in the yards for repairs. Hero and Eldin were celebrities (some might say characters of notoriety) in the sky-floating city, and of course there was a degree of chivalry in respect of the ladies, and so the captain at once agreed to the loan of certain items of ship's hardware—to wit, cannons!

In no time at all Ham's merchantmen were unloaded, armed and airborne; by then, too, the Council of Elders had agreed to lend their assistance, consisting of orders to three platoons of Regulators, all tried men and true, eager to scratch a previously inaccessible itch. As the population of Baharna gaped and gawked from its various levels down upon Regulating HQ, so those worthies had gone aboard the three sky-ships up rope ladders suspended directly over the balconies of their canal-hugging establishment, and then Ham's rescue force was fully manned and under way.

They'd come across Yath without lights, had seen the Kledans moored low over the lake. More, they'd seen the campfires and the large parties of slaves sleeping ashore, watched over by their Kledan guards. Then those guards had in turn seen Ham's ships against the stars, when but for quick thinking, the advantage were lost. Since the Kledans were quite obviously *in flagrante delicto* (keeping, selling, or otherwise using slaves was strictly forbidden now in Oriab) and since slavers were normally armed to the teeth, direct and violent action was the only recourse.

Venting flotation essence for all they were worth, the merchantmen had dropped down to the level of the Kledan vessels and opened fire on them. One of the enemy, half-crippled, had fled for Kled, another had tried it but got flanked over Yath and forced down; as for the rest of it, the questers and their ladies had seen that for themselves.

"But what," Ham then wanted to know, frowning, "did Gan want with you lot?"

"Er, p'raps he thought we were spying on him," Hero replied. "I mean, Eldin and myself. And the girls were with us, so they got roped in, too."

"But you *were* spying on him, weren't you—for meddlesome old Kuranes?" Ham frowned.

"Ah!" Eldin put in, holding up a stiff finger. And not unmindful or incapable of a measure of diplomacy: "Well, not *quite*. We were here simply to . . . to offer our services to Baharna's Council of Elders!"

"Oh?" Ham Gidduf found that just a bit suspect. He grinned a sharp-eyed grin. "And there was I thinking you'd merely been visiting my daughters—which in fact is why you *told* me you were here. Hmm! Anyway, when we're all finished here you can tell it to the Council of Elders for yourselves, for that's where I'm taking you."

And he did.

The Elders were mainly a dour lot; doddering, most of them—but to a man honest and honorable. After the preliminaries of a hearing, their spokesman asked:

"And is it your business, questers, to go interfering in the internal affairs of Serannian's neighbor states and countries? We'd have brought Raffis Gan to book sooner or later without your assistance, you know."

"Later, most likely," Eldin mumbled, only half to himself.

"Eh? What's that?" the gray-pate wasn't totally deaf.

"He said 'Of course, sir, quite right'!" Hero quickly spoke up.

Ham Gidduf, however, was more outspoken and knew nothing of diplomacy. "Hah!" he snorted. "What?

You'd have sent out warships, would you, to drag the dog back from Kled or wherever? And what of my two daughters by then, eh?"

"Merchant Gidduf," said the spokesman, raising an eyebrow, "you must surely be aware that Oriab has no warships."

"Of course I'm aware of it!" Ham was scornful. "And so is wily old Kuranes in Serannian or Celephais or wherever. So he sent these two buckoes to advise you how best to handle the affair. Spies? They're allies, and a good thing for all present, too!"

"In fact, sir," Hero added, thinking quickly, "Kuranes was sure you already knew of Chief Regulator Gan's bent—that is to say, that he *was* bent—and only sent us because of our, er, tactical experience. In the event of hostilities, that is. Before we could report to you, however, Gan picked us up."

The Elder nodded. "Hmm! Well, it seems we must thank you for these timely revelations concerning Raffis Gan. And certainly we're in your debt—you and all concerned—for the, er, *dissolution* of Yath-Lhi. But since it appears that there was no treasure, and so no more treasure-seekers, bent or otherwise, she at least is a terror that can never rise again."

"True," said Hero, blinking rapidly. "She's gone, melted away forever." But at the mention of treasure his hand twitched almost of its own accord toward his pocket . . .

"Ahem!" Ham Gidduf then ahemmed. "And now, if I may take the opportunity: I finally wish to offer the freedom of my home, of my home town Andahad, and of all Oriab—including Baharna"—he looked all round the chamber, waiting until the Councillors had nodded as one man—"to this fine, upstanding pair of utterly fearless questers!"

"Indeed! Indeed!" came reedy chirrups and dry rustles of approval.

"Also," Ham wasn't finished, "I am pleased to announce the double engagement of David Hero and Eldin the Wanderer to Ula and Una Gidduf respectively! Of course," he spoke now directly to the questers, "you've brought suitable tokens of the tryst with you?"

"Eh? Tokens? Tryst?" Eldin felt a sinking sensation in the pit of his stomach, and not solely at the prospect of appearing tokenless.

Hero gripped his elbow. "Certainly!" he replied. "Of course, there's much for us to be doing between times, but as tokens of our respect, our fidelity, our, er . . ."

"Foolhardiness?" prompted Eldin in a whisper.

"Our affection and esteem—" Hero produced from his pocket a magnificent pair of emeralds, each as big as the end of his little finger. "This one for Ula"—he handed it to the half-swooning girl—"to wear in a pendant round her neck, to lie against her breast and remind them—er, remind *her*—of me; and this one for Una, to wear in a ring upon her finger, binding her to Eldin forever!"

As one man the Elders creaked to their feet and applauded; Ham Gidduf too. They were still at it when the questers and their ladies sneaked out and away into Baharna. And because the girls were with them Eldin couldn't clout Hero, and for the same reason Hero couldn't kick the Wanderer.

*

They had their fight later—verbal, over a pint of muth—in the *Quayside Quaress*. But that was much later.

First there'd been a message to get off as quickly as possible to Kuranes (a priest at the Temple of the Elder

Gods had obliged with the loan of a pigeon), and then there'd been two whole idyllic days (and nights) spent in the company of the twins. That had come to an end when Ham, his delayed business now all done, turned up to spend some time with the girls himself. Not to be denied his jiggly-bits, however (forbidden fruits were ever juicier), Eldin had insisted that before they set sail for Serannian, they must go and pay their respects to Buxom Barba. And to her belly-dancers.

And while they sat there bickering, boozing, and never batting an eye for fear of missing something while Zuli Bazooli did many wonderful things on stage, with and without her pythons, who should park himself at their table but:

"B'gods all!" Eldin gave a start, sent his drink flying. "It's—"

"The seer with invisible eyes!" Hero gawped.

"Aye-aye!" said that worthy, winking each empty orb in turn.

"You're dead!" Eldin accused.

The s.w.i.e. looked hurt. "I may pong a bit, but—"

"You know what we mean," said Hero.

"Oh, that poisoned dart. Immune!" he told them, with a mostly invisible grin. "Well traveled in Kled, I was, as a boy. Jungle-spawned poisons can't kill me. It merely knocked me down for an hour or two."

"You didn't drown when we sank the *Craven Lobster*?" Hero still couldn't believe it.

"Do I look drowned? No, I came to draped across a barrel bobbing in the bay," the s.w.i.e. answered. "Been draped across one ever since! It all worked out all right, then—for you two, I mean?"

"Apart from a promise or two we can't possibly keep—at least not yet awhile—it worked out perfectly!"

Eldin slapped the seer's shoulder. "All's in order and we're squared up all round."

"Difficult, that," said Hero. "To be square all round."

"Ah . . . not quite!" said the seer.

"What Hero said or what I said?" Eldin wanted to know. "Explain."

"Lippy's after your blood. He's even offering a reward. To whoever breaks one of Hero's limbs, a week's free boozing on Lippy's five-star muth. Same goes for you, Eldin, except he drinks free for a month!"

"We'll worry about that later," Hero shrugged it off. "Right now we're the ones doing the drinking. And it's good stuff we're drinking, not Lippy Unth's filth!" He grinned. "Anyway, he'll get no takers on a deal like that. What, a man should work us over—hazardous exercise at best—for the dubious privilege of damaging his brain on Lippy's guk? But this"—he tapped a fingernail on the bottle on the table—"this is the *real* stuff! Will you join us?"

"Too true!" said the s.w.i.e.

"But tell me," Eldin was still curious: "I mean, we were *sure* you were dead. See, we saw you lying there, saw pictures form in your ex-invisible eyes, saw 'em bleed and flood over."

"Bleeding the poison out of my system!" the s.w.i.e. answered. "And those pictures were an eleventh hour warning to you two. These eyes of mine were looking after us, see?"

"Do you mean," said Hero, frowning, "that your eyes are only invisible when you're conscious?"

"Dunno," said the seer. "I've never looked when I'm asleep! Anyway, what are we drinking . . . ?"

All of which set the tone of the conversation for the rest of a very liquid night, which soon degenerated into a blur that none of the three would ever seek to bring into proper focus. Best that they didn't know. In the morning they woke up in a tangle of nets on the quayside, and then it was time for Hero and Eldin to be on their way again . . .

They redeemed their flotation bag, had it pumped full of essence, went the way they'd come. The wind was off the land but somewhat aslant, so they used arms and jackets as sails, guiding themselves toward *Quester* where she lay moored to the old hulk's mast.

It was as they vented essence to begin their descent that Eldin spotted a small rowing-boat close to *Quester* tethered to the buoy with the scabfish warning.

"Urchins out fishing," opined Hero, narrow-eyed nevertheless.

"Fishing for what? Scabfish?" Eldin was instantly suspicious—but too late. Essence had been vented; they were sinking lower; the rowboat lay directly between them and their small vessel.

"Boat seems to be empty," said Hero, but still his voice was tight.

"Not so," Eldin denied. "See, a spyglass glints. Something stirs!"

A figure sat up in the rowing-boat. Huge, solid, shiny as a ripe olive: Lipperod Unth, teeth bared in a savage grin. In his hands, a wicked-looking crossbow.

"All hands to the boats!" Eldin whispered hoarsely.

"Women, children and cowards first!" Hero groaned.

"Ahoy, there, questers!" Lippy yelled, gleefully aiming his weapon. "Nice day for a dip in the briny, eh?"

"Lippy," Hero called back. "The very man we were looking for."

"Oh?" Lippy feigned an idiot's gawp. "And you

guessed I'd be out here in the bay, eh? Well, well! And now that you've found me?"

"Lippy,"—it was Eldin's turn—"we know you're mad at us, and that's p'raps understandable, but—"

"What, mad at you, me?" the massive black cut him off, foam showing now in one corner of his mouth, his great expressive lips beginning to protrude. "What, just 'cos you sank my place in three fathoms of slop, near-drowned my customers, probably ruined me forever? Now I ask you, is that any reason to be mad? Mad? *I'm totally insane!*"

"Lippy!" Hero desperately called out. "We can pay for the damage."

"Hah!"

Hero fumbled in a pocket, came up with a tiny leather pouch. They'd drifted so close now to the rowboat that Lippy couldn't possibly miss; they could see, almost feel his finger tightening on the trigger. But he'd seen the tiny pouch in Hero's hand.

"Eh? Eh?" he shouted. "You couldn't cram enough gold in that to buy a plate of soup! Not that you two would *buy* soup—you'd steal it!"

Hero tossed the pouch and Lippy caught it. Curious, he put down his crossbow, opened the tiny bag into his hand. The third emerald—Yath-Lhi's belly-bauble—made green sparkles in the morning sunlight. Lippy's mouth fell open and his great lips retracted a little. "Well, now!" he weighed the emerald in his palm.

"You can buy another *Craven Lobster*, in a better part of town," Eldin called down. They were directly over the rowboat now, drifting toward *Quester*.

"True, true," Lippy grunted. He put the jewel carefully into his pocket, picked up his weapon and re-aligned it. "The injury's paid for," he stated then. "But *not* the insult!"

"I apologize for Eldin!" Hero cried. "It was the full moon, I tell you!"

And: "Forgive my young friend!" the Wanderer pleaded. "Booze is a cross he's carried all his life. Just a sip of your excellent beverages, and he was bound to—"

"Enough!" cried Lipperod Unth—and his crossbow went *twannnnggg!*

There came a loud "pop" and a ripping sound, followed immediately by the ominous *hiss* of escaping essence. Lippy roared and laughed and danced till he almost upset his boat. And down came the questers, gaunt and whey-faced out of the sky—and *Quester* the craft still a soggy twenty-yard sprint away.

Hero glanced down and gulped, saw the sea rushing up at him, saw once again the buoy's warning notice: " 'WARE SCABFISH!" and croaked: "Eldin, just one thing."

"Eh?" the Wanderer blinked rapidly, an astonished I-don't-believe-it expression on his face.

"How's your breast-stroke?" Hero asked, conversationally. And then . . .

Splash!

TALE'S TAIL

Some little time earlier, Eldin had said:

"It's a strange sea, the Southern Sea, especially here in the middle of this expanse lying between Dylath-Leen, the Isle of Oriab, and Celephais. Ships have disappeared here, lots of them. They get hailed, go for a look-see, are never seen again. Survivors, none!"

"A sort of Baharna Triangle, eh?" Hero had responded.

"A what?"

Hero had frowned, looked blank. "Nothing—a fleeting memory from the waking world . . . I think."

"Oh!" And, suspiciously: "Are you making mock?"

"Not a bit of it"—with a shrug and a raised eyebrow—"Say on, do!"

"On clear days—sometimes on still, clear nights, when the moon's full and the sea is crystal—*things* have been seen, way down deep." Eldin was being mysterious, or he was telling tall ones again.

"Oh?" Hero having finished stripping himself naked, disgustedly inspected a scattering of flaky scabs on his calves, chest and forearms. "Things? Fishes, d'you mean? Nasty fishes—like scabfish! Or just common-or-garden sea-serpents? League-long octopussies, p'raps?"

Eldin scowled through his own scabs, said: "Don't jest about things told to you by your elders and betters."

"Elders, I'll grant you," Hero glanced at the Wanderer sideways. And: "Oh, very well—what sort of *things*, exactly, have been seen on clear nights when the moon is full?"

"Horrible things!" Eldin insisted. "A sunken town or city, with a long-drowned temple or monastery on a hill. And in the courtyard a tall, terrible monolith, and tied to that ancient altar slab—head down and lacking eyes—a sailor or merchant out of Oriab, still clad in his silken robes. *That's* what's been seen!"

Hero sighed, dangled his feet in the water from the deck of *Quester*. "Eldin, it's noon of a summer's day. There's no wind to speak of. I'm hot and sticky and the sea's flat as a mirror. Now, you may sit there on your backside mumbling ghost stories, sorry-looking and scabby as a dead cat, all you want. Me, I'm for a swim. I'm overboard, to and fro for a half-hour, and lo and behold new skin will be forming before your very eyes! Clean water is the best treatment for scabfish scabs, and I happen to be the living proof of it. It was a scummy harbor and scabby fish did this to us, and it's a clear, sweet sea that's going to clean it up. I mean, look at me: except for the merest blemish here and there, I've successfully shed the horrid things; while you, who haven't been near the water since Lippy Unth sank us—"

"I may never bathe again," Eldin morosely broke in. "*Ugh!* Those scabfish! And that Lippy—he'll have cause for pouting next time I see him!"

"What? You're planning to look Lippy up? On Oriab? And Ula and Una ready to ring our noses the moment we step ashore? You're not thinking straight, old lad." And he'd gone feet-first overboard, sinking deep in cool, clear water. As he surfaced:

"All right! You win!" Eldin tossed him his belt. "Only wear this, and let me tie a line to you."

"Eh? Are you serious?" Hero trod water, fastened the leather belt around his waist. It was a good belt and he didn't want to lose it.

"Please," Eldin pleaded. "For me? Then, while you splash about, I'll be able to take a nap in peace. At least with a little peace of mind." He dropped Hero the end of a long fishing line, belayed the other end to a cleat. Hero gave a snort—but he tied the line to his belt. Anything to keep his quirky partner happy. Another snort and, feeling foolish, he'd swum off with long, clean strokes.

Eldin had watched him for a minute or two, listened to the lazy sizzling of the sun on the water (it was that sort of day), finally taken off his shirt and stretched flat on his back in Sol's cleansing rays. And in a little while he'd fallen asleep and dreamed with crystal clarity and detailed repetition all of the foregoing—and then some. The substance of his dream within dreams was this:

Hero swam. He chugged to and fro happy as a child, dived deep, let the salty sea soak into his skin and lave those few crusty blemishes which yet persisted. No scabfish here, where the waters glittered silver and gold, and beneath him nothing but deeps going down (for all he knew) interminably. *Hah!* A man would need damn good eyesight to see right down there on a moonlit night. Indeed, he'd need eyes far-sighted as those of the s.w.i.e. himself! Eldin could be a silly old duffer sometimes, giving credence to tales such as those.

So thought Hero in Eldin's dream, as he swam and cavorted, and the fishing line uncoiling on the deck, and *Quester* a motionless flyspeck on the great glittering mirror ocean . . .

It was the deep flash of silver that first attracted Hero's eye: some fish cruising a fathom or two deep, reflecting the sun's lances as it turned on its side, the better to look at the swimmer on the surface. Shark? No, not with silvery scales, surely. Leathery things, sharks. But immediately cautious, Hero stopped swimming and lay flat, peering into watery deeps. For a moment he saw nothing, then . . .

He sucked air in a huge gasp. Fish nothing! That shimmer was from the costume she wore—on her bottom half, anyway. As for her top half—she wore nothing there!

She, yes! A girl, a gorgeous girl (they all are, let's face it), was out here in the Southern Sea! Eh? But where was her boat? Fifty yards away, there lay *Quester* quite becalmed, with Eldin snoozing on the deck. Hero trod water, scanned all about. And there to the south, halfway to the horizon . . . a mast and the low outline of a deck, surely?

The girl surfaced, grinned cheekily, tossed back her yellow hair in a spray of water. She glanced toward *Quester*, put a warning finger to her lips, grinned again and turned on end, disappearing in a flash of silver. Hero dipped his disbelieving face into the water, ogled after her, saw her milky breasts and buttocks all shiny as she slipped easily into the deep. Then she was coming up again, agile as a porpoise as she turned on her own axis, seemingly displaying herself for Hero's approval. And he approved! What's more, if he could see her, she must certainly see him—all of him. And apparently she approved, too.

Again she broke the surface, green eyes full of mischief, breasts bobbing, and again that cautionary finger to her lips as she glanced toward *Quester* and the slumbering Eldin. And:

No fear of that, my girl! thought Hero. What? She should think for a minute he might want to let the Wanderer in on this? Not a chance! Let that scabby old rat catch a single glimpse of her, and the game were over before it could get started.

"Huh!" Eldin puffed up his cheeks, blew out a great snoring snort. He was beginning to perspire where the sun hammered down on him.

Hero swam, drew closer to the girl, was dazzled by her beauty; certainly by the sun, flashing from her where she stood in the water with droplets streaming from her nipples, a rainbow forming in the cascade from her hair, knowing smile permitting the merest flash of teeth like pearls. But even as he closed with her, off she went again in the direction of the near-distant mast where it stood upright from its plank of a deck. That's what it looked like, sitting there on the horizon like that: a plank with a spar lashed upright, almost in imitation of a real boat. Funny how your eyes play tricks with you when the sun's hot and the sea's cool and a gorgeous girl's teasing the life out of you.

And flat on his back on board *Quester*, Eldin dreamed all of this and began to groan, sweating profusely now. On the one hand he groaned for his young friend, and yet on the other he gloated. He sensed the other's danger, yes, but at the same time he knew it was only a dream. And it would be fun if Hero got his comeuppance, even in a dream . . .

Meanwhile, Hero was after the girl again; he'd put on

a spurt and got so close he could actually stretch out a hand and touch her flashing flank. He did so—snatched back his hand as if it were scalded! All the dazzle went out of his eyes in a moment, all the lust out of his loins, all his adrenalin *into* his system!

No costume, that silvery sheath of a nether-garment, and no warm human flesh beneath it. Oh, firm enough flesh, aye, but cold as a fish. And just as slimy! Lord, she *was* a fish after all—some sort of fish, anyway.

As he recoiled from touch and sudden, shocking knowledge both, so he felt the line grow taut where it stretched between him and *Quester*. He had reached the end of his tether. Heart hammering, he glanced back; Quester stood off from him by a hundred yards; the fish-girl (mermaid?) was now apparently tired of being chased and had decided to chase him. And at the same time he felt strange, strong hands grasp his ankles to pull him down, and finally he knew for sure that Eldin's sea-ghosts were only too real.

All oblivious of which (except that it was a dream), Eldin experienced a sort of uneasy pleasure. This would teach the daft young bugger to doubt him! Oh, it wasn't real, of course not—but still it was very satisfying. And yet it was strangely disturbing, too . . .

The male or males of the species had Hero now, webbed hands clutching, bodies slippery so that kicks skidded off. Round-eyed they were, with red gill-slits throbbing in their necks; all silver-scaled from waists to flipped feet, but softly pink toward the tops, like salmon—and in their wide-slit mouths, needle teeth! And while Hero was a good swimmer, indeed a grand swimmer—oh, but he was no match for such as these! The sea was their element, natural to them as green fields and mountains were to Hero. He could no more fight them here than they could have fought him there. But he could try.

And the man-bait female circled all three figures as Hero was dragged deeper and deeper, grinning at this man they'd fished (or possibly manned?) from the surface. She was no longer beautiful but quite definitely evil; he saw her for what she was: a scaly, slimy creature whose pearly teeth were daggers, whose blood was thin and cold as the deep, deep sea.

But because he continued to fight and because the life line still tethered him to *Quester*, they couldn't drag him straight to the bottom. Instead, the gradual, airless descent was like the swing of a very slow pendulum. Until finally Hero—lungs bursting and eyes straining from their sockets—finally he spied below his ultimate destination: brief glimpse of an aeon-sunken city, with a hill rising from the murk, a temple and courtyard, and an awful altar stone draped in weed! A single glimpse, but sufficient to stir him to greater effort, to concentrate his waning energies on one last attempt for freedom ...

Up on the surface *Quester* rocked a very little, just enough that Eldin's head turned out of the vertical (nose-up) position and lolled to one side. This half awakened him. A pigeon—yellow—one of Baharna's temple birds, completed the job. Fluttering and p-cooing, it landed on his matted chest, lifted a pink-clawed foot to display its message-cylinder. Blinking in the glare of abrupt awakening and gathering his senses, Eldin sat up, shaded his eyes, opened the cylinder and read the scrap of paper within:

ATTENTION, ELDIN!

Seer here:

Bad vibrations, unpleasant premonitions. About Hero. I've been sending (mentalistically speaking) but don't know if you've received. So I'm reduced to a pigeon. No, great clown, not physically—just the use of one! Don't know what it's all about, except you should keep him away from water. In fact if I were you, I wouldn't even let him wash his face!

> *Be scrying you—*
> *s.w.i.e.*

Eh? Water? Boat rocking? Eldin sat bolt upright, likewise the hairs on his neck. The boat rocked again. The line was taut where it disappeared over the side at a steep angle.

Eldin became a blur of motion. He snatched up Hero's knife from the heap of clothes piled haphazardly on the deck, gripped its blade in his great teeth. A moment later, his own knife strapped as ever to his calf, he was overboard in a dive which would do credit to a dolphin. And down into the not-so-benign deeps he plunged, down . . . down to where a small knot of figures looked locked in a balletic battle.

While below:

It was the end, and Hero knew it. Even in dreams a man can only dive so deep, and lungs need air asleep or waking. Exhaustion and oxygen-starvation were killing him. He strained, writhed, hauled himself a few desperate feet up the line—and was dragged back again. He threshed his body in what seemed a final frenzy. Bubbles, pitifully few and small now, streamed from his agonized lips. A moment longer it lasted, and then he gave a convulsive shudder and went limp. He hung still in the water, mouth agape and eyes blindly staring.

The fish-men and -maid were jubilant; they relaxed their holds upon him, began a closer inspection of their prize. And as they let go his ankles and came up alongside him—

Stiff-fingered, Hero drove a hand into the bulging eyes of one, smashed an elbow into the stomach of the second; and then he kicked wildly for the surface. Going up, he saw something coming down. A wonderful, even beautiful something. Eldin grabbed him, kissed him, blew air into starving lungs. *Impossible!* thought Hero, *except in dreams*. Then Eldin pressed something into his hand, and as quickly as that the balance was adjusted, scales (the other sort) were tilting in Hero's favor.

A fishy belly offered itself, and Hero obligingly sliced it open. Fish guts stained the water red and yellow, webbed hands scrabbling desperately. Eldin cut his creature gill to gill, scared off the female with a lunge of his grisly knife. Then the Wanderer looked around, sought Hero.

Hero!

The younger quester was just about all in. His feet kicked—or more nearly twitched—very feebly as he drifted surfaceward, his head tilted back and glassy eyes gazing straight up. And this time he wasn't faking it. Eldin drove his great legs as never before, grabbed Hero's hair in passing, hauled him along behind.

And looking down worriedly on Hero as he blazed for the surface, Eldin could also see into the deeps beneath—could see the horde of gill-beings even now speeding in his wake!

The surface, the blessed surface! Eldin's head broke through in glittering droplets, and a moment later

Hero's. Then the younger man was drawing air with a noise like badly-holed bellows, and Eldin scrambling aboard their vessel, crying: "Up, quick! Come on, climb up! Give me your hand, I tell you!"

But Hero simply floating on his back, too exhausted even to struggle. Eldin flinging himself on the deck face-down, grabbing Hero under the arms and hauling him unceremoniously aboard.

"Don't—*gasp!*—interrupt me—*gasp!*—when I'm breathing!" Hero complained, flopping there while Eldin thundered headlong into the cabin. A moment later came the throb of *Quester*'s flotation engine at full throttle, then Eldin storming up again on to the deck.

Hero propped himself up on one elbow. "Knackered!" he coughed, by way of explaining his inactivity.

Scaly heads broke the surface close to *Quester*; webbed hands came up over her sides; Hero was on his feet in a trice. "But not that knackered!" he gasped.

And of course, the rest of it is known.

The surface was pink where severed fingers and hands, even a fishy head or two, floated in profusion, when at last *Quester* cleared the water and drifted skyward; and only then dared the pair put down their swords and rest. After that:

A storm came up out of nowhere (conjured, perhaps, by the thwarted gods of the submarine temple?) that blew *Quester* across the sky like a tuft of thistledown. But battened in the cabin Hero and Eldin didn't give a damn between them. "Few reefs up here to strike against," the Wanderer commented, sinking muth straight from the bottle.

"I say top the bags brim-full," Hero nodded, shivering, not quite fully recovered. "Let's climb clear of the storm and only come down again when it's blown itself out. It's a mite cold up there, but safe as safe can be!"

"Agreed!" said Eldin, turning the pumps up full. "As for getting cold: why, there's booze enough in store to keep us warm for a week, even in upper atmosphere!"

And as the dreamlands fell away beneath their keel, so the adventurers started in on one of their very best binges.

THE END

But there are more dreamquests in store!

BRIAN LUMLEY

☐	51199-9 DEMOGORGON	$4.99
☐	50832-7 THE HOUSE OF DOORS	$4.95
☐	52137-4 NECROSCOPE	$5.99
☐	52126-9 VAMPHYRI! Necroscope II	$4.95
☐	52127-7 THE SOURCE Necroscope III	$4.95
☐	50833-5 DEADSPEAK Necroscope IV	$4.95 Canada $5.95
☐	50835-1 DEADSPAWN	$4.99 Canada $5.99
☐	52032-7 PSYCHAMOK	$5.99
☐	52023-8 PSYCHOMECH	$5.99
☐	52030-0 PSYCHOSPHERE	$5.99

Buy them at your local bookstore or use this handy coupon:
Clip and mail this page with your order.

Publishers Book and Audio Mailing Service
P.O. Box 120159, Staten Island, NY 10312-0004

Please send me the book(s) I have checked above. I am enclosing $ _____
(Please add $1.25 for the first book, and $.25 for each additional book to cover postage and handling.
Send check or money order only—no CODs.)

Name _____
Address _____
City _____ State/Zip _____
Please allow six weeks for delivery. Prices subject to change without notice.

FANTASY BESTSELLERS
FROM TOR

☐ 52261-3 BORDERLANDS $4.99
                 edited by Terri Windling & Lark Alan Arnold   Canada $5.99

☐ 50943-9 THE DRAGON KNIGHT $5.99
                 Gordon R. Dickson   Canada $6.99

☐ 51371-1 THE DRAGON REBORN $5.99
                 Robert Jordan   Canada $6.99

☐ 52003-3 ELSEWHERE $3.99
                 Will Shetterly   Canada $4.99

☐ 55409-4 THE GRAIL OF HEARTS $4.99
                 Susan Schwartz   Canada $5.99

☐ 52114-5 JINX HIGH $4.99
                 Mercedes Lackey   Canada $5.99

☐ 50896-3 MAIRELON THE MAGICIAN $3.99
                 Patricia C. Wrede   Canada $4.99

☐ 50689-8 THE PHOENIX GUARDS $4.99
                 Steven Brust   Canada $5.99

☐ 51373-8 THE SHADOW RISING $5.99
                 Robert Jordan (Coming in October '93)   Canada $6.99

Buy them at your local bookstore or use this handy coupon:
Clip and mail this page with your order.

Publishers Book and Audio Mailing Service
P.O. Box 120159, Staten Island, NY 10312-0004

Please send me the book(s) I have checked above. I am enclosing $ _____
(Please add $1.25 for the first book, and $.25 for each additional book to cover postage and handling.
Send check or money order only—no CODs.)

Name _____
Address _____
City _____ State/Zip _____
Please allow six weeks for delivery. Prices subject to change without notice.